LOW BRIDGE!
Folklore and the Erie Canal

LOW BRIDGE!
Folklore and the Erie Canal

Lionel D. Wyld

SYRACUSE UNIVERSITY PRESS

1962

Library of Congress Catalog Card: 62-10627
COPYRIGHT © 1962 BY
SYRACUSE UNIVERSITY PRESS
SYRACUSE, N. Y.

Third printing 1966
Fourth printing, first paperback 1977
Fifth printing, second paperback 1982

Library of Congress Cataloging in Publication Data

Wyld, Lionel D
Low bridge!

(A York State book)
Includes index.
1. Erie Canal—History. 2. Folk-lore—New York
(State)—Erie Canal. 3. Erie Canal in literature.
I. Title.
F127.E5W9 1977   917.47   77-882
ISBN 0-8156-0137-9

MANUFACTURED IN THE UNITED STATES OF AMERICA

To Norma with love

Preface

"You must have heard of it," said the narrator in *Moby-Dick*, Melville's classic novel published in 1851, and the Erie Canal probably needs little introduction to any reader. But what was the "Old Erie" really like?

Since the present book is a kind of folklorist's tour on the one hand and a literary history on the other, the folk tales that are recounted and the expressions of the life of "canawlers" that are found in the literary record will here serve, as validly as they can, to answer that question.

This book is, I think, a fair picture of the Erie Canal and of the times, for the cultural mosaic is formed as much by such facets of a civilization as by the factual histories. Diaries, journals, guide-books, folklore, drama, poetry, and critical essays —biased as well as objective—offer engaging material for the cultural historian; often, too, the fictionist, even while clothing his facts in robes of obscuring and maudlin romanticism, can come close to the real meaning and issues of the times.

In this latter regard, one should not discount the essential worth of books like Walter D. Edmonds' *Rome Haul* or Samuel Hopkins Adams' *Canal Town*. It would likewise be absurd to fail to recognize the very fine line that may separate folklore from a more conscious evolvement.

In the present volume, *folklore* is used in its natural and best sense. Differentiation is made, for the purposes of scholarship and criticism, between the purely literary and the traditional, but the former is by no means excluded as something of little value. In the final analysis, happily, folklore is more what the folk make it than what the academic folklorist may neatly sterilize and categorize.

This book owes much to the encouragement and help of Dr. MacEdward Leach of the University of Pennsylvania, for it stems largely from his suggestion that a book on the folklore of the Erie Canal would not only be an interesting task to write but also a worthwhile addition to the growing number of works which are making folklore studies available for the general, as well as for the professional, reader. Whatever value the present work has must be attributed to Professor Leach's searching but always encouraging criticism. His enthusiasm for folklore and his keen personal interest in this project are gratefully and warmly acknowledged.

Acknowledgments seem due so many persons who contributed information and criticism to this book that a general word of sincere appreciation may, in necessarily omitting many deserving names, seem not too ungracious. In particular, however, I should like to say thanks to Dr. Louis C. Jones, who allowed me free access to the facilities of the New York State Historical Association and to his personal files, putting at my disposal not only the Fenimore House Library collections and the Van Norman bibliography of New York State, but also material in the Cooperstown archives collected under his supervision; and to Mr. Richard N. Wright, of the Canal Society of New York State, who offered numerous suggestions toward an accurate and logical presentation of facts about the canal and its boaters.

Two librarians deserve special thanks: Mrs. Margaret Lewis, head of the Children's Department of the Schenectady County Public Library's Main Branch, who helped immensely with the task of tracking down the many juveniles which deal with the Erie; and Miss Catherine Buckley, formerly in charge of interlibrary loans at the Rensselaer Polytechnic Institute Library, whose willingness to tackle the myriad problems of locating and securing items far afield resulted in my counsulting almost all of the nineteenth-century primary sources in original editions.

For the criticism of colleagues and friends who read parts of the manuscript, I am especially indebted; the following list includes their names, along with those of other persons who helped in particular ways: Mr. Walter D. Edmonds, Boonville; Professor David M. Ellis, Hamilton College; Mr. Larry Hart, Schenectady *Union-Star;* Miss Ellen Kenny, Grosvenor Library; Mr. Paul McFarland, Binghamton; Professor Thomas F. O'Donnell, Utica College; Dr. Marvin Rapp, State University of New York; Mrs. Lillian Schayer, Plainfield, New Jersey; Mr. and Mrs. Jack R. Warner, Lafayette, Indiana; and Professor Douglas Washburn, Rensselaer Polytechnic Institute.

A faculty research grant by the Rensselaer Polytechnic Institute provided funds to defray some of the expenses for necessary field work and travel. This aid is gratefully acknowledged.

For an author to acknowledge the help and encouragement of his wife is a happy courtesy. To my wife, Norma, I am especially grateful, not only for the acceptance of the usual but all too frequent disturbances which writing occasions in a household of four but also for the constant and buoyant encouragement she offered as we tackled the problems of Erie water. That she typed the manuscript, readied numerous drafts, and became a willing "canaller" are but a small part of her contribution to this book.

LIONEL D. WYLD

Buffalo, New York
March, 1962

Contents

xi

York State is a country.

CARL CARMER
Dark Trees to the Wind

"Canallers, Don, are the boatmen belonging to our grand Erie Canal. You must have heard of it."

HERMAN MELVILLE
Moby-Dick

I

They Built
the Longest Canal

WHEN the first spade of earth was turned at Rome, New York, to begin the building of the Erie Canal, one of the canal commissioners keynoted the ceremonies in prophetic language. "By this great highway," he said, "unborn millions will easily transport their surplus productions to the shores of the Atlantic, procure their supplies and hold a useful and profitable intercourse with all the maritime nations of the world." [1] Yet, even this earnest statement did not anticipate the effect the canal was to have or the changes it would work. When the Erie was completed in 1825 and water flowed in one continuous "ditch" from Buffalo to Albany, William L. Stone summed it all up in words which have never since been surpassed for their epitomizing the story of the Erie. In a memorial volume prepared for the celebration which climaxed the construction of "Clinton's Ditch," Stone told fellow New Yorkers, the United States, and the world that the authors and builders of the Erie "have built the longest canal, in the least time, with the least experience, for the least money, and to the greatest public benefit." [2]

The Erie Canal has indeed been more than a historic waterway coursing through central New York State: it is a legend. And the building of the canal was more than a feat of engineering and construction (although that seemed wondrous enough as an accomplishment of the new republic); in retrospect, it appears in history and finds reflection in folklore and literature as a saga and an epic. While the Erie Canal was still three years from completion, in 1822, poet Philip Freneau penned some "Stanzas on the Great Western Canal of the State of New York." The name of the canal was impressive, but only befitting the task. It was, Freneau wrote, "a work from Nature's *chaos* won"; and he went on to tell the story in verse:

> By hearts of oak and hands of toil
> The Spade inverts the rugged soil
> A work, that may remain secure
> While suns exist and Moons endure.[3]

It is not difficult to become acquainted with New York State's "eighth wonder of the world" and the circumstances which brought it from idea to reality, for both the building of the Erie and the story of the major background events have been told in scholarly and popular histories, and in factual accounts and historical novels. They range from Noble E. Whitford's monumental (and by far the most complete) *History of the Canal System of the State of New York* to the widely read juvenile Landmark book, *The Erie Canal*, by Samuel Hopkins Adams.[4]

Talk about a waterway connection between the Great Lakes and the Atlantic can be traced back at least to the early 1700's, when the colonial leaders saw the possibilities for a continuous water route across what is now New York State. The Mohawk Valley offered a travel route for both Indian and white. Navigation up the Hudson River to Albany and beyond provided no obstacle. Westward from the Albany area a chain of natural waterways—including rivers, creeks, and a lake—led across the state to Lake Ontario. The falls at Cohoes, where the Mohawk River had its confluence with the Hudson, presented a formidable portage at all times; another, of about a mile, around the "Little Falls of the Mohawk," and an especially trying overland link from the Mohawk to Wood Creek presented difficulties to travellers. Even in colonial times, connecting these barely separated elements to lessen the problems of western travel seemed a highly sensible idea.

The region was the home of the Iroquois confederation, and doubtless the waterways from the Mohawk to the Finger Lakes helped bind together that powerful league. As early as 1700, Richard Coote, governor of the Province of New-York, was concerned with travel conditions in the area. He instructed His Majesty's Chief Engineer in America, Colonel Romer, to observe, during the colonel's visit to the Iroquois, the geographical features of the area, "and to take particular note of the two carrying places and to report . . . how much they would be shortened by clearing and cleansing the creeks from the woods, so as to make those creeks navigable for boats and canoes." [5] In 1724, Cadwallader Colden, surveyor-general for the colonial governor, pointed out the advantages of a water route in a monograph, *A Memorial concerning the Furr-Trade of the province of New-York;* and that same year a survey was instituted to determine a possible route from Albany to Lake Cataqui (Lake Ontario). After the French and Indian War, certain "improvements" were made in the Mohawk River–Wood Creek–Oneida Lake water transportation route. In December 1768 Governor Sir Henry Moore, emphasizing the beneficial effects of France's Languedoc Canal, recommended improving the Mohawk River for use, especially between Schenectady and Fort Stanwix; but no action was taken by New York's General Assembly.

George Washington, touring the State of New York in 1783, suggested the possibilities for developing the region for east-west water traffic. As a result, the first true canal survey was undertaken. In 1784, the legislature commended a plan by Christopher Colles, an Irish engineer who had emigrated to this country in 1765, for removing obstructions to the navigation of the Mohawk River. In November of that year they deemed public expenditure for the purpose outlined by Colles "inexpedient" but on April fifth of the following year Colles received an appropriation—of $125!—to implement his plan. With this sum New York State began the long climb to its Parnassian position as the very home of "canal engineering."

Unfortunately, Colles and his associates failed, but Colles did publish the proposals (1785), stressing the advantages of inland navigation between Albany and Oswego. Colles had taken a survey of the obstructions in the Mohawk River as far as Wood Creek. He published the results in a pamphlet in which he proposed the establishment of a company with a capital of £13,000 to complete inland navigation at Cohoes, Little Falls, and Fort Schuyler, about seven miles of canals in all. The next year Jeffrey Smith, Long Island assemblyman, introduced "an act for improving the navigation of the Mohawk River, Wood Creek, and the Onondaga River . . . and for extending the same, if practicable, to Lake Erie." [6] The language of this bill, as Noble Whitford points out, is significant since for the first time Lake Erie is mentioned in connection with inland navigation; it does not appear again in legislative action until a resolution calling for surveying the route which later became the Erie Canal is promulgated in 1808. The "long canal" idea, however, was gaining momentum.

In the years intervening between the initial committee appropriation for Colles and the final legislative action in 1816 which initiated the construction of the trans-state canal, the history of the Erie is one of almost continual agitation, although to be sure not all of the proposals or schemes were in agreement either as to how to proceed or where to construct "canal communications." Minor improvements were voted, and navigation of the Mohawk was aided in some areas. In 1792, General Philip Schuyler contributed to the Erie's development by forming the Western Inland Navigation Company, a company later associated with the final Erie project. The company actually started construction, having been chartered to open navigation from the Hudson River to Seneca and Ontario Lakes. By 1796, when the Western Company secured a $15,000 loan from the state, they had built canal links in and around Little Falls; and they opened in that year, for boats of up to sixteen tons, a route from Schenectady to Seneca Falls.

Touring the West in 1797 with an English engineer, William Weston, Schuyler talked of furthering the water communications between the East and the West by canals which would cross the state. Gouverneur Morris, in a letter to John Parish, December 20, 1800, remarked that ships might be made to "sail from London through Hudson's River into Lake Erie" for one-tenth the expenditure for a British campaign.[7] In 1803, he told the surveyor-general of the state, Simeon DeWitt, his plan for "tapping Lake Erie . . . and leading its waters in an artificial river, directly across the country to the Hudson River."[8] DeWitt felt that the honor of first conceiving the Erie Canal idea "unquestionably" belonged to Morris, one of whose more bizarre schemes put the canal on an inclined plane of uniform slope from Lake Erie to the ridge between Schenectady and Albany. (At some points en route this canal would have been on embankments one hundred and fifty feet high!) James Geddes, later one of the famous canal engineers, also tended to give credit to Morris; but there were other claimants.[9]

Meanwhile popular opinion was marshalling for a canal or canals. The comments of numerous advocates of a continuous east-west waterway are to be found sprinkled in diaries, letters, journals, and newspaper accounts. The journal of Elkanah Watson, who toured the western part of the state in 1791, "partly by land but chiefly by water,"[10] probably influenced General Schuyler in his own canal-directed planning. Colles, long before he and his associates convinced the legislative committee that they should be allowed to do $125 worth of surveying, spoke in New York City on the improvement of waterways and in 1772 gave a series of public lectures in Philadelphia on lock navigation. But credit for concentrating public opinion on an Erie Canal project probably belongs to Jesse Hawley, who claimed "the original and the first *publication* of a project for the overland route of the Erie Canal, from Buffalo to the Hudson."[11] In a series of articles signed "Hercules" which appeared in the Genesee *Messenger* during 1807–1808, Hawley advocated the commonsense need and practicality of the canal. Others began commenting similarly in letters and pamphlets, urging the canal as a boon to trade. "It would do much more than double the value of produce in the State of Ohio, and it would add at least fifty per cent to the value of produce in the western part of the State of Tennessee," one writer remarked enthusiastically.[12] The assurance that New York would continue its rise as the nation's greatest metropolis was being forecast. It is unnecessary, the same writer continued, "to use many arguments in proving, that if the projected canal should be perfected, New-York would become one of the most splendid commercial cities on the face of the earth." [13] The influential *Weekly Register* (later *Niles' Register*) backed the canal idea. Later, a "New-York Corresponding Association" was formed with the purpose of acquainting the Union with "that noble and munificent spirit of enterprize" leading to internal improvements. In direct attack on those who would abandon the Western Canal, the Association kept interest in the Erie active.[14]

Thomas Jefferson, on the other hand, during his term of office as president of the United States, would not release federal funds for an Erie Canal project: he thought the idea a hundred years premature and the task completely impractical. In March 1810 proposals were put forth by Thomas Eddy and Jonas Platt to induce the legislature to appoint a commission to examine the whole route from the Hudson River to both Lake Erie and Lake Ontario, with a view to making an independent canal, rather than simply extending the work of the Western Inland Lock Navigation Company, using the rivers as feeders only. Jonas Platt offered the resolution in the senate, with DeWitt Clinton seconding it, whereupon it passed that body unanimously. Seven commissioners (Gouverneur Morris, Stephen Van Rensselaer, DeWitt Clinton, Simeon DeWitt, William North, Thomas Eddy, and Peter B. Porter) were appointed to study the possibility of a trans-state route. At the same time, $3,000 was appropriated for expenses. Prior to this, Judge Joshua Forman had, in February 1808, introduced a resolution in the assembly for a canal joining the Hudson River with Lake Erie; and James Geddes, who was later to be named one of the Erie engineers, made a survey of the entire range. The Geddes report for a canal route was entered January 20, 1809. The commissioners again tried to enlist support from the federal government and from other states and territories, but failed. They reported to the legislature that "sound policy demands that the canal should be made by the State of New York alone, and for her own account."[15] Some money was raised for starting construction, but the outbreak of the War of 1812 postponed the canal project.[16]

In 1815, with the lessons of the war and its effects on transportation and prices in the foreground, Eddy, Platt, and Clinton—who had secured the first canal commission appointment in 1810—now took up the battle anew, seeking public sentiment as well. Following a well-attended meeting in New York City on December 3, 1815, Clinton, then mayor of New York, and several others were appointed a commission to prepare a memorial to the legislature. The document, the "New York Memorial," is the work of Clinton; it proved to be the catalyst needed. Former and alternative schemes were abandoned, and the idea of an "Erie Canal" took precedence in public and legislative comment. On March 8, 1816, the final report of the board of canal commissioners, created by the act of April 8, 1811, and deprived of funds in 1814, urged nonetheless immediate commencement and vigorous prosecution of a canal from Lake Erie to the Hudson (and also on a route to Lake Champlain). They furthermore recommended employing American engineers.

After still further legislative wrangling and debates, a bill was passed on April 17, 1816, appointing Stephen Van Rensselaer, DeWitt Clinton, Samuel Young, Joseph Ellicott, and Myron Holley as commissioners. Their charge was "to consider, devise, and adopt such measure as may or shall be requisite, to facilitate and effect the communication, by means of canals and locks, between the navigable waters of Hudson's River and Lake Erie, and the said navigable waters and Lake Champlain."[17] This time $20,000 was appropriated for expenses. In May the commissioners met in New York and appointed Clinton as president, Young as secretary, and Myron Holley as treasurer. The Erie canal-to-be was divided into three sections, with an engineer in charge of each. James Geddes was assigned to the western section (Lake Erie to the Seneca River); Benjamin Wright had charge of the middle section (Seneca River to Rome); and Charles C. Broadhead

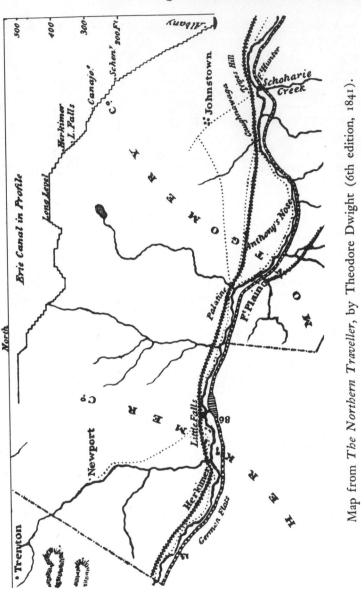

Map from *The Northern Traveller*, by Theodore Dwight (6th edition, 1841).

supervised the eastern section (Rome to Albany). The Buffalo area presented certain singular problems in geography, and William Peacock was named to determine the most feasible route for the canal in that area. Colonel G. Lewis Garin was to direct the Champlain division.

Construction of the Erie Canal began on the Fourth of July, 1817. The site chosen—Rome, New York—was a wise one, for there the digging was easy and the greatest progress could be made in the shortest time. Then, too, working "both ways to oncet," as Yorkers later drawled out pridefully, they knew the opposition would have a more difficult time breaking up operations. When completed, the canal ran 363 miles from Albany to Buffalo; in this distance eighty-three locks compensated for the various levels, twenty-seven of them in the first fifteen miles or so between Albany and Schenectady around the Cohoes Falls. At Lockport the famous *combines*—five pairs of double-locks—were the marvel of the engineering world; but the dimensions of the canal channel itself, compared with its length and the immensity of the over-all task, seem, in retrospect, almost negligible—40 feet on the surface, 28 at bottom, with a depth of water to but four feet. It seemed to be little more than a wet ditch, yet it was indeed, as one enthusiastic historian of the canal cogently put it, "from the beginning a golden cord, a bind, in our national existence." [18]

The achievement of this Erie Canal becomes even more remarkable when one considers the state of engineering in this country in 1815. Civil engineering as a profession was unknown. To a large extent, also, the Erie project created the over-all profession of engineering in the United States.[19] With ingenuity matched only by pioneering courage, the Erie engineers coped successfully with countless problems and overcame numerous difficulties. A legislative report in 1958 put their story in romantic and enthusiastic tones:

The whole question of hydraulics and locks, a waterproof cement, a stump puller and men who could stand the damp and disease of the Montezuma swamps had to be solved. . . . The rock-cutting through the mountain ridge near

Lockport was accomplished by DuPont's new blasting powder; the swift waters of the Genesee spanned by a waterbridge of Roman arches; on the 70-foot embankment over the Irondequoit Valley was seen "the sublime spectacle of boats gliding over the hill tops"; hordes of bog-trotting Irishmen left their famine-stricken island to dig in waist-deep mud and water through the mosquito and malaria infested Montezuma marshes; the Mohawk River was crossed by two mighty aqueducts, the Schoharie Creek by a dam crossing; and finally, the level of the Hudson was reached by a flight of 16 locks.[20]

The engineering lay largely in the hands of a few relatively untutored and almost completely inexperienced men. Three names are prominent in this early canal history: James Geddes, Benjamin Wright, and Canvass White. Geddes and Wright had a little surveying in their backgrounds. White went to England where he walked along two thousand miles of towpaths to study English canal construction. "Few men," remarked the president of the American Society of Civil Engineering in 1882, "have ever accomplished so much with so little means." [21]

The Erie Canal opened officially in October 25, 1825, and the ensuing events celebrating the occasion have become an important part of Erie legendry. Not the least were the cannon, placed the length of the canal and down the Hudson River to New York, to carry by successive firings the news of the canal's opening from Buffalo to Manhattan. The festivities ended in New York City on November 4, 1825, when the triumphant procession of canal boats reached New York harbor and were welcomed with one of the greatest spectacle displays in American history.

The Aquatic display transcended all anticipations, twenty-nine steam-boats, gorgeously dressed, with barges, ships, pilot-boats, canal-boats, and the boats of the Whitehall firemen, conveying thousands of ladies and gentlemen, presented a scene which cannot be described. Add to this, the reflections which arise from the extent and beauty of our Bay—

the unusual calmness and mildness of the day—the splendid manner in which all the shipping in the harbour were dressed, and the movement of the whole flotilla. Regulated by previously arranged signals, the fleet were thrown at pleasure, into squadron or line, into curves or circles. The whole appeared to move as by magic.[22]

This was written by Cadwallader D. Colden, whom the city fathers had charged with preparing an appropriate *Memoir* for the occasion, a monumental work in its own right, and one which remains important as a repository of contemporary accounts and commentaries of the canal as well as of the celebration which feted its completion.

The *Seneca Chief*, with DeWitt Clinton and a highly diversified cargo aboard, led the cavalcade down the Erie Canal from Buffalo. On board as it left for Albany and New York was a cargo of pot ashes, from Detroit, Sandusky, Erie, and Buffalo; white fish, from Lake Erie; flour and butter, from Michigan, Ohio, and Buffalo; and some bird's eye maple, and cedar wood, ordered by the Corporation of the City of New York (to make boxes to hold the medals to be struck for the occasion). The *Young Lion of the West* carried flour, butter, apples, cedar tubs and pails "of very excellent workmanship," some new brooms "of a superior quality," and a deckside menagerie of wolves, foxes, raccoons, and other forest life. The entourage, escorted from Albany by a fleet of steamers, arrived in New York City on November 4, where a gala fete had been arranged in reception. Two kegs of water had been brought from Lake Erie, the contents of one of which was ceremoniously poured into the Atlantic at Sandy Hook. This now-famous "Wedding of the Waters" ceremony, in the words of DeWitt Clinton, was

intended to indicate and commemorate the navigable communication which has been accomplished between our Mediterranean Sea and the Atlantic Ocean in about eight years, to the extent of more than 425 miles, by the wisdom, public spirit and energy of the people of the State of New York;

and may the God of the Heavens and of the Earth smile
most propitiously on this work and render it subservient to
the best interests of the human race.[23]

Then, Dr. Sam Mitchell poured forth into the sea the bottled
waters from every part of the globe—the Nile, Ganges, Indus,
Thames, Seine, Rhine, Mississippi, Columbia, Orinoco, and La
Plata—symbolically opening commercial intercourse with all
the nations of the world.

When the canal opened, England had more than a hundred
canals, but no one canal independent of branches extended a
hundred miles. Russia had a 4,500-mile water route, including
lakes, but no one canal reached more than half the length of
the Erie. France's then-famed Languedoc Canal, impressive
as it was, stretched a mere 115 miles. In America, the "Canal
Era" began in earnest. Building canals became an overnight
mania. Pennsylvania developed a network of them into the
largest system in the country, but the Erie remained the
longest, and the most successful. Every state revived half-
completed projects, or turned previously desultory efforts into
enthusiastic ventures in canal engineering. "All of them," recalled Edward Everett Hale in his *Memories of a Hundred
Years*, "took on new life with the triumphant success of the
Erie Canal." [24]

The Grand Western Canal's steady and prideful growth
from a mere ditch became an important part of York State
history, with an almost incalculable influence. Freight rates
dropped to one-tenth of what they had been—and even lower.
Business boomed all along the towpath. Within a decade after
its opening, the Erie Canal had paid revenue into the state
treasury exceeding the initial outlay for its building. Even
before 1830 the state realized more than eight per cent annually
on its loan, and the canal had increased the value of real estate
in New York State by millions of dollars.

Although the canal was not made to accommodate passenger
traffic, early Erie history is filled with travellers' tales; and
packet boats—the "aristocrats of the Old Erie," as Edward
Hungerford called them—cut a fancy pace through central

New York. They offered the tourist or other traveller an inexpensive, leisurely mode of conveyance. One of the popular guidebooks of the times gave the following "Description of a Canal Packet Boat" in 1828:

> The length is 60 or 70 feet, a large part of which is devoted to the dining room, where two rows of tables are set. At night, mattresses are spread on the seats each side, and another row above them on cots suspended from the roof. The ladies are accommodated with births [*sic*] in the cabin, which is usually carpeted, hung with curtains, and in other respects more handsomely furnished. The kitchen and bar are conveniently situated; and the tables are spread with an abundance, and often a delicacy, which may well surprise those not accustomed to the cheapness of travelling in this part of the country.
>
> A small library, a number of newspapers, &c. will serve to make the time pass agreeably, even if the traveller be a stranger, or the weather not inviting. In many places, the view from the deck is highly interesting. . . .[25]

The heyday of the packet boat was relatively brief, however, for the stage coaches, though they rocked and pitched, made far better time than did the boaters going their couple of miles an hour. More particularly, of course, railroad trains seemed to foredoom the Erie from the very beginning. The original "Old Erie" remained roughly the same to the Civil War, although the first "enlargement" was begun in 1835. Subsequent enlargements pointed toward the eventual Barge Canal System of the twentieth century. During its first forty years the Erie Canal made transportation and commercial history, and for a short time after the Civil War, in the early 1870's, freight traffic gave the Grand Canal a period of its greatest use. The subsequent decline, despite the abolition of tolls in 1882 and the fervent support of faithful canal backers, came about inevitably. Railroad mania proved to be as infectious a malaise as had canal building; the Iron Horse permanently supplanted the canal boat.[26]

One can see today in a few scattered sites the "old" and the "new" along the way of the Erie Division of the New York State Barge Canal. The "old" seems especially romantic and not a little tinged with nostalgia now. Certainly, its saga is part of what once was called "the American Dream." That the Erie Canal had a heyday filled to overflowing with richness and color hardly needs emphasizing. That it represented a significant achievement for the nation—and more particularly for the State of New York—needs no elaboration. Prophetically, the words of the eminent English engineer William Weston, included in a letter to the canal commissioners, had expressed it fittingly as early as 1814. "Should your noble but stupendous plan of uniting Lake Erie with the Hudson, be carried into effect," he had written, "you have to fear no rivalry. The commerce of the immense extent of country, bordering on the upper lakes, is yours forever, and to such an incalculable amount as would baffle all conjecture. Its execution would confer honor on the projectors and supporters, and would in its eventual consequences, render New York the greatest commercial emporium in the world. . . ."[27] The Erie made men and engineers. It opened the West.[28] It unleashed a commerce greater than had been suspected, revolutionized transportation, and made economic history. The canal guaranteed the supremacy of New York City as the largest port and the commercial capital of the country. New York State became indeed the Empire State and the canal the "pathway to empire." Across the state towns and cities sprang up, owing their growth, as well as their very birth in some instances, to the canal. "The Erie Canal," said Francis Kimball, "rubbed Aladdin's Lamp. America awoke, catching for the first time the wondrous vision of its own dimensions and power."[29]

II

"Low Bridge!"

WHEN it comes to touring the Erie Canal, even via the folk-lore or history route, there is a whole new world of terms and expressions to explore. Like many another area, New York State has some peculiar talk which is a part of its regionalism. Take the word *Yorker* itself. To the upstate New Yorker of an earlier age, the "New" was customarily dropped: his was *York State,* and he and his neighbors were either *Yorkers* or *York Staters.* The whole fascinating canalization period in American history contributed many now-forgotten terms to nineteenth-century speech; the Erie Canal contributed an impressive number in its own right.

"Lo-o-w bridge!" became a rallying cry for canallers who wanted to attract other boaters. It was a call to which any loyal son of the Grand Erie Canal would unhesitatingly respond if he were within earshot. It seems, also, that the phrase found its way into local vaudeville parlance, joining such prior American terms as *doxy* and *rambler* in denoting (in this instance) the former canal cook who tried to go "society" by dressing in furs, long gloves, lorgnette, and plumed hat, but who instinctively ducked at the call, "Low bridge!" [1]

David Harum, that venerable York Stater in the Edward Westcott novel of 1899, made a point socially as well as semantically about the Old Erie when he remarked at a New-port society banquet that if all the society gentlemen c'd be

15

brought together and someone were to yell "Low bridge!"
nineteen out o' twenty 'd duck their heads! ² Not only had
many persons doubtless worked on the towpath, including
Harum's "society gentlemen," but all canal travellers knew
the danger of which the canal boater's cry of "Low bridge!"
warned. The story goes that the numerous bridges across the
canal were built because the State of New York promised
farmers whose land the canal severed that they would be
provided with bridges for cattle crossing and pedestrian traffic,
but the economy-minded state did not feel obliged to build
them very high!

The Erie experience gave rise to many such colloquialisms
and regional expressions, making the average boater's vocabulary colorful, to say the least. It also had a quite nautical flavor,
impressing upon the non-canalling public the kinship the
Erie canaller felt with his maritime colleagues. While folklore
carries the average canal man's delusions of a higher nautical
status for his calling to an intense degree, there seems little
doubt that some of the sentiment was real. While the tempest-
tossed sea imagery of such ballads as "The Raging Canal" is
but delightful mock-heroic, the sheer length of the canal man's
great "inland water communication," as the local press continued to call the Erie, made it seem worthy of including in
Neptune's domain. The canal packet boats were named after
the sleek sailing craft of the Atlantic service—little matter that
their speed on the Erie was restricted by regulation to *four
miles an hour!* The captain of an Erie packet could proudly
array himself in full seaman's regalia, and his stovepipe hat
and badge of service became to the youth of the times an
appealing and hoped-for goal in life. If he were especially
sporting in his attire, the Erie captain might be called a *ship-
shape macaroni,* a nautical dandy in the most romantic tradi-
tion.³ Towns along the route of the canal were "ports," many
of them of course surviving to this day, dotted throughout
central and western York State: *Gasport, Spencerport, Mid-
dleport, Newport, Port Byron, Brockport,* and—the most
notable of all—*Lockport.* (At Lockport the Erie engineers
and mechanics dropped the Big Ditch over the Niagara escarp-

ment by a group of five pairs of locks, or *combines*, that were
from the beginning a world-renowned tourist attraction, the
famous *Lockport Five*. And, equally impressive, at the western
end of Lockport, was the *Deep Cut*, where nearly two miles
of canal trough were cut through solid rock with an excava-
tion of 1,477,700 cubic yards.[4]) A boater meeting another on
the canal might use a customary greeting from the mariner's
world, "Full freightings, Captain!" and he would refer to his
tour of duty (or that of his help) as a *trick*. At night he slept
in his *cuddy* on the canal boat, a nautical term referring to the
sleeping room or cabin abaft and under the poopdeck on a
ship. The word is thought to have derived from *cubby*, meaning "snug" or "close," and, since the canal boat had but one
cabin the cuddy was especially "close." As a matter of fact,
decorum usually went to the winds and canal boaters and their
cooks more often than not shared this "closeness" to an inti-
mate degree. Canal fiction, particularly in the hands of Walter
D. Edmonds, has recaptured some of this aspect of the Old
Erie and the times when cook's agencies for bachelor boaters
were commonplace in towns along the towpath.

A dictionary of "canalese" probably ought to begin with
some basic words for the canal buff's vocabulary, words and
terms which were in use on the Erie as well as on other canals
in the nineteenth century. The canal itself consisted of a *berm*
side (*berm-bank*, one dictionary suggested, was "actually used
only in U.S.A." [5]) and a towpath side. Sometimes the side opposite the towpath was called the *heelpath*.[6] *Feeders* conveyed
water into the canal to maintain proper level; *waste weirs*
helped to dispose of excess water from the canal. *Tumble-bays*
were sluices which ran around the locks to carry water.[7] At
the canal locks, of course, *locktenders* (or *lock-keeps*, as they
might also be called) opened and closed the gates to let traffic
pass from one level to another. On the Erie, a lock-keep used
his shanty as a kind of combination office and home. At times,
because of the fighting tradition of the average canaller, they
doubtless served as referees as boats jammed together impa-
tiently waiting lockage. At other times the locktender tried
his hand at selling, offering cures for men and mules, in com-

petition to the higglers or peddlers who travelled about selling their wares. Sometimes he operated a grocery; sometimes he ran a saloon. At all events, the lock-keep was a prodigious American type cut from the mold of Benjamin Franklin and the Yankee trader.

At places a lateral canal connected the main channel with an adjacent river, stream, or other canal; this was called a *side-cut*. Probably the most famous side-cut of all, that which connected the Erie in what is now Watervliet to the Hudson River, gave its name to the area. To all canallers it was known as "The Side-cut," a riproaring, notorious place indeed, where fights were even more frequent than was ordinarily the case elsewhere. There was another notable, if less boisterous, side-cut at Little Falls, which brought boats across the Mohawk River into the village. A *long level* denoted a stretch of canal where considerable uninterrupted passage between locks obtained. On the Erie Canal, historically, two "Long Levels" appear in writings about the canal. The longest of these, sometimes called the "Rome Level" or the "Utica Level," was that from Salina to Frankfort, a distance on the Old Erie of sixty-nine and a half miles without locks. Later, when the canal was enlarged and deepened, a lock was placed at Utica and part of the Long Level was straightened at several points, reducing its length to fifty-six miles. The "Rochester Level," which originally extended for about sixty-five‑miles without locks and was not much reduced by the enlargement, became the new Long Level, although the name continued in popular use for the Syracuse-to-Utica run.[8] Erie literature speaks also of the "Genesee Level," the "Fairport Level," and others.

Canallers usually referred to themselves as *boaters*, although writings about the canal in both fiction and nonfiction prefer the former term, sometimes spelled with one "l." *Steersman* also crops up now and again, even in supposedly accurate histories; but there is no evidence to support its use. The man at the tiller bar was, if not a *helmsman*, simply a boater. A canal itself, and particularly the Erie, is spoken of as a *canawl* throughout the literature, whether in story or history, and this term must be assumed to have been used. William Dunlap's three-act comedy of 1828, *A Trip to Niagara*, suggests the peculiar rendering comes from the Palatinate Germans. Others feel it is of Irish or Dutch origin.[9] Fictionists of the towpath invariably tend to use *canawl* and *canawler* with abandon, as they do *hoggee*, that term for "driver-boy" which has become a stock item in the canal buff's dictionary. The term is an inseparable part of Erie Canal lore. Most fictional treatments of the Erie have accepted *hoggee* (rarely *hoggie*) as standard canalese, although contemporary record is not very helpful. One dictionary, using the historical principles approach, even cites as its authority Edmonds' serialized novel, *Red Wheels Rolling*, a document hardly of the nineteenth century and fiction to boot.[10] A *hogler* was "a field laborer of the lowest class" in early England, and there is a Scot diminutive, *hoggie*, which otherwise has the conventional meaning of the word.[11] In British usage, *hog* was also a term for a sixpence and in America for a ten-cent piece. It is possible that a driver-boy, being paid pitifully low wages if at all, earned the epithet *hoggee*. The derivation must be conjectural, however; no nineteenth-century dictionary places it in contemporary canal usage.

In Erie fiction hoggees come in for horrible treatment at the hands of unscrupulous Scrooge-like captains, but in real life some canal workers deserved the wrath of the boat-owners. *Trippers* were a case in point. These were long-haul workmen who went back and forth between the eastern and western terminals of the canal. "If you was to discharge a tripper between ports he'd think it was terrible," complained one captain, "but they quit you any time they please. They're makin' the best of wages all summer, and in the fall, which is the time when freighting on the canal is most rushing and profitable, we have to pay 'em three or four dollars a day and board. . . . A good many are supported in cold weather by the taxpayers. They go to jail purposely—get drunk, you know, and create just enough disturbance to be sent up till spring." [12] Working on the canal produced its own jargon, as one might suspect, some words of which (like *tripper* above) seemed obvious enough. Other expressions, like *Fog-gang*, referring to the workers who cleaned out the canal as an annual routine,[13] are

less decipherable. In the days when the Erie was under construction the canal laborers often had a boy whose job it was
to supply them with whiskey at appropriate intervals during
the day. They called him the *jigger-boss,* and the boy had the
task of doling out half-gills of whiskey to each workman sixteen times a day. Other boys were employed as *runners* to seek
out passengers for the packet trade. The runners, according
to history and legend, contended so vigorously for business
in the Schenectady area that one strip along the canal there
for a long time was referred to as "The Battleground." Somewhat later, when freight hauling largely supplanted passenger
trade as the chief traffic on the Erie, agents concerned with
the assignment of cargoes might find themselves called *scalpers*
by the boaters, and the term finds a place in the play, *The
Farmer Takes a Wife,* made from the original Edmonds' canal
novel dealing with the 1850's. It had the same general connota-
tion as "ticket-scalping," an Americanism which has come down
through canal and railroad parlance to the present day. Immigrant and non-native workers on the canal might be called
foofoos, which Samuel Hopkins Adams called "good Erie lingo
for a foreigner." [14] "Don't you know what a Foo-Foo is?"
asked one of the characters in Bartlett's *A Glance at New
York:* "Well, as you're a greenhorn, I'll enlighten you. A FOO-
FOO, or an outsider, is a chap who can't come the big figure." [15] The "big figure" in this case was three cents for a glass
of grog and a night's lodging.

   Grog meant alcoholic refreshment of various kinds. This
particular term is, of course, not American and certainly not
canalese, but its origin is interesting, since it stems from the
nickname ("Old Grog") given to a British admiral who introduced the drink about 1745, originally as rum diluted with
water. By the time of the Erie Canal, *grog* had a more generic
meaning. Grog, or a tankard of ale (which went by the colloquialism of *foamer*) might in the Erie Canal days be pur-
chased by a Yorker *fip,* a coin worth varying amounts in the
American colonies and states, but usually the equivalent of
about six cents. (The term was an abbreviation and a corruption of *five-penny* or *fi'penny,* denoting a Spanish half-real.)

A canaller's wages could be expressed as "four shillings and found," meaning that the workman received, in addition to a cash stipend, board and lodging as a digger. Ready money or cash he often spoke of as *rhino*, and a person who had a great deal of ready money was *rhino-fat*. During the building of the canal, some workmen were paid in *canal scrip*, IOU's which were backed by the state government and the canal commissioners. Worthless money or banknotes whose credit was gone were called *red dog notes*. They "barked" (today we would speak similarly of a check as "bouncing"); a canaller "couldn't buy a chaw of tobacco with five dollars of 'em." [16] Food in general was called *prog*, boiled or baked potatoes were *pritties* (cf. the Irish *praties*), and buttermilk was *skimmagig*.

The Erie Canal itself had a number of aliases. At first it was known as *Clinton's Ditch*, but gradually, as the project was completed, the term *Big Ditch* stuck and became a term more of awe than of contempt. Even before its completion, however, the canal was being referred to in literature as well as by the public as the *Grand Western Canal* or simply the *Grand Canal*. (Western New York, it should be noted, in 1825, was "the West" to most people.) As the years wore on and enlargement of the canal resulted in changes, the original Clinton's Ditch came to be known as the *Old Erie*, a term which now seems to evoke a sense of nostalgia for the early days of the canal.

Bullhead boat, from a sketch in *Rochester and Its Early Canal Days*, by Capt. H. P. Marsh.

The vessels that rode Erie water were not limited to the simple barges or tankers which became so common a sight on the twentieth-century Barge Canal System. The sleekest craft were the *packets*, which ran for the passenger trade. (See, in the section of illustrations, the broadside advertisement for the Red Bird Line.) *Lineboats* were operated by a transportation company—i.e., a "line," hence the name—and mixed freight and passengers. Both packets and lineboats operated on the same principle as the stage coaches, with changes of horses prearranged along the way. The packet usually had a large cabin amidship, which displayed a row of curtained windows "from stem to stern at each end, and a great bulk of barrels, bales, and boxes" in the middle section.[17] A *freighter* carried no passengers ordinarily, and was far less trim than either a packet or a lineboat. Other miscellaneous craft that frequently travelled Erie water included the *bullhead boats* (thought to have derived their name from a corruption of *ball-head*, since their prows were rounded), *shanty boats* (hovel-type houseboats often anchored on the Erie's setbacks), and the long, clumsy *Durhams*. Riding one of these latter boats, wrote Edmonds, "was almost as slow as dragging heavy wagons through deep ruts"; their crew, he said, were "a hard crowd, and no sensible traveler shipped alone on a Durham boat if he had any money or a decent coat on his back." [18] The *hurry-up* boat has firmly established itself in fiction about the Erie, and while the name seems logical enough as a canal colloquialism, the contemporary record provides no clue regarding the authenticity of the term. Within the narrow channel of the canal and the relative shallowness of the water, it was common enough for canal boats to raise a swell which could damage the earthen sides of the canal. The generally squared fronts of the barges and boats, and the tendency to exceed the four-mile-an-hour limit imposed by the canal commissioners, did not help. Then, too, canal berm could get broken unexpectedly by rains swelling the canal and its feeders, and by rodents and muskrats digging away. The hurry-up boats came to the rescue in such cases of breached berm. ("When they're wanted, they're wanted in a hurry," says a captain in one of the canal novels.[19]) According to some accounts—in the fiction, that is—all other canal boats had to "lay to" for a quarter of an hour after the hurry-up boat had passed on its way to the break. Frequently, as a result of its passing, canal boats were *mudlarked*, that is, grounded or mud-stuck because of an insufficient water level in the canal.

Squeezer and *hoodledasher*, two of the more colorful terms in canalese, have in common the idea of boats in tandem. A squeezer was a two-section canal boat, or a "double-barge." Similarly, the hoodledasher was a hookup where two or more cargoless boats were tied to a full-cargo boat, so one span of mules or horses could draw them all. The latter term in more recent times refers to powered boats which push one barge and tow one or two others behind. How the terms originated no one seems to know.[20]

Gossip travelled "along the tow-line" and one canal wife might well tell another that she "heard it by the towpath news." If she told something she shouldn't, the appropriate phrase was "spill the nosebag"—not unlike today's "spill the beans." While not necessarily restricted to the Erie Canal or New York, fibbing in the nineteenth century went by the curious expression "stretching the blanket," and "hit the logs" referred to the unfortunate state of the corduroy roads in early America. The canaller's oath, "Well, I'll be spavined!" doubtless derived from his frequent distress at having to contend with the disease of the hock of his mules and horses, an enlargement of the leg bone as a result of strain (common, of course, among towpath animals). Mules, in Erie parlance, said one informant, were "long-eared robins." [21] Steam packet men later called them "hayburners." A towpath driver, especially one who signed on to work his way across the state, could refer to his situation as "walkin' passage." "Look for a post!" was a common canal shout having reference to the snubbing posts at intervals along the canal bank where the boats tied up to change horses or to load and discharge passengers and freight.

Numerous words and expressions, like "Low bridge!" and *Brainard barrow* (for a new and efficient wheelbarrow "wonderfully improved, so that its oldest friends hardly knew it" [22]), derived specifically from the Erie situation, while others —*berm*, *locktender*, *towpath*, and *cuddy*, for example—were in use on canals in general. Still others, like *shunpike* (by which travellers avoided tolls by detouring around turnpike toll-houses) and *younker* (or *youngling* or *young 'un*) were a part of Yorker speech without reference to a canal setting. Some words and expressions remain in the language to this day. All of them can be met by anyone reading the abundant literature which deals with nineteenth-century York State. The more spiced of them are met when travelling the Old Erie.

III

The Eighth Wonder
of the World

ALMOST before the proud State of New York could memorialize the completion of the Erie Canal with the grand celebration of 1825, when the "wedding of the waters" inaugurated a new era, travellers—of all classes and countries—seemed eager to be aboard a canal boat.

True, the opening of the canal created a cheap and more convenient means for "getting West," and a host of emigrants to western New York and the Ohio territory poured into the Hudson terminus seeking passage. A chief use of the canal manifested itself also in hauling operations, for the canal offered an inexpensive highway for the shipment of products of a tremendous variety—from salt, foodstuffs and handicrafts, to fuels and fertilizers. These were a part of the history of York State's contribution to economic progress. The bona fide tourist, on the other hand, contributed a great deal to popularizing the canal as a mode of travel; through his accounts the world soon learned of the great American achievement, and, although readers and listeners heard of the torturous sleeping conditions generally found aboard an Erie packet, they came to know the Erie Canal as something to be admired. The derision of "Clinton's Ditch" had inevitably given way before this admiration: far and wide the Erie became known as the Grand Western Canal. A kind of eighth wonder of

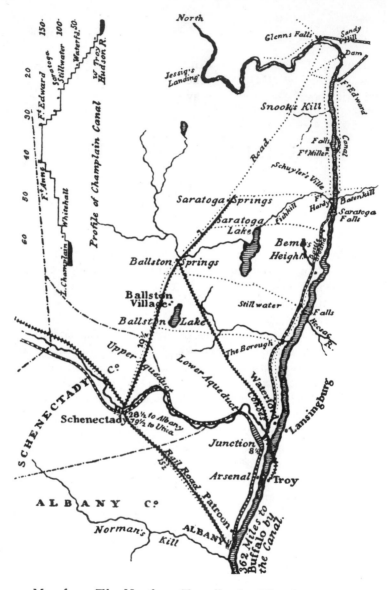

Map from *The Northern Traveller*, by Theodore Dwight
(6th edition, 1841).

the world, it was available to all who could fit a ride on a canal boat into their New York State itinerary.

Before long, such a trip on the Erie Canal became a "must," the American counterpart of the "grand tour" of fashionable European capitals.[1] One traveller, making his first "voyage" on Erie water, discovered this avid interest in the canal. "The truth is," he stated, "the canal is in everybody's mouth." He found words inadequate: "It is not possible for me," he said, "to convey any adequate idea of the pleasure and wealth which floats upon this canal . . . nor of the advantages which are experienced from it by the people who live upon its borders, and to those more remote settlements throughout the entire region of the Northwest."[2] G. M. Davison of Saratoga Springs surmised canal travel more suited to business interests, but he gave a candid and withal favorable appraisal of the Grand Western in his first tour-book to include the Erie, published so opportunely in 1825. Under the heading "CANAL PASSAGE," the note said:

Of the sources of gratification to the tourist, during the canal passage, that of the novelty is perhaps the greatest. To the man of pleasure, it will be considered, perhaps, too little diversified with incident to be repeated; but to the man of business this objection will probably yield to the united considerations of the convenience, safety, and rapidity of this mode of conveyance.[3]

Colonel William Stone, who travelled to Niagara in 1829, thought his packet, *The Superior*, "splendid,"[4] and John Fowler, an Englishman touring in 1830, found that passenger boats "comfortably and conveniently fitted up, are generally preferred to the stage,—are no doubt much easier. . . ."[5] He added, it perhaps should be noted, ". . . but give me land, however bad, or if it *must* be water—the ocean—no 'dull canal with locks and chains.' . . ."

But native Americans generally swelled with genuine pride when they rode on Erie water. According to one manuscript, which first appeared in *The Ariel* of Philadelphia in 1829, a

touring Pennsylvanian remarked that he felt "pleasingly ele-
vated at the thought of travelling on the *Grand Clinton Canal*
for the first time." He marvelled at the economy of the transportation afforded by the canal: "The captain actually en-
gaged to take us to Utica, a distance of 89 miles, for one cent
and a quarter a mile!! a York shilling for each meal extra, and
to make no charge for births [*sic*], which are a very necessary
accommodation, as the boats run day and night." This American tourist had nothing but good words for the Erie. After
"enjoying a pleasant confab" with his fellow travellers, he retired to his "birth," while (he said) "our boat skimmed its
peaceful way along this artificial and wonderful water communication." [6]

Numerous notables toured York State early after the opening of the Erie, and most of them travelled at least part of
the way to Buffalo by canal boat. For those taking the "little
grand tour" of central-western York State, the up route generally went by canal, with the return by stage. In most instances all travellers entering from the Hudson River area took
the stage from Albany to Schenectady, since the twenty-
seven locks over the Cohoes Falls in the few miles between
the two cities made the journey by canal boat impractical.[7]
The stagecoach route, following the turnpike and the old
Mohawk trail, did it in a brief fifteen miles. From Schenectady,
which boasted one of the world's most remarkable bridges at
the time, tourists boarded the packets for Utica and points
beyond. More often than not, a stopover was made at Utica,
at any rate, in order to digress to Trenton Falls, which was
said to out-Niagara Niagara.[8] From Utica either canal boat or
stage was available, some persons definitely preferring the latter after exposure to the sleeping problem aboard an Erie
packet.

On that one issue—sleeping accommodations (or, rather, the
lack of them)—rested many a traveller's feeling of misgiving
for having chosen canal transportation. British actor Tyrone
Power, who made an extensive tour of the United States in
the early 1830's, boarded his first canal packet at Buffalo, an-
ticipating, as he later wrote, "a couple days' quiet travel, which,

if a little monotonous, would be at least unattended by the fatigue and dust of a stage journey" between there and Utica. To his dismay the hot and humid temperatures proved stultifying, with the heat, he said, increasing as the night closed in. He slept "tolerably sound" the first night but awakened "anything but refreshed." The following night he "found it impossible to look upon the cabin. . . . A hotter atmosphere," he said, "can hardly be imagined," so he asked the captain to allow him a mattress on deck. Told that this arrangement was forbidden by existing regulations, he was determined, nonetheless, "not to sleep within the den below, which exhibited a scene of suffocation and its consequences that defies description." Instead he filled his hat with cigars, planted his feet firmly on deck, and resolved, "malgré dews and musquitoes, to weather it through the night." [9]

Conditions did not improve, even after packet boats had years of service and experience. DeVeux' travellers' guide for 1841 considered packets a great relief from the fatigue of railroad cars or the swing of post coaches, but cautioned that "the lodging part, if there are many passengers, cannot be favorably spoken of." Scotsman Patrick Shirreff found his canal packet crowded all the way from Buffalo to Schenectady. "Few things in America seem more extraordinary than the sleeping accommodations of the packets," he noted, adding that the passengers, suspended in rows when in bed, reminded him of strings of onions in a green-grocer's shop.[10] Philip Hone, who was mayor of New York shortly after the Erie opened, confided to his diary that while he found conditions of Erie Canal travel generally quite favorable, "my hammock, to be sure, was rather narrow and not very soft, and my neighbour overhead packed close upon my stomach." [11]

The sleeping situation proved no more tolerable to the American novelist and short story writer, Nathaniel Hawthorne. "I was inclined to be poetical about the Grand Canal," Hawthorne wrote, but his trip on the Erie soon turned to one of "overpowering tedium." A night on the canal boat did not help. With twenty other persons in the cabin, which became the bedchamber when a curtain was lowered between ladies and gentlemen and tiered shelves drawn down for berths, Hawthorne tried vainly to rest. Here is the picture he gave his readers in "Sketches from Memory":

> For a long time our various incommodities kept us all awake except five or six, who were accustomed to sleep nightly amid the uproar of their own snoring, and had little to dread from any other species of disturbance. It is a curious fact that these snorers had been the most quiet people in the boat while awake, and became peacebreakers only when others ceased to be so, breathing tumult out of their repose. Would it were possible to affix a wind instrument to the nose, and thus make a melody of a snore, so that a sleeping lover might serenade his mistress or a congregation snore a psalm tune! Other, though fainter, sounds than these contributed to my restlessness. My head was close to the crimson curtain,—the sexual division of the boat,—behind which I continually heard whispers and stealthy footsteps; the noise of a comb laid on the table or a slipper dropped on the floor; the twang, like a broken harpstring, caused by loosening a tight belt; the rustling of a gown in its descent; and the unlacing of a pair of stays. My ear seemed to have the properties of an eye; a visible image pestered my fancy in the darkness; the curtain was withdrawn between me and the western lady, who yet disrobed herself without a blush.
>
> Finally all was hushed in that quarter. Still I was more broad awake than through the whole preceding day, and felt a feverish impulse to toss my limbs miles apart and appease the unquietness of my mind by that of matter. Forgetting that my berth was hardly so wide as a coffin, I turned suddenly over, and fell like an avalanche on the floor, to the disturbance of the whole community of sleepers. As there were no bones broken, I blessed the accident and went on the deck.[12]

Once on deck, Hawthorne had to admit that the scene—a cloudy sky, an intense darkness on the canal, save for the lanterns at each end of the boat—was an impressive one.

A versatile German tourist to America, Frederick Gerstaecker, had similar feelings about the canal, for he found
that daytime travel on the Erie was comfortable enough but
the evening was hopeless. In an amusingly candid, on-the-spot
account of his trip from New York to Buffalo, he related an
incident which seems to have been all too typical in the
narrow-shelf sleeping "saloon." He awoke in the night with
"a dreadful feeling of suffocation" and cold perspiration on
his forehead. Hardly able to draw breath, he felt a "weight
like lead" on his stomach and chest. When he could not move
the "colossus," as he termed it, he managed to wiggle out his
cravat breastpin, which he proceeded to press "with a firm
hand in the mass above. . . ." The incident concludes:

> A stout heavy man, who slept in the upper frame without a
> mattress, was too much for the well-worn canvas; during
> his sleep it had given way under the weightiest part of his
> form, which descended till it found support on my chest.
> The thrust of the breastpin . . . gave me that opportunity
> of making my escape I so gladly seized.[13]

Charles Dickens had similar problems with the sleeping situation, but, unfortunately for literary historians of the Erie,
chose to do his packet-riding on another canal.[14] But other
writers did travel Erie water, including William Cullen Bryant,
E. E. Hale, Frances Trollope, Fanny Kemble, and Caroline
Gilman, a prolific Southern writer who was one of that "d—d
mob of scribbling women" Hawthorne complained about.

Typical perhaps of the nineteenth century's travelling female, Mrs. Caroline Howard Gilman is of particular interest
to York State by virtue of her having taken passage on an
Erie canal boat, sampled among other forms of transportation
during a "northern excursion" in the late 1830's.[15] Like many
other writer-travellers, Caroline Gilman recorded her impressions and published them. Fortunately—and unlike many of
the diary-writing tourists of the times—she could wield a pen
fairly well and her prose style is sometimes engaging. Her
poetry, on the other hand, is often poetry in name only; but

she called her little book of impressions *Poetry of Travelling*.
Poetry might be an appropriate title at that. Her first impression of the canal, at Cohoes Falls, is almost lyrical:

> I have never seen canal navigation before, and here the very
> majesty of canal-ism dwells, wielding his lazy sceptre over
> the Erie and Champlain channels. There is a remarkable
> variety of objects along this little region. The cars whirl by
> on the Troy and Ballston rail-road, mocking the slow canal
> boats, that peep up from the banks like tortoises; while small
> boats—for no craft of importance can navigate here—glide
> over the diminished Hudson, seen among the emerald isles
> that diversify its tranquil stream.

She boarded a packet at Schenectady, after making a duti-
ful stop at Troy to visit the famous lady educator, Mrs.
Willard, at her female seminary. The traveller admitted to trying the canal out of curiosity. Some random excerpts from
her journal provide an insight, as typical as any on-the-spot
accounts of tourists, into canal boat travel.

> We saw nothing of Schenectady, passing directly into a
> canal boat, which, being a novelty, we wished to test. Up-
> wards of forty persons were crowded into this small space,
> there being no restrictions as in stages. Why not? Why
> should these boats be crowded indiscriminately? Fortunately
> for us the company were respectable. . . .
> Everything connected with this mode of conveyance
> . . . [is] disagreeable, but . . . [w]hen it is possible to be
> on deck, canal navigation is pleasant enough. I do not at all
> object to bobbing one's head down at the bridges—it is some-
> what exciting. . . . When we are all prostrated, I always
> peep about to see how comically everybody looks. . . .
> [T]hen what a change to our cabin, three tiers deep, with
> berths on each side! But the difficulty of moving an elbow
> was mitigated by the perfect good humor of the com-
> pany. . . .

This "good-natured feeling" Mrs. Gilman found somewhat to her surprise. "Are the scenes I have witnessed," she asked in her journal, "really among the same population which English travellers have described? Am I dreaming, when I find only courtesy among the cultivated and quietness among the other classes?" Caroline Gilman, it should be noted, was a proslavery Southerner touring New York and New England with something of aristocratic condescension. Like most informed writers she had doubtless read widely in the abundant literature of travel, published in large part by English tourists who did not often find Americans—or the Erie Canal—to their liking.

Her journey on the Erie produced the inevitable poem. After a rather maudlin entry in her "Notes," she admitted to a feeling of melancholy induced by the "loneliness and dejection" of the route between Schenectady and Utica; the sinking of the sun as she stood on deck added to her inspiration. Here are a few stanzas of the result, to which she gave the title "Music on the Canal":

> I was weary with the day-light,
> I was weary with the shade,
> And my heart became still sadder,
> As the stars their light betrayed;
> I sickened at the ripple,
> As the lazy boat went on,
> And felt as though a friend was lost
> When the twilight ray was gone.
>
> The meadows in a fire-fly glow,
> Looked gay to happy eyes;
> To me they beamed but mournfully,
> My heart was cold with sighs.
> They seemed, indeed, like summer friends;—
> Alas, no warmth had they!
> I turned in sorrow from their glare,
> Impatiently away.
>
> And tear drops gathered in my eyes,
> And rolled down my cheeks,

And when the voice of mirth was heard,
  I had no heart to speak.
I longed to press my children
  To my sad and homesick breast,
And feel the constant hand of love
  Caressing and carest.

There is no evidence that Caroline Gilman ever again rode a canal boat on the Erie Canal, but she did reach a sufficient prominence as a belles-lettrist to be included among other references in Davidson's *The Living Authors of the South* and Hart's *Female Prose-Writers of America*. At Utica, she was happy to be off the canal. She took a stage coach to her next stop.

When the celebrated Shakespearean actor Charles Kemble came to America in 1832, he brought with him his daughter, actress Fanny Kemble, who became an immediate sensation on the New York stage. In her *Journal*, kept during this American tour, the young lady seemed to have nothing but compliments to pay to the country which had received her so warmly. At one point in her itinerary she went from Schenectady to Utica on the Erie, confiding in her *Journal*, "I like travelling by canal boats very much"; the valley of the Mohawk was "beautiful from beginning to end." [16] The only disquieting features of an otherwise fully pleasant journey for her were the "nuisances" of low bridges (being obliged to prostrate herself on deck she called "humiliation") and the prospect of sleeping in "the horrible hencoop allotted to the female passengers."

But this trip on the Erie Canal provided the Kemble troupe nonetheless with enjoyable diversion from the rigors of stage travel: the canal boat was slow, but "infinitely preferable to the noise of wheels, the rumble of a coach, and the jerking of bad roads."

Another "Fanny"—Frances Trollope, mother of the English novelist Anthony Trollope and something of a literary personage in her own right—seems to have found her junket on the Erie Canal unpalatable even as a diversion. "I can hardly imagine any motive of convenience powerful enough," she

declared firmly in her *Domestic Manners of the Americans,*
"to induce me to imprison myself again in a canal boat under
ordinary circumstances." Her reasons she stated forthrightly:

> The accommodations being greatly restricted, everybody,
> from the moment of entering the boat, acts upon a system
> of unshrinking egotism. The library of a dozen books, the
> backgammon board, the tiny berths, the shady side of the
> cabin, are all jostled for in a manner to make one greatly
> envy the power of the snail; at the moment I would will-
> ingly have given up some of my human dignity for the
> privilege of creeping into a shell of my own. To any one
> who has been accustomed to travelling, to be addressed
> with, "Do sit here, you will find it more comfortable," the
> "You must go there, I made for this place first," sounds very
> unmusical.[17]

Yankees and Yankee speech caught the traveller's interest.
In a transcript of an overheard conversation, Mrs. Trollope
indicated her amusement that Yankee talk just "got nowhere"
—the two conversing persons "went on, without advancing or
giving an inch, 'till I weary of listening." Her chief amusement during the trip, however, derived from the names given
to canal towns, especially to such incongruous naming as
"Port Byron" for a "town" consisting solely of a whiskey store
and a warehouse!

About the only memorable event in an otherwise oppressive
and tedious trip for Mrs. Trollope was the traditional side-tour
to Trenton Falls. She thought this—in contrast to canal boat
travel—"a delightful drive" in "a very pleasant airy carriage."
The Falls were impressive, and the pleasure of the trip was
heightened by her discovery of an inscription, "Trollope, England," which had been scrawled into the rock among the
numerous tourists' autographs. "The well known characters
were hailed with such delight," she said, "that I think I shall
never again laugh at anyone for leaving their name where it is
possible a friend may find it." (Mr. Trollope and a son,
Thomas A. Trollope, had visited the area in 1829; Fanny's

account of the side-trip is one of the fullest of the travellers'
accounts of Trenton Falls.)

She had very little of good to say for the Old Erie. She
did find the "little falls of the Mohawk . . . a lovely scene,"
however, and actually considered the town of Little Falls a
beautiful village. At the western end of her trip, she remarked
upon the beauty also of the Oneida and Genesee country,
but hastened to add that "had we not returned by another
route [i.e., by stage] we should have known little about it."

"From the canal," Mrs. Trollope concluded, "nothing is
seen to advantage, and very little is seen at all."

Another English literary figure, the novelist Captain Frederick Marryat, took things more in stride, perhaps because he
found to his complete pleasure that "the American women are
the *prettiest* in the whole world." [18] Going to Utica by way of
Saratoga—the longer but fashionable way—Marryat proceeded to Oswego via canal boat: "a very small affair," he
said, "about fifty feet long by eight feet wide"; but the captain of the packet interested him:

> The captain of her was, in his own opinion, no small affair;
> he puffed and swelled until he looked larger than his boat.
> This personage, as soon as we were underweigh, sat down
> in his narrow cabin, before a small table; sent for his writing-
> desk, which was about the size of a street organ, and, like
> himself, no small affair; ordered a bell to be rung in our
> ears to summon the passengers; and then, taking down the
> names of four or five people, received the enormous sum of
> ten dollars passage-money. He then locked his desk with a
> key large enough for a street-door, ordered his steward to
> remove it, and went on deck to walk just three feet and re-
> turn. After all, there is nothing like being a captain.

He admitted that parts of his *Diary* might be slow reading.
"I get on very slow with my description, but canal travelling
is very slow," he apologized.

Duke Bernhard, of Saxe-Weimar Eisenbach, touring Erie
country in 1825–26, appeared to have a typical European con-

descension toward anything American. The canal was completed, he wrote in his *Reise durch Nord-Amerika*,[19] "without calling to aid the great experience possessed by other nations." The Erie Canal does "the greatest honor to the genius of its progenitor," he admitted, adding, however, that "one who has seen the canals in France, Holland, England, will readily perceive, that the water works of this country afford much room for improvements." Thoroughly pessimistic about American canal engineering, he commented that the wooden aqueducts and the locks would probably soon need repairing, and "the gates also lock badly, so that the water which percolates forms artificial cascades."

During a stopover at Schenectady he found Givens Hotel "excellent" but he thought Union College from "its decaying appearance . . . not in a very prosperous condition." Boarding the packet *Samuel Young* for Utica, he suffered that night from the usual want of decent sleeping berths, but remarked, upon reaching his destination, that Utica was the "most flourishing town in New York." He especially liked the Utica taverns, for being "perfectly comfortable, and proportionately cheap." Despite all his feelings, the Duke concluded that "Americans, in general, are quiet people"; he distinctly *liked* one thing: the fact that tipping in an American inn or tavern was not an obligation as in European hostelries.

Doubtless the most vigorous voice raised against Americans by an Erie Canal traveller in these early days of tourists was that of Captain Basil Hall, whose *Travels in North America* caused, according to Frances Trollope, "a sort of moral earthquake." [20] Captain Hall reported candidly, to be sure, and some readers, judging from the controversy which raged about this bestseller, felt he purposely failed to see the country to any advantage whatsoever.[21]

Taking, he said, the road-book *The Northern Traveller* as his guide,[22] he contracted at Albany with a stage company for a private coach to take his family to Niagara. Hall thus began his tour with little thought for canal boat travel, but he found the arrangements did include canal transportation as well. At Schenectady he discovered the canal basin to be a beehive of activity. "I have seldom seen a more busy scene," he observed. "Crowds of boats laden with flour, grain, and other agricultural produce, were met by others as deeply laden with goods from all parts of the world, ready to be distributed over the populous regions of the west." He commented favorably on Watervliet, where he found the Arsenal City, with fifty thousand stand of arms, in good order against any national emergency; but he disliked the "scraggy meal" his party was served in Troy. En route to Caughnawaga by packet, his first experience with "low bridge—everybody down" was a novelty at first, "amusing to hop down and then to hop up again," but this became "very tedious" after a while. Sleeping berths he thought "extremely ingenious" aboard the canal boat and, unlike most of his contemporaries, he did not enter in his record a lengthy vituperation against the accommodations.

His chief criticism was not of the canal—or indeed of any American institution—but rather of the American passengers themselves. He found them, like most other tourists, indifferent to the beautiful scenery. They were travelling—unless for business reasons—more for the sake of saying they had done it than for any enjoyment of the travel itself. "There was, I grant," he remarked, "a great deal of talk about such things; and we had seen in their road-books and other writings much about the extraordinary wonders, and the natural beauties of their country; but, as yet, generally speaking, we had met a perfect insensibility to either, on the part of the inhabitants." [23]

The Erie Canal in Captain Hall's pages fares not too badly, however, for he was not so critical of the great waterway as he was of other facets of American civilization. As a matter of fact, canal traffic intrigued him, and at one port he became particularly amused "by seeing, amongst the throng of loaded boats, a gaily-printed vessel . . . with the words CLEOPATRA'S BARGE painted in large characters on her broadside." He thought the great span across the Genesee River at Rochester a "noble aqueduct"; Utica he also liked because, compared with other towns in the state, it was a step higher in the "progressive scale of civilization," among other reasons because there was located "at no great distance an institution, called Hamilton College, intended, I was told, for the higher branches of science." [24]

Another Englishman, John Shaw, taking what he called a "ramble" through the United States, Canada, and the West Indies, frankly acknowledged that he felt the United States "a truly go-ahead country," but he despaired having one's "brains knocked out by passing under bridges so low in construction" while travelling on American canals. This singular and "extraordinary neglect of parties at the head of affairs grossly neglecting to apprise passengers of the danger" proved intolerable to him. Mr. Shaw did not travel on the famed Erie, however, but made his trip on a branch canal.[25]

In sharp contrast to those who complained, other foreign visitors found touring by canal, if not thrilling, at least pleasurable enough. A number of travellers even felt the Erie tour memorable in some respects. The revolutionary hero, Marquis de Lafayette, travelling on the canal during his triumphal tour of the twenty-four United States in 1824–25, marvelled at the aqueducts over which the Erie Canal "pursued an aerial route" sometimes "for more than a quarter of a mile, at an elevation of 70 feet." His secretary Levasseur, who kept a journal of the trip, remarked that "the horses and the tow-path were excellent, we travelled rapidly and comfortably; for the boat [the *Rochester*] that carried us, was much more convenient and better provided with the comforts of life than would have been supposed." Levasseur commended the engineering as well, adding, "The bridges are usually of an elegance and boldness of execution that is inconceivable." [26]

Another Frenchman, Michael Chevalier, whose *Society, Manners and Politics in the United States* presented a study in the Alexis de Tocqueville manner, considered the Erie Canal, while not especially noteworthy as an object of art, certainly an object of admiration. It contrasted sharply, he reminded his fellow Europeans, with the Old World's engineering accomplishments:

From our canals, which are navigated by heavy and clumsy boats slowly and painfully dragged forward . . . , you can get no idea of this great channel, with its fleet of light, elegant, covered barks gliding along at a rapid rate, and drawn by a powerful team. Every minute boats are passing each other, and the boatman's horn warns the lock-master to be in readiness. Each moment the landscape varies; now you traverse large new towns, fine as capitals, with all their houses having pillared porticos and looking externally like little palaces; it is an admirable spectacle of life and variety.[27]

Foreign tourists on the Erie Canal often remarked upon the characteristic democracy of the canal region. Frenchmen like Chevalier generally commented favorably regarding both the people and the engineering of Canal Era America. An occasional Englishman, like James Stuart in *Three Years in North America* (1833) saw the "utter democracy" as a continuous fascination;[28] but ordinarily the English tourists, particularly those from aristocratic or Tory backgrounds, looked upon the average American as unrefined; and Nordic nobility like Duke Bernhard could hardly have been expected to appreciate something so remote to their circumstances as the American experience. They all—including Fanny Trollope and the Basil Halls—had to admit that individual Americans did impress them favorably from time to time, but on the whole the English were perhaps too close to the War of Independence and the affair of 1812 to travel with an unjaundiced eye on even so renowned a waterway as the Grand Western Canal.[29]

But the travellers did come, and in great number, proving the world's awareness of the young nation's accomplishment —actually of one state's accomplishment. "The packet-boats of the Erie Canal," said Edward Hungerford, "represent a pleasant phase of the romantic era of American travel about which much can be said."[30] Much *was* said, and tourists on York State's grand canal made a rather large contribution to Erie literature. Fortunately for the historian of the Erie, they seem almost always to have had pen in hand.

IV

The Old Erie:
Canal and Canallers

LONG before the Erie Canal joined the Great Lakes to the Hudson, York State had acquired a considerable legendry. Much of it, of course, was aboriginal—like the stories of Occuna, the young Seneca killed at the Falls of Cohoes, and the "Thunder-water" tales of Niagara; and some resulted from the colonial and early national experience—such as the "Baker's Dozen" which originated in Albany, the composing of "Yankee Doodle" across the Hudson at Fort Crailo, and the birth of "Uncle Sam" at Troy. The Erie Canal gave Yorkers a new bounty of stories, legends and other lore to add to an already impressive heritage.

The two valley systems which the Erie utilized and united— the Mohawk and the Hudson—offered a locale already made fertile by history and tradition. "Most storied of our New World rivers is the Hudson," wrote Charles Skinner in *Myths and Legends of Our Own Land*. "It had its source in the red man's fancy, in the spring of eternal youth; giants and spirits dwelt in its woods and hills." [1] Shatemuc, "king of streams," the red men had called it. And the Mohawk River appeared no less favored. To the Indians it was Te-non-an-at-che, "the river flowing through mountains." The noted British actor, Tyrone Power, reflected the thoughts of countless other nineteenth-century travellers and tourists when he remarked that

"no valley in the world can present charms more varied or
more beautiful." [2] When General George Washington toured
the Mohawk Valley in 1782 and 1783, he felt it would become
the "pathway to empire," and the Erie Canal implemented the
fulfillment of that prophecy.

The effect of this heritage—traditional and historic—was
pronounced; and Erie lore, legends, stories, tall tales, songs,
and folk characters provided a considerable deposit of folk
materials. The folklore of the Erie Canal has antecedents both
indigenous and universal in nature, for the Old Erie, while
spawning many a canawler who could claim a towpath unique-
ness, gave rise to a number of Erie tales which are recognizable
hero tales and *Sagen*, known to folklorists around the world,
having their counterparts in other areas, even in other countries,
apart from towpath and berm.

At the Erie Basin in Buffalo the Old Erie met with Lake
Erie, a principal source of its water and its commerce. Here
the lore of York State is intertwined with that of the Great
Lakes, and the tales that are told often are more "lake" than
"canal," like that of the storm-hag carcagne, held to be responsible for the disappearance of ships on Ontario and Erie;
or stories involving smuggling ships called *owlers*, by which
canallers (as well as other shipmen) dealt in contraband with
Canada.[3] From Buffalo the original Erie Canal ran to Black
Rock, then along the Niagara River bank, following Tonawanda Creek to the mountain ridge. Here was the country of
the Niagara frontier, where Indian legend tells of Heno, the
Thunderer, who long ago held forth his arms to save a beautiful maiden from death in the Falls. And at the famed Niagara
Falls themselves, a mecca for newlyweds, the "Maid of the
Mist" still dwells, according to legend, in a crystal heaven far
beneath the swirling waters.[4]

At Lockport the great combines lowered the canal down
from the Niagara escarpment and evoked immediate admiration
from everyone who saw this marvel of American engineering.
Even those less inclined to praise Americans in this early period
felt, as a German tourist put it some time later, that the

famous Lockport Five was "a noble work for so young a country." [5] The accomplishment at Lockport, one of the final tasks undertaken on the original Erie project, seemed inspiring to everybody. "Here," wrote a noted Southern traveller in the 1830's, "the great Erie Canal has defied nature, and used it like a toy; lock rises upon lock, and miles are cut in the solid stone." [6]

From there the canal took an easy course to the Genesee country and to Rochester, over one of the long levels, where for about sixty miles traffic flowed smoothly, uninterrupted by locks. A few miles east of Lockport, where the Genesee Level began, lay Gasport, a typical and thriving canal community in the nineteenth-century Erie days.

> It lay in a prosperous farming community. The better-class houses were owned by merchants and retired farmers. There was one business street, with the bridge, which separated the prosperous side from the poorer class. On this street, and on the prosperous side of the bridge, were the general store, the drug store, the butcher shop, the feed store, the undertaker, and strange to say, the saloons. Nearby, along the side streets, among the stately elms, on the prosperous side of town, of course, were the churches and the residences of the church trustees. There was social rank in Gasport, and the trustees of the church were also the pillars of the state. Some of them were narrow and bigoted in religion and very strict as to the observance of the Sabbath, but in politics and business they were not so particular. [7]

Medina, between Gasport and Albion, once made Ripley's "Believe It or Not" columns for its road running *under* the canal, a byway appropriately called "Culvert Road." Named for the sacred city of Mohammedanism, Medina began its prosperous growth when Clinton's Ditch opened the Brockport-to-Lockport section in 1824. At the end of the first decade of the Old Erie, Medina boasted "the most pretentious hostelry in the region." This landmark, topped with a gilded bird on its belfry, was the Eagle Tavern, built smack beside the canal. [8]

The Genesee River was crossed at Rochester on an impressive stone aqueduct. When completed in 1823, the Grand Canal Aqueduct—804 feet long with nine Roman arches—was the longest stone arch bridge in America. Built of red Medina sandstone, with a coping of gray limestone, it lasted for nineteen years.

The "Young Lion of the West," as Rochester was called, owed its success to the Erie. "It was a broad river and power-packed waterfalls that gave Rochester being," wrote Rochester newspaperman Arch Merrill, "but it was a narrow shallow ditch that made it great. The tumbling waters turned the mill wheels but the slow, steady flow of the Clinton Ditch carried Genesee flour to the markets of the world." [9] Within ten days after the opening of the canal, Rochester had shipped 10,000 barrels of flour. The town that was "Rochesterville" a decade before, with a population of some 300, almost overnight became a burgeoning canal town, with nearly 8,000 residents by 1826.

From Rochester, the Erie Canal ran through Fairport and into Wayne County, named for "Mad" Anthony of history and ballad; it passed through drumlin country with its hillocks formed by prehistoric glacial drift. Eastward lay Palmyra, "Pal" to the canawlers and to natives, the town depicted in Samuel Hopkins Adams' novel *Canal Town*. Near by, on the "Hill of Cumorah," Joseph Smith received the golden plates of the Book of Mormon, and Mormonism got its start. Some refer to Smith as "The Prophet of Palmyra." Near Palmyra, too, Spiritualism came into being in the spring of 1848, when the Fox sisters at Hydesville heard the knockings which they felt obliged to interpret for the world. They demonstrated for such notables as Bryant, Cooper, Bancroft, and Carlyle; and even when the fraud was exposed, Spiritualism as a movement kept on, continuing to almost deify the Fox sisters.[10]

Beyond Palmyra, the canal stretched out over the drumlin country through Newark, the rose center of New York State; Lyons, already twenty-two years old when the canal work began; and Clyde, both town and river named by a Scot who remembered his homeland, even christening the main street

"Glasgow Street." Then through relatively level land the Big Ditch passed through Montezuma, which gave its name to the notorious marshlands, to Port Byron, where an obscure cobbler, Henry Wells, went on to fame as one member of the Wells-Fargo transportation partnership that helped shape the West, and where Isaac Singer built his first sewing machine. A little south of the canal, at the tip of Owasco Lake and joined to the Grand Western by the Owasco Creek feeder, lay Auburn, which, according to one longtime resident "swapped its chances of the Erie Canal for the solider State's Prison and got the worst of the bargain." [11] Sam Adams should know, for he was, without doubt, a veritable son of the Erie Canal; and from "Wide Waters," the old residence at Auburn, came many stories and novels about Erie country and the days of the wondrous canawlers.

Salt and the Erie made Syracuse; near that city lay one of the greatest salt deposits in the United States, known from colonial times. Early trade in salt centered in the two areas around Salina, in central York State, and Pittsburgh, in western Pennsylvania. When the Erie provided Syracuse (just south of the old Salina) with hauling facilities, the salt market languished in Pittsburgh, chiefly a distribution point; and Syracuse salt, needed in western settlements, helped to develop the Niagara frontier as a transfer and trans-shipment area.[12] In Syracuse today stands what was until recently the last state-owned canal building, the Weighlock Building, dating from 1850. The building has been converted into a canal museum, opened in 1962.

North of Syracuse, on the route of the Erie division of the later Barge Canal, Three Rivers marks the heart of the state, where the Oneida and Seneca Rivers join to make the Oswego. The Oswego River, and later the Oswego Canal, provided from this point a link with Lake Ontario.

As the early canal boats moved eastward, passing south of Oneida Lake and entering Rome, New York, the Erie was finally done with the long cut through western New York State; from Rome, the Erie Canal followed the Mohawk Valley. In later years, as the fabulous days of the Canal Era passed into fond memory, the New York State Barge Canal was confined more and more to the channels of the Mohawk itself; and the old towpaths, locks, and berms became drydocked markers overrun with crabgrass and moss, or filled in, like Canal Street in Watervliet, or Erie Boulevard in Schenectady and in Syracuse, to make roadways for growing cities. At Rome (where the first "Stars and Stripes" had flown in battle) the first spadeful of earth was turned to begin the building of the canal on that Fourth of July in 1817. Later, down from the north country, the Black River Canal—with its great lock system—brought its tremendous commerce into confluence with the Erie at Rome.

As has already been mentioned, Rome seemed a natural place to begin construction of the Erie Canal. If the canal backers had started at Albany, the opposition might have been able to show that it did not pay. But Rome was situated on what would be one of the Erie's "long levels" which ran uninterrupted by locks from Frankfort to Salina. Beginning there, the progress could be immediate. It was. On October 22, 1819, a little over two years after the first spadeful of earth was turned at Rome, the first canal boat, named *The Chief Engineer* as a compliment to Benjamin Wright, made the trip from Utica to Rome in four hours. A section of the Grand Western Canal had opened, and boat trips gradually became longer as the canal itself was built farther and farther in both directions from Rome.

In Utica, as in other canal towns, the Erie brought prosperity and growth. "It is clear," said William Cullen Bryant's *Picturesque America,* "that the impetus of the city is not derived from the river, but from the Erie Canal; for the streets are all built in the proximity of the latter, and the former is outside of the town altogether." [13] Not until 1918 was the old canal abandoned and the canal lands turned over to the city for filling in. The city fathers in 1923 removed one of the more memorable landmarks: a hideous bridge across the canal. The biggest of many bridges over the canal in Utica, this one had been painted green and appropriately dubbed "The Green Elephant." [14]

Eastward from Utica, where after 1836 the 97-mile-long Chenango Canal joined the Erie, the Big Ditch passed through towns rich in colonial and Revolutionary legends—Herkimer, Frankfort, the "German Flatts," and Little Falls. It had meanwhile passed over seven creeks by aqueducts of various lengths. At Little Falls, a lengthy aqueduct stretched across the Mohawk River, connecting the Erie with the village. Canal boats could take this "siding" into Little Falls or through boats could continue on in the main canal on the south side of the river. This region, at the "Little Falls of the Mohawk," had been one of the first portage areas discussed by the early canal advocates, even in colonial days; "improvement work" was begun as early as 1793 in the vicinity, and the first locks were operative in 1796. Rising on the south side of the Mohawk a steep hill called "The Rollaway" could be seen, at the foot of which the canal ran on a channel blasted out of solid rock. Near by, tourists and visitors could see "Profile Rock," which *Picturesque America* in 1874 called "one of the institutions of the place," a landmark "where the stone has been so mauled, and had its stratification so handled, that the very fair likeness to a human profile has been washed out." [15]

In the Fort Hunter region canal traffic encountered Schoharie Crossing, a formidable test, at times of high water, of a canaller's skill and patience. Here the Erie Canal crossed Schoharie Creek on a long dam. Walter D. Edmonds shows in one story something of the canaller's attitude toward the crossing.[16] When boats went over the dam with the flood waters, sometimes more delay than serious harm resulted; often they were not badly damaged, but, as Edmonds put it, "they had to float them down the river as far as Schenectady to get back into the canal!"

Just to the west of Schoharie Creek, some of the German Palatinates had settled. They were freeholders, unlike the tenant farmers of the Hudson Valley patroon system. In ancient times, the "Palatine Bridge Fairies" dwelt in the region; stemming from Indian legend, the fairies gave a hunter game any time he needed it, and could appear and vanish at their pleasure.[17] Also, in this area, according to the half-fact, half-fic-

tional recollections of Samuel Hopkins Adams, the "Palatine
Doiches" created the first school outhouse. Thus, as Adams
so appropriately put it, "was the little red schoolhouse aug-
mented by the little white outhouse." [18] Near by, on the route
of the canal, lay Auriesville, where in 1656 Catherine Tek-
akwitha, the Indian Catholic "lily of the Mohawks," was
born, and where today in her honor stands the Shrine of Our
Lady of Martyrs.

Schenectady, which an Edmonds character called "the
Dutchest damned town in this country," was the crossroads
of New York State, the real gateway to the Mohawk Valley.
From here the colonial roads, and later a turnpike, led westward. Across the river enterprising Schenectadians had built
what they boastingly referred to as "the biggest bridge in the
world," a marvel commented upon by townsfolk and travellers alike.[19] Old Dorp (as Schenectady was called because of
its Dutch heritage) grew with the Erie Canal, despite the fact
that in 1825 its citizenry—along with Rome's—refused to
enter into the jubilant celebration which commemorated the
canal's completion. (Rome's disappointment stemmed from
the canal planners' routing the canal outside the village; Schenectady felt that the canal, by robbing Schenectady of the
Mohawk terminus and carry to Albany, would cause a setback
to the city's prosperity.[20]) Yet by 1829 competition among
packet boats for passengers had reached such a keen pitch that
their runners turned one strip of the canal into "The Battleground," a name it retained for a considerable time. In 1831
the first train from Albany came into Schenectady on the
new rail line; this locomotive, ironically, was named "DeWitt
Clinton," in honor of the father of the Erie Canal, long the
railroad's staunchest rival.

Curving toward Cohoes, the canal went through twenty-
seven locks before it reached Albany, only fifteen miles away
by the overland route. At Niskayuna, near the site of the
canal, Charles P. Steinmetz, the "wizard of electricity," la-
bored, and a stone from the old Erie aqueduct near by provided a base for a Schenectady plaque honoring him. Near
by, too, General Electric Company engineers designed "elec-

tric mules" for hauling canal boats, but experiments proved them not feasible. At Crescent, an aqueduct over 1,100 feet long carried canal traffic back across the Mohawk as it neared Cohoes. The falls of "Cahoos" provided perhaps the most formidable obstacle for the canal engineers; yet, where William Weston had prophesied that it would take two years, Erie contractors and Irish laborers finished the job in far less time, overcoming the falls by a series of locks that were the marvel of the engineering world. Cohoes, already a manufacturing center, became the "Lowell of New York," its shirts and woolens making, this early, a bid for leadership in the world market.

Turning south, the canal cut through Watervliet, called the "Arsenal City" from the location there of a U.S. government arsenal. Originally "West Troy," Watervliet was more familiarly known to canallers as "The Side-cut," so called because of the lateral canal, or side-cut, connecting the Erie with the Hudson River and, hence also, with Troy on the east bank. The wild character of a few square blocks, notorious for the number of saloons, gave the area a rough-and-tumble reputation. Troy, on the Hudson's east bank, doubtless owed its economic prosperity to its location at the confluence of the Hudson and Mohawk rivers and of the Erie and Champlain canals. According to Trojan conjecture, Uncle Sam, the symbol of America, was born there; and it was Troy's *Sentinel* for December 23, 1823, which published anonymously the Rev. Dr. Clement Clarke Moore's "Account of a Visit from St. Nicholas," which made the jolly gentleman and his "eight tiny reindeer" a permanent part of Christmas lore. Troy industry boasted the largest water wheel in the world and, with the success of the Erie forecast, Trojans, with more enthusiasm than common sense, proposed in 1825 building a canal from Troy to Boston! [21] The detachable collar, "invented" in Troy, gave "The Collar City" its commercial nickname.[22] By 1850, because of its commercial prominence, Troy had numerous boat lines—like the Troy Tow-Boat Company (131 boats and barges, 840 men, 500 boys, and 1,000 horses)—operating on the Erie, Champlain, and Hudson waterways.[23] Perhaps, as far as the Erie Canal is concerned, the most important thing Troy had to offer was Rensselaer Polytechnic Institute, founded (November 5, 1824), so it is said, largely as a school for educating engineers for the canals of New York State. The first graduating class, with George Clinton a member, took a scientific "botanizing expedition" on the Erie Canal in 1826.[24]

Some 360 miles from Buffalo, the Grand Erie Canal coursed along the Hudson's banks from Watervliet to the great basin at Albany. Here was the capital city of the state and the eastern terminus of the canal. In 1825, when the canal opened, bread could be had for a penny a loaf and the canaller's skimmagig for two cents a quart. When the original Dutch settlers lived there, folklore tells us that, in Baas Volchert Jan Pietersen Van Amsterdam's bake-shop on New Year's Eve in 1654, the legend of the baker's dozen was born; today an annual tulip festival—complete with *Kinderkermis* (a children's parade), Dutch costuming, and Holland-bulb tulips—recreates each spring something of the Dutch life which influenced the city.[25] Long known as *Fort Orange*, Albany still retains this name in familiar parlance among many people of the capital district area.

Most visitors found old Fort Orange impressive. "The Americans," wrote an Englishman stopping in Albany in 1840, "know how to build towns as they ought to be built," and he praised Albanians for having "nothing to do with . . . unwholesome narrow streets" as he "walked down that noble one, called State Street" and over the bridge "thrown across the basin of the great Erie Canal." [26] (At the top of "noble" State Street hill today sits the State Capitol building, its "million dollar staircase" made of great blocks of Medina-quarried red sandstone, hauled to Albany by canallers on Clinton's Ditch.) The canal basin at Albany had a pier enclosing the basin on the river side: "a place of deposit," so the guide-books of the times stated, "for vast quantities of lumber." [27] When everyone was preparing for the opening ceremonies of 1825, Albany built a pier where 2,000 canal boats could be handled; in 1831, nearly 15,000 of them arrived and departed from New York State's capital.

The historic upstate region from Buffalo to Albany sprang into a hustle-bustle of life with the opening of the Erie. Men and women of various sorts were molded into a new kind of being—the canaller, or *canawler*, as they seemed to prefer it along the towpath. Their work and lives, in an area already rich in folklore and traditions, added to the cultural deposit of the upstate regions. Of these canallers, many developed into folk characters, some achieving nearly legendary status as their stories were passed along the towline. And there were others—local eccentrics, for example, and boatmen in love, or hucksterish locktenders selling liniments and oils for men and mules.

Such folk characters who derived from the Erie context provide one index to the influence of the Grand Canal on folklore. They might be classified roughly into three general categories: first, the canallers themselves, who lived and worked on the canal; second, those persons who can perhaps best be described as "marginal" Erie folk characters; and, third, the folk hero transplanted to Erie water, usually by literary means, from some other locale set in more authentic folk tradition.

The first of these types—the indigenous canawler—probably had no sophistication whatever, and only in an instinctive way recognized any group or class loyalty. Yet as a group the canallers possess compelling characteristics of interest to the folk historian. The canaller and his culture represented a rather definite, separate social grouping, one apart from the mainstream of society. He was both mobile and caught; unlike the gypsy who roamed rather freely (if on a kind of circuit), the canaller had a limited mobility on and along the waterway. Often it was not really the full extent of the canal; he lived and worked on the "narrow ribbon of water," on the main Erie, occasionally on side canals, sometimes on the Oswego to Lake Ontario, sometimes (in the early days) down the Hudson River to New York. All non-canallers were "outsiders" who rarely if ever understood the inner feelings of the canaller or appreciated fully his code. For the canaller did have a code, peculiar to the canal; it bound all canalmen together and made them the social group they were. Just as with other, more well-defined minority segments of the population, they were bound together by particular mores, ethics and morality, and *modus vivendi*. (The canaller on the Erie fits into this pattern of social grouping more easily than does his counterpart on other waterways—in Pennsylvania, for example, where the canals were more numerous but extended relatively few miles each, the canaller was forced more frequently into contact with the general population and did not live as fully "on the canal" as his New York State fellow.) Fiction dealing with the Erie is filled with the problems which this group status engendered whenever the canaller stepped off the towpath, or later when the Canal Era began to pass, when he felt progress encroaching upon his life and livelihood.

To Jake Beales—"part water, part sand, part wind . . . [but] all canawler"—it seemed that most of Europe and all of the east coast gushed into Buffalo, walking or riding on and along the Erie Canal. Beales turned a wasteland of wrecked and half-sunken canal boats and other craft into habitable quarters for emigrants and other people moving westward; the area became known as "Bealesville" until it was destroyed by a severe lake storm in 1844.[28] Another canawler, John Mueller, fell in love with a locktender's daughter. The story of this towpath driver's romancing at Jacksonburg Lock in Herkimer County became the subject of a ballad sung by canallers who kept the episode alive: "John Mueller was a mule driver/On Erie's verdant shore . . . [and] the lockman's lovely daughter/Had for him a passion strong. . . ."[29] Myron Adams, the story-teller in his grandson's *Grandfather Stories*, worked the Big Ditch himself, and if even half of what Sam Adams related of the canaller's exploits is unvarnished, the venerable gentleman deserves mention in his own right. Adams Basin, near Spencerport, was named after the Adams' clan, for their contribution to building the Erie. Samuel's Erie-laden tales abound in canalside characters of diverse shades, many of them authentic reminiscences. In the "based-on-fact-fiction" realm, too, are such other canawlers who figure in

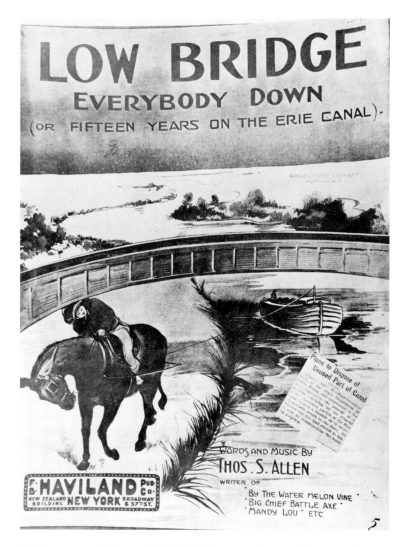

Title page of "Low Bridge" (From a photostatic copy in the Grosvenor Library, Buffalo, New York)

ROCHESTER

AND

ALBANY.

Red Bird Line of Packets,

In connection with Rail Road from Niagara
Falls to Lockport.

1843. 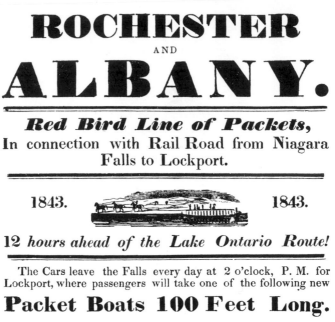 1843.

12 *hours ahead of the Lake Ontario Route!*

The Cars leave the Falls every day at 2 o'clock, P. M. for
Lockport, where passengers will take one of the following new

Packet Boats 100 Feet Long.

THE EMPIRE!

Capt. D. H. Bromley,

THE ROCHESTER

Capt. J. H. Warren,

and arrive in Rochester the next morning at 6 o'clock, and can
take the 8 o'clock train of Cars or Packet Boats for Syracuse and
Albany, and arrive in Albany the same night.

☞ Passengers by this route will pass through a delightful country, and
will have an opportunity of viewing Queenston Heights, Brock's Monument,
the Tuscarora Indian Village, the combined Locks at Lockport, 3 hours at
Rochester, and pass through the delightful country from Rochester to Utica
by daylight.

N. B.---These two new Packets are 100 feet long, and are built
on an entire new plan, with

Ladies' & Gentlemen's Saloons,

and with Ventilators in the decks, and for room and accommoda
tions for sleeping they surpass any thing ever put on the Canal.

For Passage apply at Railroad and Packet Office, Niagara Falls.

September, 1843. T. CLARK,
J. J. STATIA, } Agents

TYRONE POWER.

In the Character of Major O'Dogherty

In the Drama of S.ͭ PATRICK'S EVE, written by himself.

Published by C. SHEPARD. 262 Broadway N.Y.

J. T. Bowen's Lith.

One of the Erie's famous tourists in the 1830's, the British actor, Tyrone Power, shown here in costume for Major O'Dogherty (Library of Congress)

Opposite page: broadside advertisement of the Red Bird Packet Line (Courtesy Canal Society of New York State)

Canal boat *Buffalo* in the Erie Canal at Little Falls. From an old glass negative. (Courtesy Buffalo and Erie County Historical Society)

Opposite page: scenes from the Fox film, "The Farmer Takes a Wife," starring Henry Fonda and Janet Gaynor

Scene from the Fox film, "The Farmer Takes a Wife," starring Henry Fonda and Janet Gaynor

View of the enlarged Erie Canal showing horses on the towpath pulling canal boats in "hoodledasher" fashion (Courtesy Buffalo and Erie County Historical Society)

View at the mouth of the Buffalo River, Fort Porter, showing canal boats with towing horses. From a drawing (1873). (Courtesy Buffalo and Erie County Historical Society)

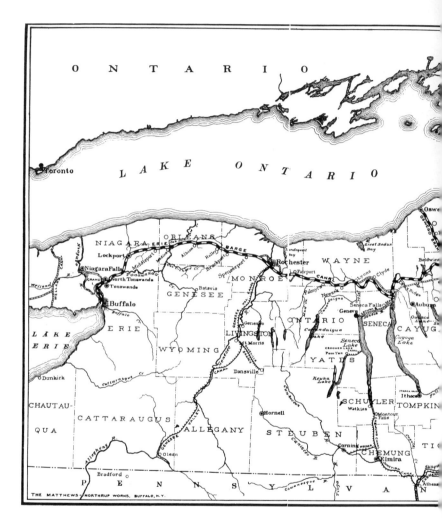

THE MATTHEWS-NORTHRUP WORKS, BUFFALO, N.Y.

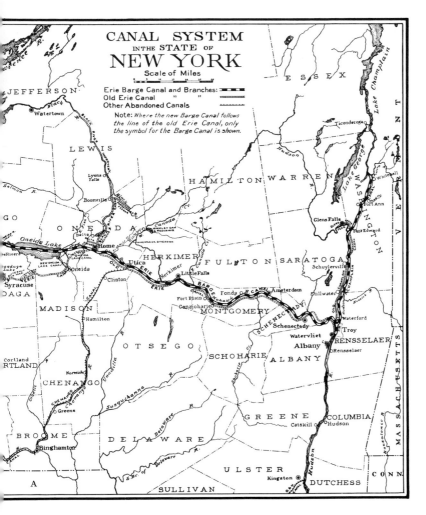

CANAL SYSTEM
IN THE STATE OF
NEW YORK
Scale of Miles

Erie Barge Canal and Branches:
Old Erie Canal   "   "
Other Abandoned Canals

Note: *Where the new Barge Canal follows the line of the old Erie Canal, only the symbol for the Barge Canal is shown.*

Reproduced from Buffalo Historical Society Publications, XII (1908)

Sig Sawtelle's circus boat winters next to the Farmer's Market in the Erie Canal at Syracuse, New York (1891). Beyond Clinton Street bridge the ice on the canal has been cleared for skating. (Courtesy Canal Society of New York State)

Rochester Aqueduct in the days of the Old Erie
(Courtesy Arch Merrill and the Rochester *Democrat and Chronicle*)

"Entering the Lock," watercolor by E. L. Henry (1899) (From the original in Albany Institute of History and Art)

Advertising poster of the 1880's showing (among others) prizefighter Paddy Ryan, who operated a saloon on the notorious Side-cut (Library of Congress)

View of the Erie passing through East Frankfort (Print from *History of Herkimer County, N.Y.* (1879)

View of Lockport, New York, about 1836, showing the famed combines, or double locks, a major tourist attraction and engineering marvel of the times (Library of Congress)

Staffordshire china plate, *circa* 1825, showing entrance of the Erie Canal into the Hudson River at Albany (From the china collection in Buffalo and Erie County Historical Society)

Walter D. Edmonds' *Mostly Canallers,* and the "created" legendary types which spring full-grown—like Philetus Bumpus, an Albion tavernkeep whom Carl Carmer put into tall-story tradition as a former canawler turned innkeeper because of a frightening experience with an oversize sturgeon.[30] And other canawlers, with names like O'Brien and McCarthy, have become legendized in tall tales told in Erie country.

Many Erie characters had highly evocative nicknames. "The Hawk," "Stubbie," and "Footie" frequented West Troy; the latter's name derived from his habit of taking long walks. "The Jumper" was especially appropriate; he could run and jump second to no man on the canal. But he was lightfingered as well as swiftfooted, and one day, cornered by a local sheriff on one side of the Side-cut Lock, "Jumper" leaped across the lock and escaped.[31] (He may have been the same person Harold Thompson cites as Watervliet's "Jumpy" Burke, whose "favorite exhibition was to leap across a lock with a pair of heavy dumb-bells in his hands.")[32] Moritz Jagendorf in *Upstate, Downstate* mentions a canaller known as "The Black Bully," who could "leap clear across the widest part of the canal";[33] but Samuel Hopkins Adams discounts all of these. No man ever spanned that forty-foot breadth, said Adams, although, he says, many made a "creditable attempt."[34]

Other canallers were known collectively as the "Cisco Chasers" or the "Longlevellers," depending upon whether they boated from the Oswego Canal to Syracuse (where Cisco fish were common) or hailed from the 60-mile long level which ran from Syracuse to Utica. The "Gum Chewers" (because of an association with the gum of trees?) hauled lumber down from the Black River country.[35]

Canallers had their share of ghosts, witches, and other such superstitions and spirit-lore, especially the Irish, who, according to Marvin Rapp, "buried their pixies into the canal with loving care."[36] Old-timers along the Erie towpath told of one mule driver who battled a ghost in Rome swamp—a spirit with "a horrible face and great flashing teeth." The canal man struck it again and again with a stick, but the stick landed on

nothing solid. Other canawlers recounted tales like that of a
cook's ghost crying out on the anniversary of her murder,
and there were other weird shenanigans.[37]

At Herkimer, a macabre tale of love and murder goes the
rounds. The locktender near there loved his wife deeply,
and she, young and very pretty, found innocent pleasure in
talking with the passing canallers who waited near their shanty
while the boats were in lockage. Jealously the locktender for-
bade his wife's conversing with the canallers and he made her
a virtual prisoner. When he saw her packing one night, he became enraged at the thought she might be leaving him for one
of the young canallers, like the one even then tied up for
lockage. In his jealous rage he killed her, weighted her body
down, and dumped it into the lock. Others had heard the wife's
cries, and the local constable soon had the demented locktender
in custody. The body, however, never was found, though the
lock was drained the next day. The strangest part had yet to
come. Subsequent locktenders never slept easily in their predecessor's shanty, each of them finding depressions (like the
shape of a head) on his pillow at night, or wet spots on the
linen. Only when a third locktender finally insisted upon a
new shanty did the "Ghost of Lock Herkimer" seem gone for
good. (The informant for this story, John O'Brien of Herkimer, told of another similarly macabre tale of a locktender's
murdering his wife at Black River's lock 67.) [38]

Such a story may have been "stretching the blanket" a little, but canallers, and not alone the Irish, had their superstitions. Children especially wished on four-leaf clovers, hay
loads, and first stars, and towpath drivers forecast the weather
by the droop of a mule's ears. Witches and witch-hex superstitions—like the twitching of a broom when a person enters
the room as a sure sign a witch is present, or the thought that a
witch could ride best on a stolen broom—were numerous.
Many canallers believed in the Pennsylvania Dutch defense
against witches, and carried a new broom on the bow of the
canal boat to ward them off. Other people believed firmly that
a witch could be hired to put a hex on them, a belief fostered
by those who unscrupulously wanted to do "hoo-doo black-

mailing." Canallers stood in awe of witch-hexes and, along with other elements of the population, of the roving bands of gypsies who once used to frequent the highways and fields. (Witch Crego's admonition in the novel *Canal Town*, that fever came "when the black moskeeter stands on her head," and the "feverbirds" of Samuel Hopkins Adams' gypsy folklore, had their counterparts in authentic folk tradition.) Aside from malarial fever, the all-too-common "miasma" brought persons down with chills and fever, and a superstition along the canal blamed its occurrence on the sacrilegious tampering with the wilderness as the canal cut through the state.[39]

The Irish brought their leprechauns and pixies with them to Yorker territory and put them on and around the canal they dug. The true Irishman could "jure" up one of these spirits day or night. New driver boys used to be initiated by the Irish hoggees in "rites" during which the hoggees used their power to bring forth the good and the bad spirits. The initiate could without much difficulty find himself finally face to face with the awful swamp ghost:

> So terrible was this creature from the bogs . . . that the sight of him would turn every hair on the head of the beholder snow white and the scream that tore itself deep from the throat of the victim on the sight of the ghost would be the last human sound he would ever make. As the new driver boy sat stiff and white with fear the older boys would slip away one by one. . . . [E]erie sounds and weird movements came at precisely the right time from the dark edge of the firelight . . . accompanied by a moan which issued forth from the woods. With that, a white shape would float up from the swamp in full sight of the scared driver. With a Yess!!! the driver boy would run for the boat, head down, eyes shut, mouth open.[40]

The Irish have come in for perhaps more than their share of the ribbing of foofoos, on the canal as well as off it, but they were, by and large, well respected as the backbone of canal construction. Imported largely to serve as laborers, the

Irish proved to be the greatest of boons to the digging of the Ditch. They turned "Clinton's Folly" into the Grand Western Canal. Few people could stand the conditions which the Irish tolerated. Local inhabitants, Pennsylvania Dutch, and Negroes from the South were all tried, but the Irish bog-trotters proved always the best of the lot. They had stamina and they had grit. Some of the Irish, like Paddy Ryan of prizefighting fame, made names for themselves after they left the canal behind; but the bulk of the Irish made their contribution as diggers and construction help. And, among their other qualities, they had a sense of humor, as the tales about them will testify.

When the canal was being dug, they used to live in shanties thrown up along the canal site. The natives of the region did not often welcome the "fightin' Irish" and the two groups —the Irish workers and the townspeople—rarely mixed well. Great stories went around about how the canal builders got drunk and beat their wives. One time the Irishmen, when they heard of it, planned a little party for the local folk who used to come up on Sundays to see how the canal was progressing. On one such Sunday, when the Irish decided a large enough crowd had gathered, some of the women came out screaming from their shacks pursued by the husbands with clubs. Their children, too, set up a commotion. After a while, when they thought the "act" had lasted long enough, they went back into their shanties and laughed their fool heads off.[41] When the Tonawanda-Buffalo leg of the canal was under construction, Irish diggers provided the "sidewalk superintendents" with something to remember. At intervals along the path of the red stakes the Irish workmen placed barrels filled with beer. As they dug a stretch of the canal and reached a keg, the workers drained its contents in hearty draughts, then moved earnestly to the next—the "fastest diggin' and drinkin' the canawl has ever seen," as one writer put it.[42]

Once, so one story goes, a canawler was taking a boatload of Italians to Syracuse. They had all been living on macaroni and were so starved for fresh meat that every time they saw a woodchuck one would jump ashore after it. Beyond Utica the steersman spotted a big skunk in a field along the canal and yelled out, "Look—a black and white woodchuck!" With that, about fifteen of the Italians jumped ashore and surrounded that skunk. He sprayed them with his perfume, but that did not discourage the immigrants. They killed the skunk, made a stew out of it, and told the steersman it was one of the best woodchucks they ever ate.

"But," concluded the teller of this tale, "they smelled my boat up so much that the mules wouldn't come aboard, and I had to use one team all the rest of the trip." He also had to give up passengers for a while and take to hauling paving blocks instead.[43]

Those folk characters who might be called "marginal" Erie types—figures like Sam Wilson, Paddy Ryan, and Sam Patch —found fame or fortune as a result of events in their lives which occurred in Erie country. Paddy Ryan began his career in Watervliet and Troy, training under Troy boxing master Jimmy Killoran to beat the English prizefighter Goss and become, as Harold Thompson put it, "King of the Erie Canal and Champion of the World." [44] As a youth he worked as a locktender, and in true folk-hero fashion Paddy once saved a young lass from drowning in the Erie Canal. Another Trojan, "Uncle Sam" Wilson, according to many persons was the prototype for the American national character-symbol. Uncle Sam—whether Troy's native son or not—arrived on the scene about the time of the War of 1812 and naturally concerned himself with the big York State enterprise of the next decade. One of his "biographers" put it this way:

One day when America was a little older, but still quite young, Uncle Sam found himself on the towpath of the Erie Canal. Irishmen, with brogue as thick as buttermilk, had dug it. Uncle Sam loved a paddy from the Old Sod, just as he loved good men everywhere. He knew all about St. Patrick's achasin' the snakes out of Ireland and he knew all about Ireland's "little people." Uncle Sam smiled to hear boatmen singing:

> I've got a mule, her name is Sal,
> Fifteen miles on the Erie Canal.
>
> .   .   .   .   .
>
> Low bridge, ev'rybody down!
> Low bridge, for ye're going through a town,
> And you'll always know your neighbor,
> You'll always know your pal,
> If you've ever navigated on the Erie Canal,

"America is doing all right," chuckled Uncle Sam and moved on.[45]

Sam Patch found fame in failure in Rochester at the Falls of the Genesee, near the great Erie aqueduct. On Friday the thirteenth, in November of 1829, Patch, an exhibitionist who had performed numerous daredevil feats at Niagara and elsewhere, apparently fainted during an attempt at the Genesee, before several thousand spectators. He died in the fall, a 96-foot drop. According to Samuel Hopkins Adams, his grandfather Myron witnessed the "fearsome leap," and Sam Patch, he said, "was celebrated for years in song and drama." [46] It was true. During the 1830's Sam Patch's fame grew, as the stories about him magnified his stature and his accomplishments. Poems, children's stories, and plays utilized Patch legendry; he became *Sam Patch; or, the Daring Yankee* to the American theater. Even William Dean Howells, years later, worked Patch into one of his novels, when Basil and Isabel March visit Rochester, commenting upon the Erie Canal en route, in *Their Wedding Journey* (1872).

A town character in Lockport, during the building of the Erie, did not benefit from the Erie project but rather was caused considerable anguish by the Big Ditch. Another of the marginal Erie characters, he became known far and wide as "the rattlesnake hunter who was the enemy of the whole reptile race." His Rattlesnake Oil—the natives, of course, pronounced it "Ile"—which he made and sold as a result of his tremendous snake-chasing activities, was a great remedy in the Lockport region for the "rheumatiz" and gout. The canal brought an end to his business, however, for progress—and settlers—meant rattlers would disappear. They did. "No use countin' on snakes in the future," he bemoaned. "Already canawlers thicker'n the trees used to be. I wish I had never heard of a canawl, or that I hadn't settled short of Michigan." [47] The local press, the Lockport *Union-Sun*, reported in the 1850's that his predictions proved true:

> In another year his trade in oil was ruined. Some years later it was heard that he had moved beyond the great Lake Michigan, where he lived for twenty years. The last tiding of him was that he had moved to the foot of the Rocky Mountains in consequence of a contemplated canal which would run within ninety miles of him! [48]

While such indigenous eccentrics as these characters lived in—or escaped from—canal environment, better-known folk heroes may have plodded along the Erie towpath as well. But if such is the case, folk memory is not especially helpful here. On the other hand, literary liberties sometime effect interesting transplantings; Catskill John Darling, for example, wrested from his southern New York habitat, seems quite at home on Erie water in a story Carl Carmer tells. In it, Darling is a "canal boatsman superhuman and fisherman beyond all get-out," who at the age of 11 split tree stumps with a plow drawn by his two pet steers, and who, on one occasion, Paul Bunyan-like, shingled a fog twenty feet above the chimney of his house. John Darling proves to be not only champion buckwheat pancake eater of the world and best sugarbush operator of the north country, but one of the state's greatest fishermen as well. For the latter feat, he wins the hand of no less a maid than Erie Sal.[49] While stories of Darling place him in various parts of Sullivan and Orange counties, New York, as well as in Ireland,[50] Carmer alone seems to have placed him in Erie country. It seems more than likely that Carmer's imagination is not the first to have grafted literary shoots to a folklore stock and that other writers will one day "find" a story placing Johnny Appleseed along the towpath planting his seedlings (there is a story already of the state legislature authorizing canallers to plant a strip of *corn* from Buffalo to Albany along the canal), or one in which Paul Bunyan lets Babe the Blue Ox pull an Erie canal boat even faster than Lake Erie sturgeon are reputed to have done.

V

Canalside Sports
and Diversions

THE AVERAGE canaller seems to have been a combination of perennial adolescence and hearty, frontier-type masculinity. Like any major artery of traffic, the Erie Canal was by nature democratic, and the canallers' amusements, like their language and customs, were those of American pioneers living in the open and thrown upon their own resources. During its heyday the Erie Canal was anything but the "dull utility" it became later as it was forced into the pattern of a progressively urbanizing New York State. Towpath and berm teemed with activity, diversional as well as essential. As an erstwhile canaller put it, "What a moving marvel of humanity was the old towpath!" [1]

The record shows that canallers would fight at the drop of a hat, but it also shows them to have been friendly and convivial. They were, of course, without societyish restraints and refinements, but their brawling, although frequent, seldom had real malice in it. While some of their sports involving animals would be regarded as cruel today, it was not until the second half of the nineteenth century that reforms of the treatment of animals were undertaken in America. On the basis of some of the material following in this chapter, the term "fun-loving" applied to canallers may seem euphemistic, but less so if they are judged by the standards of their times.

61

Canalside sports and contests were doubtless not unique to Erie water, but representative of activities found along other towpaths as well, and, indeed, in areas apart from canal regions. Races between cockroaches, grasshoppers, bedbugs, and frogs were common. Walter D. Edmonds tells a delightful tale about caterpillar-racing, apparently a sport which developed no small following along the Erie. The story is told by a canal-family lad, and there were rules and protocol to be observed. "The way we raced caterpillars," he said, "was to set them in a napkin ring on a table, one facing one way and one the other. Outside the napkin ring was drawed a circle in chalk three feet acrost. Then a man lifted the ring and the handlers was allowed one jab with a darning needle to get the caterpillars started. The one that got outside the chalk circle the first was the one that won the race." [2] "Red Peril," the real hero of the tale, and "the fastest caterpillar in seven counties," proved to be a real champion. His trainer, a known "connesewer" in caterpillar-racing, found Red Peril scared of but one thing—butter, a trauma effected by his having once been immobilized in it. His last race was against the "Horned Demon of Rome," a race he won valiantly, by expiring on the chalk line.

Cockfights were popular with canal men. One chief gathering place seems to have been Leonard's saloon on the "Dyke," or lower Cohoes, where canallers frequently paid off their debts in fuel, keeping the enterprising saloonkeeper in winter supply. The sport of cockfighting finally became illegal in New York State, and by 1880 newspapers carried accounts of raids on the cockfight "arenas." Bulldog fighting used to be another sport which an S.P.C.A. would not have tolerated. The haunches of the dogs were sandpapered until they were raw, in order to get the dogs fighting mad and cause them to tear into each other.

Betting, whether on cockfights or other game contests, was part of the canaller's diet. They literally "bet on anything." Schoharie Crossing, where the canal passed over Schoharie Creek, often proved to be a particular source of dismay in rainy weather. Since it was a highly dangerous undertaking, few canallers, including the most experienced, would venture to cross the feeder until the weather cleared and the waters abated. Any fool who tried to tempt fate by failing to wait it out would immediately draw heavy betting from the onlookers regarding his chances.

A canaller who stopped by the McClare Hotel in Rexford bet the barkeeper a dollar he could down a gallon of hard cider without taking more than three breaths. When the barkeeper took him up on it, the canaller excused himself for several minutes, then returned, gave the jug a full tilt and emptied the contents. The bug-eyed bartender handed over a dollar, shaking his head that he had not thought it could be done. "T' tell the truth, neither did I," said the Erie canaller, wiping his sleeve across his mouth, "till I ran down to the neighbor tavern to find out!" [3]

Gambling and liquor, needless to say, provided almost constant diversion for canallers of all sorts. One captain, writing to his relatives in 1882, confessed that he had "sined the pledge" and "dont shak any dice or play any more gambling games." The man found ample reasons for the wisdom of his changed ways. In his letter he commented, "There was a Capt of a boat Drowned a little while ago by the name of mike Heart left a Wife and six Children Caused by being drunk and falling in between to Boats." [4]

"I have seen enough of that kind of business so that I am satisfied to leave all intoxicating liquers alone," he concluded.

This was written during a winter layover, when the Hudson River ice was eight inches thick. Three years earlier, in Rome on the Erie, a combination of freezing weather and snow closed the canal. Under date of "november 21, 1879" the canaller wrote: ". . . Well we lay about one mile and a quarter from Rome West there is about fifty or 100 boats between here and the feeder it is all Blocked in with snow and ice So the boats cannot move the ice breaker has not worked at it yet. . . . I think it will be doubtfull weather we get through rome or not this fall it is fearful Coald weather I froze my rite ear last night and it is freezing hard to night Pa says it acts just as it did that fall we froze in here. . . ."

Two situations—this being "froze in" and encountering washouts or breaks—often caught canallers in ports not of their own choosing and made them turn to the communities for diversions (or to think up their own) to while away the time, in the one case usually until the spring thaw, and in the other until a repair crew again opened the canal to traffic. Sometimes the initiative of the canallers manifested itself commendably. An upstate newspaper report upon two major breaks ran the following account.

THE RAGING ERIE CANAL

A WASHOUT ON THE BLACK RIVER AND A CRACKED WALL AT FRANKFORT GIVE COOKS TIME TO HAVE PINK TEAS AND CREWS LEISURE TO FORM LITERARY AND POLITICAL CLUBS

The break in the canal early last Sunday morning gave a few hundred canal men a rest they didn't want, and cost them a lot of money they couldn't afford to lose.

The lay-up came in the way of a bonanza of restfulness to horses and crews, but it was as welcome as sulfuric torments to the owners who saw drivers and steersmen with healthy appetites for corned beef and cabbage and horses eating their heads off in solemn ease with their noses buried in hay or oats.

It costs from $10 to $15 a day to run an ordinary horseboat and, while canal captains are a philosophical lot, it takes more than a commonly philosophical mind to see the bottom dropping out of his pocketbook and his money floating off as fast proportionately as the muddy water rushing through the sewer and off to the ocean.

It was all right for cooks who could go visiting other cooks, getting up pink teas and five o'clocks for their friends. And it wasn't bad for the drivers and deck hands who could form literary and socials, organize silver clubs and meet for the discussion of theological problems, but the poor owner had to pay the piper for the dancing and he looked as sour as if he had been condemned to a diet of green persimmons and young apples and expected to endure aches and pains eternal.[5]

The press commented on the fact that, due to the economy-minded canallers, stores in town did not make money by the disaster. Even the "liquor repositories" near by, continued the reporter, got little additional profits, "for the navigator, when he is navigating, doesn't carry cash, and his bibulous tendencies are laid aside for indulgence in one wild bath of beer when the season is over."

Both canallers and townsfolk came in for commendation under the circumstances.

It might have been thought that potato patches and henneries would have suffered under the visitation of a couple of thousand canallers, but they didn't, and they impressed the community with the fact that they are as superior to temptation as anything human between the great fresh lakes and the blue salt sea.

Perhaps the most astonishing feature in connection with this involuntary assembling of two great fleets is that it was not taken advantage of by any of those who might have seized the opportunity. No missionaries from the Volunteers or the Salvation Army went on a peregrination to save sinners; no peddlers with things to sell which no rational being would be without visited them; no insurance men went up there or down the other way to write policies on life or underwrite the boatmen for compensation in case of accident. Like a lot of Sir John Mores they were left alone in their glory, and the chances are they're glad of it.

Races between canal boats were frequent and enthusiastic. When gasoline engines were in prospect for the Erie, Cap'n Hanks of the *Tilly Schlitz* lamented the passing of the old days. "They ain't no races on the canal now," he remarked, "like they was in the old passenger packet days, 'long about '53. Boats carried from 40 to 50 people—nothin' else—and would skim out from Albany to Buffalo in less 'n six days. That was goin' it some, eh? Six horses drawed 'em along at a dead gallop, a rider on the wheel horse, so t'speak, lashin' 'em for twelve miles, when they was changed for fresh horses.

"Even th' meules that drawed the freight boats was goers in them days," said the salty Erie captain. "I had one named *Rub 'er Heels* that could show 'er tail to lots of thoroughbreds on the Speedway today. Fact is that leaving out her ears an' tail . . . [you] couldn't tell her from a runnin' horse. She was a full daughter of Starbuster and was dammed by Gazelle Umpleby, and, in a manner of speakin', by every boat driver that ever tried to curry 'er unannounced. She indeed was quite some goer!"

Cap'n Hanks recalled one Erie captain who would "git so het up over a race, leanin' out over the bow an' shoutin', that near every day he fell overboard from excitement." This was Captain Jason, "who allus wore a uniform like a rear admiral." As Hanks told the story, "he yells t'me one day as we drawed down the stretch t' Albany, 'if you beat—' (an' here he leans out too far an' goes over) 'that Jackson boat t' th' lock,' he resooms as his head comes to the surface, 'I'll git you a new suit of clothes in Albany.' "

Hanks got the suit.

" 'Nother time," said Hanks, "I was steerin' between th' Lockport locks 'bout dusk.

" 'Hard a-port!' yells Cap'n Jason of a sudden from the bow. I thought he meant starb'd, but I throwed 'er to port as ordered, an' we skinned twenty feet of new plankin' off on the rocks.

" 'Damn it!' he yells, 'don't you know I mean starb'd when I say port?' "

"They don't grow men like Cap'n Jason now," concluded Hanks.[6]

Choosing the name for a canal boat must have been an interesting chore, although, to be sure, as with motel nomenclature today, originality often seemed lacking. *Sea Gull* and other sea-and-ocean imagery appeared frequently. Some names, like *Rub 'er Heels* mentioned by Captain Hanks, were at least different, and by and large canal boats on Erie water did have colorful and evocative names. *The Chief Engineer* was the first of many of that name. *The Seneca Chief, The Young Lion of the West* (named for the city of Rochester), and *Noah's Ark* made the trip to New York City in the celebration entourage of 1825. Boats were named for love, for pride, and for patriotism. The names ranged from the uninspired and conventional *Floating Library* (for an Erie "book boat") to the more exotic and imaginative *Breath of Cashmere.* The salty Erie sailors, with more romance than realism, christened them *Western Wave, Seaman's Fancy*, or simply *Spray.* An old circus boat, *Kitty* of Utica, became in 1893 the *Good News*, a "Gospel boat" manned by workers of the Rescue Mission of Syracuse.[7] The *Rambler*, out of Rochester, was well named: University of Rochester students used to charter it to go to Hamilton College football games, nine miles from the canal port of Utica.[8]

When the Old Erie was in its last days, a wealthy family built a beautiful craft and people often wondered how it got its unorthodox name. The husband and wife could not settle on a name, so after arguing bitterly they decided to ask somebody on the street in town, agreeing in advance, no matter what he answered or how oddly, to paint that name on their boat. When they put their question to a passerby, his answer was, "Damned if I know!" and so they painted on the side of the boat "DAMFINO."

Children and adults alike played games like cockshy or duck-on-the-rock, and group activities were common along the towpath as elsewhere in the country. Greased pig and greased pole contests were popular, particularly at gatherings where whole families and groups participated. One account recalls a field-day fete held near Oneida Lake, with 150 canallers and their families. The greased pole climbing contest was the chief sport, and the canaller who finally managed to outwit the other contestants and win a five-dollar prize had been clever enough to fasten currycombs around his knees facing each other.

Pie-eating contests, like corn-husking bees and flapjack-

eating sessions, seem to have faded from the American scene.
Pie-eaters drew considerable crowds and betting was usually
vigorous. The contests ran as either endurance tourneys or time
races. In the former, as with the flapjack fanciers, a winner
was declared when his opponent was glutted and quit. With
the timed contest, each entrant began at the end of a row of
pies and made his way forward, the first who finished a
stipulated number of pies being declared the winner and
champion. Pie contests were run "wet" or "dry" by mutual
consent, depending upon whether water, cider or other liquids
might be taken en route to the finish line; and the pies themselves might be either "hard" or "soft" as the contest stipulated, a hard pie having double crusts, while a soft pie—like
custard and lemon meringue—having but one.

Myron Adams of East Bloomfield, New York, served as
judge in the bout between The Great Alexander and Forty-
Pie Hoskins, typical if half-fictional characters among the
reminiscences of the old canawler. It was a wet match, with
$50 at stake to go to the first to eat through a side of twenty
hard pies. The challenger, Alexander, ate straight apple; his
opponent, who claimed the New England championships both
soft and hard, preferred to alternate apple with rhubarb. The
techniques of the two contestants were decidedly different,
for the challenger was a steady muncher, who started at the
apex of a cut of pie—all pies were quartered before the contest began—and ate persistently through crust and filling. Hoskins, on the other hand, used his cavernous jaws to great advantage. His was the gulch-and-gobble technique: "uncomely,"
observed Adams, "but it covered a deal of pie." [9]

Canallers had more than adequate training for this sort of
thing. One of the most remarkable things about life on the
Grand Western Canal was the size and variety of the table at
mealtime. Breakfast was especially bountiful, as numerous
travellers, tourists and emigrants noted in their diaries, letters
home, or published accounts. "An American breakfast is something astonishing," wrote Frederick Gerstaecker, as he sat
down to the morning meal aboard an Erie canal boat travelling
westward. The European, he observed, "beholds in surprise

coffee, pork, pickled gherkins, potatoes, turnips, eggs, bread, butter, and cheese, all on the table at once; but as soon as the stomach has become accustomed to this strange assemblage, I must honestly acknowledge that it suits a hungry Christian man much better than dry bread and weak coffee." [10]

His countryman, Duke Bernhard of Saxe-Weimar, found similar fare in Utica taverns en route, during his tour in the 1820's. "You find upon a table," he wrote, "beef-steaks, mutton, broiled chicken, or other fowls, fish, and boiled potatoes, which are of a very superior quality." [11]

Most of the fictionists sailing Erie water have taken the huge breakfast as typical. A canal bride, jotting in her diary ostensibly in 1827 or 1828, noted that her captain and crew were "sufficiently victualed to appease the men's appetites." They had had considerable.

> The meal may consist of a pike or bass, fresh caught upon my overnight trawl line, a steak, bacon, sausage, and ham; a platter of scrambled eggs, baked pritties, boiled cabbage and squash, bread, both corn and white, pancakes, both wheat and buckwheat, with sorghum, maple or honey to choice; and, to wash all down, coffee, tea, milk, skimmagig, and cider.

"Dinner," the good canal wife observed, "will be heartier." [12]

"Hearty" describes the typical Erie canaller, his very life as well as his appetite. It has become a commonplace of Erie literature to speak of the "fighting canawler," and certainly the sons of the Grand Western loved their brawls and wrangles. Much of such tradition has been made, however, by authors like Walter D. Edmonds, who provided, in his very first novel, a climactic fight between the hero and a "typical" canal bully. This established a pattern that has itself become almost a convention for fictionists working the towpath. Numerous situations within novels, and sometimes whole short stories, have been woven around fighting, brawling, and general mayhem-making.[13]

Such traditions as are logged in the historical fiction appar-

ently had worthy precedents, amply documentable in the more
factual literature. Occasional comments of dissent from this
view are found. "If you ask an old canaller about the heroic
fights which Mr. Edmonds has made so vivid," stated one of
Harold Thompson's informants, "the reply will usually be:
'Oh, there wasn't much fightin' in my time,' or 'all the fightin''
was at Buffalo and West Troy, when the men had nothin' else
to do.'" Yet this same individual remembered when "Chippy
Connolly was known as Champion of the Erie Canal," who
"wouldn't hire a man who wasn't a fighter." [14]

Canal boat captains very often signed on their men more
for their fighting prowess than for other skills. Crew to boat,
and (against outsiders) canallers to canallers, Erie boaters were
intensely loyal. Runs made on time meant money in their
pockets, and delays at lockage could mean the difference between maintaining or losing a contract. Rules notwithstanding
—the down boat legally had the right-of-way—the first boat
through a lock became first by jockeying for position in terms
of the strength of its crewmen and their willingness to fight for
a position at the head of the line. They were usually quite
eager. The explanation, to those of us today at a comfortable,
twentieth-century distance, is not hard to comprehend, for
fighting provided the necessary diversion in an almost intolerable routineness of the canal boat's progress at one and a half
miles per hour. Outdoorsman and man of brawn that the average canaller was, he could hardly be expected to remain docile
when the slightest opportunity for stretching his muscles presented itself. In the very nature of the times the myth of "the
fighting canawler" became legend. Walter D. Edmonds and
those who followed him simply capitalized on the basic folklore which existed, giving it the polish of romance. The "bully"
was the working of natural selection, which had its counterpart in numerous cultures—from the primitive tribal chieftain
to the frontier gunslinger of the American West who remained
"on top" only so long as he could outfight or outdraw a challenger. On the credit side, the bully could have been a forerunner of the prizefighter of a later generation. "One of the

great days of Erie history," said Alvin Harlow, "was when Ben Streeter, the Rochester bully and one of the noted fighters of the canal, fought the bully of Buffalo for one hour in the Old Rochester Arcade, and licked him." [15]

Certainly one of the more colorful—as well as respectable —figures on the Old Erie *was* a prizefighter. Paddy Ryan, who came to Watervliet from Tipperary at the age of eight, defeated the English champ, Joe Goss, in a memorable 86-rounder on June 1, 1880. After an hour and twenty-eight minutes, the so-called "King of the Erie Canal" became world champion, and "Paddy Ryan's Victory" found its way into balladry. About six years earlier Ryan opened a bar in the Side-cut, doubtless finding his prizefighting talents of considerable value in that rough neighborhood at canalside. Later, after challenging the American champion Jimmy Dwyer (who left Ryan the title by default), he went on to Goss and greater fame. Ryan the boxer gave his title up to John L. Sullivan in 1882; Ryan the bartender gave "Tom and Jerry"—named for two brothers-in-law—to the thirsty world at large.

Watervliet, especially in the latter half of the nineteenth century, had many bars besides Paddy Ryan's—at one time, twenty-nine saloons within two blocks, as a matter of fact! The notorious Side-cut area became known as "the Barbary Coast of the East," with a reputation in the 1880's for "a hundred fights a day, a body a week found in the canal." [16] The brawling Side-cut has been compared to Dawson City and the Klondike, where sightseers who were not content merely to gape at the saloons often came out of them minus their pocketbooks and with a battered skull for good measure. An immigrant from Ireland who arrived in Watervliet with five sovereigns in his pocket found his lot reduced after an evening on the Side-cut, where he tried to remain an innocent stranger. The Troy press reported, "The victim thinks that the fee charged for initiation into the mysteries of Whitehall Street is inexcusably large." Many of the saloons had names which should have been suggestive enough to make the "innocent" wary—the *Black Rag*, for example, or the *Tub of Blood*.

Others, like Peter McCarthy's *The Bank*, were more enigmatic. Rowe and Lang's establishment was deceptively inviting; the sign at the entrance proclaimed it *The Friendly Inn*.

The Side-cut had its humorous side, too. Once a tart was taken off a canal boat very much intoxicated and hauled before a local magistrate. When he asked her where she came from, she replied, "I slid down from Buffalo on a plank." The judge's response was appropriately pointed. "Well," he said, "to the jail for 180 days so you can pick the slivers out of your ——!"

Chief among the factors that helped to make Watervliet so riotous was that it served as a paying point, just as did Buffalo at the western end of the canal. Here boaters had *rhino*. It was at the Side-cut that the heavy-laden barges, filled with lumber, coal, and apples, abandoned the Erie Canal and started for New York via tug boat. The steersmen and hoggees were usually not paid until they reached West Troy—Watervliet—and they would start out with seventy to a hundred dollars to spend for entertainment. They headed first for the barbershops. After rehabilitating their dirty, unkempt appearances with a shave, shampoo, and mustache trim-and-dye, they would head for the saloons. They consumed cheap whiskey, lost most if not all of their money one way or another, and fell eventually into sleep, a fight, or the canal—sometimes all three.

It was common to refer to the Side-cut as "notorious." Incidents like that in the *Peg-Leg House* when a murder was committed with a whippletree help us to see why. In one fight, a boatman was reported to have had a portion of his ear bitten off. After another Side-cut brawl the local press commented, "The physician states that the only thing that saved the man's life was the unusual quantity of hair on his head, which in connection with his hat, broke the force of the blow." This report referred to a fight in which a canaller had heaved paving blocks at a locktender.

From the beginning of the Erie Canal, locktenders seem to have come in for special dislike. Many oldtimers insist they were natural enemies of canallers. Locktenders could be temperamental and they often were opportunists. A wise captain would tip one when he went through the lock because an experienced locktender could cause a swell that could help a boat through. If, on the other hand, a locktender wanted to settle a score—or to remind a boater that he had forgotten to tip on a previous trip—he could cause a canal boat to collide roughly with the sides of the lock, which in turn could produce a mean hole in the boat's siding.

Besides the hostility of locktenders, a second major aggravation to the canaller was the log raft, chiefly because it jammed the canal. It could hold up traffic in the mainstream and, of course, at locks, where temperatures ran high anyway. Timber rafts were made up of shots or cribs which were required by law to go through lockage separately, alternating with other boats in line. Later—after passing through the lock—shots were lashed together again in order to continue the trip as a unit. A story collected from a Macedon informant tells of "one of the biggest, riproaringest fights" ever held on "The Roaring Giddap," as he called the Erie. It occurred a week or so after the opening of the season one spring, when a group of log rafts from Buffalo arrived at Macedon locks. While these were going through a double-lock into the one-mile level, traffic from the other direction had to wait at the opposite end. The boatmen rebelled after 131 boats tied up, waiting for the load of logs to go through. They complained to the locktenders, who simply quit working and went into town when they realized the impossibility of the situation. It took two days and three nights to clear up the impasse, and professional fighters of the canal boats had considerable exercise for a few days.

A canaller who was a line-boat captain of some years' service told a missionary of the American Bethel Society in 1845 that he had some hands "who would rather fight than eat." Known as "the fighting captain," he told the missionary that "we used to do pretty much as we pleased, for we could whip any boat's crew on the canal." He took a pledge not to fight, however, and began praying and offering a blessing at mealtime. At Little Falls, another boat captain crowded his craft past, taking the ex-fighting captain's rightful lockage. The locktender couldn't believe what he saw.

> "You are the last man, captain, I should think, who would let any one force himself by and take your turn. Why did you not whip him?"
>
> I replied to him that I had done fighting, and instead of whipping men, I prayed for them.
>
> "What!" said the lock-tender, "would you pray for that scoundrel who took your lockage away from you?" I told him I would.[17]

Occasionally, Erie boatmen did give up the diversion of fighting for gentler activities.

The E-RI-E
in Song and Ballad

IF FIGHTING was a major diversion for the average canaller, singing certainly had as much a place in his life. Erie balladry, richly laden with the lore of the times, speaks for itself. That canallers as individuals and as a lot were singing men seems an easy inference for the folk historian to make. The outdoor character of their work and lives, and the nature of the times, would indicate this. The Erie Canal, the pride of the State of New York, found its way early into the songs of the people who dwelt along its banks and worked its course. For a time at least, the Grand Western and the life of the canawlers furnished material for Yorker songbags, and there is every indication that in two or three of the canal ballads America has something to rival the stirring verses of British literary and folk song tradition.

Songs and ballads serve, along with folk literature of all sorts, as indices to the character of a civilization; that they may be indices, of course, to the unsophisticated aspects of the history goes without saying, but they are perhaps the more valid markings on the cultural mosaic that does indeed evidence a *civilization*. The Erie Canal left some such markings. A few Erie songs—unfortunately too few—still find expression in the twentieth century. Thanks largely to well-known popularizers like Carl Sandburg and John and Alan Lomax, the contemporary public recognizes a ballad usually referred to as "The Raging Canal," another called "The E-RI-E," and a quite popular song generally known as "Low Bridge, Everybody Down," subtitled "Fifteen Years (or Miles) on the Erie Canal." Even of these three, only the first two can rightly be considered folk songs (and the one called "The E-RI-E" as popularly known is a refinement); the third, "Low Bridge," while it certainly had its inspiration in the Erie experience, owes its recognition by the modern public more to Tin Pan Alley publishing than to folk tradition.

To a rather large extent, this can also be said for other Erie song materials extant. Still, Erie songs and chanteys—for much of the Erie songbag reflects the feeling the Erie canawlers had that theirs was a sailor's life—have found a place in several collections and in at least one important regional miscellany. The latter, Harold W. Thompson's *Body, Boots & Britches* (1940), gives considerable space to a number of them, many collected as a result of Professor Thompson's teaching at Albany's New York State College for Teachers and later at Cornell University. John and Alan Lomax included a chapter on the Erie Canal in *American Ballads and Folk Songs* (1934), and Carl Sandburg's *The American Songbag* (1927) presented versions of the three songs which are cited above. Burl Ives and Bill Bonyun have put the Old Erie on records, and New York's Frank Warner pioneered with "Hudson Valley Ballads" (1946), a 78-rpm scarcity now, which contains two Erie songs collected from upstate New York.

The literary historian finds little usable material published in times contemporary with the Erie, however; and the tape-recorder method of today's field folklorist does not often bear fruit in this modern era so far removed from the bustling Erie days. With the canal gone (or at least that kind of canal with which folklorists are concerned) and its successor the railroad dieselized, the inspiration for the songs and the need to pass them on in oral tradition has vanished with the times into the more mechanized period of modern transportation. The nineteenth-century record is not a voluminous one, for few of the Erie canaller's apparently wide repertoire were printed in contemporary songbooks. One can only surmise that the reason for such song material going unpublished lay in the nature of the songs themselves and in the hearty, often scurrilous and earthy, language they employed, typical of the salty canawler's speech. Such songs belong on the canal, their natural habitat; they would hardly do for a songbook meant for general use.

Erie Canal song material logically falls into several categories. First, there are those songs which were about the canal and sung by the canawlers themselves. Such songs are of primary importance to the folklorist. Next, there are those songs which were current in the inns and taverns along the towpath, songs which Erie boatmen sang and took back with them onto the canal, expropriating them, as it were, by substituting their own words for the non-canal words they may have learned "ashore." Third, there were those songs sung on the canal for the same reasons they were sung elsewhere. Many Irish songs fall into this latter category; Irish laborers brought with them, for instance, "The Ballad of Johnnie Troy." [1]

No study has yet appeared which organizes or attempts to classify Erie songs and ballads; as with most folk materials, they often appear as variants of familiar tunes or as additions to former verses. "Most of the early Erie Canal ballads," said Professor Thomas O'Donnell of Utica College, "were composed to be sung to traditional English airs, tunes that had been widely popular for generations first in England, then in America." [2] Sometimes songs were written to fit the music of a new and popular song, for sheet music sold well in canal stores from Albany to Buffalo. Well-known melodies, like Stephen Foster's (which were popularized by the famous Christy minstrels of Buffalo), had Erie words assigned to them—one "Erie Canal Ballad" uncovered for the Lomaxes by an Ohio State University professor was sung to the tune of Foster's "Old Black Joe." [3] Songs like "Dark-Eyed Sailor," known to be a favorite on the Ohio River and elsewhere, and comic ballads and verses of York State's D and H Canal and other waterways, doubtless travelled Erie water as well. [4]

Published folk song collections are themselves sometimes

among the greatest obstacles to a meaningful study of Erie
song materials. In two books John A. Lomax includes a "Ballad of the Erie Canal," consisting of some nine stanzas picked
up in almost as many states. It obviously had never appeared
as a single song in any other context than the Lomax volumes: this kind of accretion is, of course, the sort of which
folk songs are made, but, apart from the context of the canal,
it becomes artificial and more than a little *ersatz*.[5] Others have
taken similar liberties. Some few Erie songs have become
known principally in the "invented" versions of an Edmonds,
whose canawlers in *Rome Haul* sang "Drop a tear for Big-Foot
Sal, the best damn cook on the Erie Canal," in preference to
eulogizing a towpath mule as in the traditional song.[6] Other
writers reprint a number of songs faithfully from informants,
but some of these are hardly consistent renderings of the original canal folk songs. Unfortunately, no one seems to have
toured the Erie Canal country in the way Cecil Sharp roamed
the Appalachian regions of Virginia, Tennessee and Kentucky,
and in the days when Erie song material was still collectable
under authentic or near-authentic conditions.

It was inevitable that the completion of the Erie Canal
should be memorialized in song. Respectfully dedicated to
DeWitt Clinton and sung at the Grand Canal celebration in
New York, "The Meeting of the Waters" commemorated the
event appropriately. The words, by S. Woodworth, were new,
although they had their inspiration in Thomas Moore's Irish
melody, "The Meeting of the Waters," which dated from
1807, and which in turn drew its tune from a prevailing Irish
folk air, "The Old Head of Dennis."

Here, from the original sheet music in Grosvenor Library,
are the words of "The Meeting of the Waters of Hudson
& Erie," as published in 1825:

> There is not in the wide world a Valley so sweet
> As that vale in whose bosom the bright waters meet;
> O the last rays of feeling and life must depart
> Ere the bloom of that valley shall fade from my heart.

Let the day be forever remember'd with pride
That beheld the proud Hudson to Erie allied;
O the last sand of Time from his glass shall descend
Ere a union, so fruitful of glory, shall end.

Yet, it is not that Wealth now enriches the scene,
Where the treasures of Art, and of Nature, convene;
'Tis not that this union our coffers may fill—
O! no—it is something more exquisite still.

'Tis, that Genius has triumph'd—and Science prevail'd,
Tho' Prejudice flouted, and Envy assail'd,
It is, that the vassals of Europe may see
The progress of mind, in a land that is free.

All hail! to a project so vast and sublime!
A bond, that can never be sever'd by time,
Now unites us still closer—all jealousies cease,
And our hearts, like our waters, are mingled in peace.

From the inception of the Erie Canal, the Big Ditch got into song. The rigors of canal construction gave rise to songs about the building of the canal. Among the memories of the late Samuel Hopkins Adams, whose grandfather was a canal contractor on the original Erie project, are stanzas sung by the workers as they pushed the narrow ditch through the Montezuma marshlands.

SONG OF THE CANAL [7]

We are digging the Ditch through the mire;
Through the mud and the slime and the mire, by heck!
And the mud is our principal hire;
Up our pants, in our shirts, down our neck, by heck!
We are digging the Ditch through the gravel,
So the people and freight can travel.

We are digging the Ditch through the gravel,
Through the gravel across the state, by heck!
We are cutting the Ditch through the gravel
So the people and freight can travel,
Can travel across York State, by heck!

We are digging the Ditch through the mire,
Through the mire, the muck, and the mud, by heck!
And the mud is our principal hire,
In our pants, up our sleeves, down our neck, by heck!
The mud is our principal hire!

"Digging the Ditch" became a stirring theme in the epic
growth of America, and workers for the Erie Canal were drawn
from far and near. Since many of the laborers on the canal were
Irish, it was inevitable that they should find a place in the songs
of the Erie. While it did not mention New York's canal by
name, "Paddy on the Canal" may be assumed to have referred
to Clinton's Ditch where, like so many of the Irish, Paddy (in
the words of the ballad) "learnt the whole art of canalling."
The verses below appeared in *The American Vocalist* of 1853.

PADDY ON THE CANAL

When I landed in sweet Philadelphia,
    The weather was pleasant and clear;
I did not stay long in the city,
    So quickly I shall let you hear,
I did not stay long in the city,
    For it happened to be in the fall,
I never reefed a sail in my rigging,
    'Till I anchored out on the canal.

Chorus:
So fare you well Father and Mother,
    Likewise to old Ireland too;
So fare you well Sister and Brother,
    So kindly I'll bid you adieu.

When I came to this wonderful vampire [empire?]
    It filled me with the greatest surprise,
To see such a great undertaking;
    On the like I never opened my eyes
To see full a thousand brave fellows,
    At work among mountains so tall,
To dig through the vallies so level,
    Through rocks, for to cut a canal.

> I entered with them for a season,
>   My monthly pay for to draw,
> And being in very good humor,
>   I often sung Erin go Bragh.
> Our provision it was very plenty,
>   To complain we'd no reason at all,
> I had money in every pocket,
>   While working upon the canal.
>
> I learned for to be very handy;
>   To use both the shovel and spade;
> I learnt the whole art of canalling:
>   I think it an excellent trade.
> I learned for to be very handy,
>   Although I was not very tall,
> I could handle the "sprig of Shillelah,"
>   With the best man upon the canal.
>
> I being an entire stranger,
>   Be sure I had not much to say,
> The Boss came round in a hurry,
>   Says "boys it is grog time a-day."
> We all marched up in good order,
>   He was father now, unto us all,
> Sure, I wished myself from that moment,
>   To be working upon the canal.
>
> When at night, we all rest from our labor,
>   Be sure, but our rent is all paid,
> We laid down our pick, and our shovel,
>   Likewise, our axe, and our spade,
> We all set a joking together;
>   There was nothing our minds to enthral,
> If happiness be in this wide world,
>   I am sure it is on the canal.[8]

The building of the Erie Canal affected, of course, more than just the State of New York. It had a great deal to do with filling the western territories with the first of the large population influxes that transformed a young republic into a transcontinental nation. As a result of the Erie, emigrants poured into what is now the Midwest. The Erie's influence was

recognized especially in Detroit, where (as City Histori-
ographer Silas Farmer reported it) "an average of three steam-
boats a day, with from 200 to 300 passengers each" demonstrated the value of the canal in opening the West. "At one
time," wrote Farmer in 1884, "it seemed as though all New
England was coming. The emigration fever pervaded almost
every hamlet of New England, and this song was very popular,
and is known to have been largely influential in promoting
emigration." [9] "This song" to which he referred is "The Song
of the Wolverines," one of the earliest songs to tell the Erie
story. In addition to New York's lines—with their testimony
of the "mighty ditch"—verses were also given over to Maine,
Massachusetts, Ohio, Indiana, Illinois, and "Varmount."

THE SONG OF THE WOLVERINES

Come all ye Yankee farmers who wished to change your lot,
Who've spunk enough to travel beyond your native spot,
And leave behind the village where Pa and Ma do stay,
Come follow me, and settle in Michigania,—
Yea, yea, yea, in Michigania.

Then there's the State of New York where some are very rich;
Themselves and a few others have dug a mighty ditch,
To render it more easy for us to find the way
And sail upon the waters to Michigania,—
Yea, yea, yea, to Michigania.

Next to Irish workmen, the young lad turned to canalling
probably had as much right to become a subject for canal ballads as anyone. Harold Thompson, among numerous songs in
Body, Boots & Britches, tells of one which depicts the canal
boy's lot as happier than it was ordinarily known to be.

I WAS A BOATSMAN'S BOY

When I was young and about sixteen, none was more light and
          gay;
I gamboled nimbly on the green or sported in the hay;
The bloom of youth was on my cheeks, my heart was full of joy.
How happy were those days to me, a merry boatsman's boy!

For I was a boatsman's boy, for I was a boatsman's boy.
Johnny, get your mules fed; Johnny, get your mules fed,
   For I was a boatsman's boy.

I loved to use a pocket-knife before I went to school,
And soon I learned the mysteries of that wasteful, magic tool.
I hoarded cents I prized so high—I gladly gave to own—
And soon I learned the magic art to whet it on a stone.[10]

If he were a driver-boy, chances are that his life was far less tolerable. In addition to the rigors of the long trick, he might have had to listen to the taunts of "Hoggee on the Towpath":

   Hoggee on the towpath,
   Five cents a day.
   Picking up horseballs
   To eat along the way! [11]

Variants of this one, which was hollered from bridges along the canal in the 1880's, are many. These and other songs—or "shouts"—were sung *at* the boaters and canal workmen rather than by them. Informants generally agree that shouts like "Canawler, Canawler" were common "up and down the old canawl." Here are two versions:

CANAWLER, CANAWLER [12]

Canawlers, Canawlers, you'll never get rich;
You work on Sunday and you die in the ditch.

   Canawler—Canawler
   You son of a bitch
   You'll die on the towpath
   You'll be buried in the ditch
   Canawler—Canawler
   You work on Sunday
   You'll never get rich.

It goes without saying that such verses were heard on other canals than the Grand Erie.
   Working on some of the boats on the Erie provided more

than the usual element of danger from low bridges. One type
of canal boat was rounded rather than blunt-ended. Nicknamed
"ball-head" boats at first, they later became known as "bullheads." Such canal boats often had no place for the helmsman
save on the cabin roof and, as the following ballad indicates,
"Many canawlers now are dead/Who had no place to drop."
There was little ducking room on a bullhead. Here is a vivid if
tongue-in-cheek picture of life on such a craft:

BOATIN' ON A BULL-HEAD

I was sleepin' in a Line-barn
   And eatin' beans and hay,
While the boss was kickin' my starn
   Ev'ry night and ev'ry day.

So I hired out canawlin'
   As a horny hand of toil,
Drivin' mules that kept a-bawlin'
   'Long the towpath's smelly soil.

But my feet raised corns and blisters
   While the mules but raised a stink,
Roped my feet and threw some twisters
   Plump into the dirty drink.

So I thought I'd give up drivin',
   For the captain thought so too,
He said, "Hire out at divin'
   Or go bowin' a canoe."

I was dryin' on the heel-path,
   Watchin' boats haul up and down,
A-shiverin' from the first bath
   I'd got since I left town,

When a boat tied in the basin
   At the wood-dock for the night,
And I lost no time to hasten
   'Round the bridge to ask a bite.

They filled me up with beans and shote
   And lighted me a cob.

They asked me if I could steer a boat
  And offered me a job.

The next mornin' I was boosted
  To the stern-cabin's roof;
With the tiller there I roosted
  And watched the driver hoof.

Now the boat she was a Bull-Head,
  Decked up to the cabin's top;
Many canawlers now are dead
  Who had no place to drop.

(When the bowsman he forgot to yell,
  "Low bridge, duck 'er down!"
The Bull-Head steersman went to hell
  With a bridge-string for a crown.)

We were loaded with Star Brand Salt;
  The Cap, he was loaded too.
I wouldn't say it was his fault,
  But what was a man to do?

The bridge was only a heave away
  When I saw it 'round the bend.
To the Cap a word I didn't say
  While turning end over end.

So canawlers, take my warning:
  Never steer a Bull-Head boat
Or they'll find you some fair mornin'
  In the E-ri-e afloat.

Do all your fine navigatin'
  In the Line-barn full of hay,
And *Low Bridge* you won't be hatin'
  And you'll live to Judgement Day.[13]

Canallers kept alive in ballad form other aspects of canal
life and incidents which they cherished. When a mule driver
fell in love with a locktender's daughter, the romantic episode
went into song. In the fragment below, a hint of the usual feud
between boaters and locktenders can be seen.

BALLAD OF JOHN MUELLER
AND THE LOCK TENDER'S DAUGHTER

John Mueller was a mule driver
On Erie's verdant shore,
His walk was humble, but his gait
Was something to adore.

The lockman's lovely daughter
Had for him a passion strong;
Although she was both short and small,
She vowed she'd love him long.

Her father's haughty castle
Stood beside the proud Mohawk;
He did not lock her in the keep,
But kept her in the lock.[14]

Canallers would memorialize in song their loves, their boats,
and their horses or mules with equal fervor. The following
song speaks of a team with all the introductory gusto of Vergil
in his *Aeneid*.

Attend all ye drivers, I sing of my team;
They're the fleetest and strongest that ever was seen.
There is none will toil with such speed down the crick
Or start at the word of the driver so quick.

There's Dandy, my leader, looks boldly ahead
With his tail raised aloft, and majestic his tread.
He has a bright, shining coat of a beautiful bay;
His eyes sparkle bright as the sun at noon-day.

.   .   .   .   .

The three altogether in motion outdo
Any team of their age, the whole canal through.
Should any company try to go by us,
We'll show them our steam whenever they try us.

While Baker and Walbridge their packets run daily,
Proud Dandy and Jimmie and Charlie so gaily
Will waft all the passengers through the canal
In spite of all others, and in style, so they shall.[15]

Prosodically it seems reminiscent of that Christmas poem by
Dr. Clement Clarke Moore published in Troy, New York,
in 1823, with Dandy, Jimmie and Charlie having become the
canawler's counterparts for the more familiar reindeer.

If Erie canallers were "sailors" by courtesy only, they generally made the most of it. A whole series of songs pictured
the Erie Canal as a stormy body of water not unlike one of the
Seven Seas in its dangers for the sailing man. "The Raging
Canal" seems to have been the foremost of these songs and the
forerunner of many like numbers. The cover for the sheet
music (as illustrated) depicted a two-masted ship battling
furious waves on a stormy Erie Canal. In addition to the first
verse which appears in this book with the illustrated melody,
the following verses are taken from a Grosvenor Library
copy of the song as "Written & Sung by that Most Celebrated
Comic Singer, P. Morris."

> When we left New York harbor it was the middle of the year,
> We put our helm hard aport and for Buffalo did steer,
> But when we got in sight of Alba'y we met a heavy squall,
> And we carried away our mizen mast on that Raging Canal.
>
> She minded her helm just like a thing of life,
> The mate got on his knees uttering prayers for his wife,
> We throwed the provisions over board it was blowing such a
>   squall,
> And we were put on short allowance on that Raging Canal.
>
> It seemed as if the devil had work in hand that night,
> For our oil it was all gone, and our lamps they gave no light,
> The clouds began to gather and the rain began to fall,
> And we had to reef our royals on that Raging Canal.
>
> Loud roared the dreadful thunder, the rain in deluge showered,
> The clouds were rent asunder, by lightning's vivid powers,
> The bowsman gave a hollow, and the cook she gave a squall,
> And the waves run mountain high on that Raging Canal.
>
> The Captain came on deck and then begin to rail,
> He hollowed to the driver to take in more sail,
> The driver knocked a horse down and then gave a bawl,
> And we scudded under bare poles on that Raging Canal.

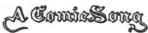

From the original in Grosvenor Library, Buffalo, New York.

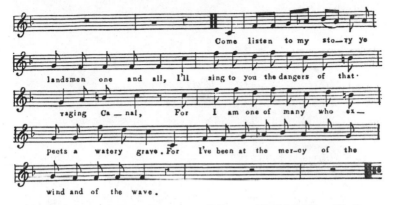

Come listen to my sto—ry ye landsmen one and all, I'll sing to you the dangers of that raging Ca—nal, For I am one of many who ex—pects a watery grave. For I've been at the mer—cy of the wind and of the wave.

From the original in Grosvenor Library, Buffalo, New York.

This Erie Canal song inspired others, and its popularity is demonstrated by the use of the tune as the "air" for other songs, such as the whimsical ballad, "The Girl from Yewdall's Mill," reprinted as it appears on a broadside in the collections of Union College.

THE GIRL FROM YEWDALL'S MILL.

BY JIMMY SMITH.   Air: "The Raging Canal."

It is of a girl at Fairmount, that I am going to sing,
Her cruel, sad misfortune tears to your eyes will bring;
She loved a gallant boatman who always dressed to kill,
She was a cotton-dolly, and she wrought in Yewdall's Mill.

He feasted her all winter, they had a merry time;
He took her to balls and dancing-school, until he spent every
    dime.
At length the spring-time came around, the canal began to fill,
He was forced to leave this charming girl that wrought in Yew-
    dall's Mill.

Oh! when it came to parting, that was a cruel task,
They hung to each other's lips like a toper to a flask;
The tears that run down their cheeks a washtub they would fill,
It was hard to part with this charming girl that wrought in Yew-
    dall's Mill.

He says, farewell, my love, I am going o'er the deep,
And for a love-token here is a nickle for you to keep;
And when the season is over, why marry you I will.
If you don't, I will spend it all for snuff, says the girl from
    Yewdall's Mill.

The captain called to him at last, and he was forced to go,
So he shouldered his feed trough and jumped on board the tow.
While sailing down the river, he gazed on Fairmount hill,
Where he saw the shaker bonnet of this girl from Yewdall's Mills.

No tidings did she get from him and the summer near passed away,
At length by a traction express she received a note one day;
Saying he had been kicked by a mule up at Phoenixville,
He was a damn fool to go near the mule, says the girl from Yew-
    dall's Mill.

He was a gay deceiver, for soon the news came down,
That he had married a big Dutch girl that weighed three hundred
    pounds;
And was keeping a lager beer saloon up on Ginea hill,
And quite forgot the doffer he had left at Yewdall's Mill.

Oh! when she heard that he was false, she says I will stop my
    breath,
She spent that five cents all for snuff and rubbed herself to death;
And every night at twelve o'clock, on top of Fairmount hill,
The ghost on [of?] Bedelia may be seen gazing on Yewdall's Mill.

Stephen Foster recognized the popularity of "The Raging
Canal" by including it in his nineteenth-century potboiler,
"The Song of All Songs." Published by the Oliver Ditson
Company, Foster's was a curious jumble of now-forgotten song
titles. The second verse ran:

There was "Abraham's Daughter" "Going out upon a spree,"
With "Old Uncle Snow" "In the Cottage by the sea";
"If your foot is pretty, show it," "At Lanigan's Ball";
And, "Why did she leave him" "On the raging canal"? [16]

Mark Twain also found "The Raging Canal" sufficient inspiration to produce a considerable number of lines concerning a

pilot man who saved a tempest-tossed craft on the stormy
Erie Canal. Twain called his piece "The Aged Pilot Man"
and included it among the reminiscences in *Roughing It*
(1872).

The version of "The Raging Canal" below is taken from a
broadside now in the Library of Union College, Schenectady,
New York:

RAGING CANAL

Come listen to my story, ye landsmen, one and all,
And I'll sing to you the dangers of that raging Canal;
For I am one of many who expects a watery grave,
For I've been at the mercies of the winds and the waves.

I left Albany harbor about the break of day,
If rightly I remember 'twas the second day of May:
We trusted to our driver, altho' he was but small,
Yet he knew all the windings of that raging canal.

It seemed as if the Devil had work in hand that night,
For our oil it was all gone, and our lamps they gave no light,
The clouds began to gather, and the rain began to fall,
And I wished myself off of that raging Canal.

The Captain told the driver to hurry with all speed—
And his orders were obeyed, for he soon cracked up his lead;
With the fastest kind of towing we allowed by twelve o'clock,
We should be in old Schenectady right bang against the dock.

But sad was the fate of our poor devoted bark,
For the rain kept a pouring faster, and the night it grew more
      dark;
The horses gave a stumble, and the driver gave a squall,
And they tumbled head and heels into the raging Canal.

The Captain came on deck, with a voice so clear and sound,
Crying cut the horses loose, my boys, or I swear we'll all be
      drowned;
The driver paddled to the shore, altho' he was but small,
While the horses sunk to rise no more in that raging Canal.

The Cook she wrung her hands, and she came upon the deck,
Saying, alas! what will become of us, our boat it is a wreck!
The steersman laid her over, for he was a man of sense,
When the bowsman jumped ashore, he lashed her to the fence.

We had a load of Dutch and we stowed them in the Hole,
They were not the least concerned about the welfare of their soul;
The Captain went below and implored them for to pray,
But the only answer he could get was, Nix come Ruse, nix fis staa!

The Captain came on deck with a spy glass in his hand,
But the night it was so dark he could not diskiver land;
He said to us with a faltering voice, while tears began to fall,
Prepare to meet your death, my boys, this night on the canal.

The Cook she being kind hearted, she loaned us an old dress,
Which we raised upon a setting-pole as a signal of distress:
We agreed with restoration, aboard the boat to bide,
And never quit her deck whilst a plank hung to her side.

It was our good fortune, about the break of day,
The storm it did abate and a boat came by that way,
Our signal was discovered, and they hove along side,
And we all jumped aboard and for Buffalo did ride.

I landed in Buffalo about twelve o'clock,
The first place I went to was down to the dock;
I wanted to go up the lake, but it looked rather squally,
When along came Fred Emmons and his friend Billy Baily.

Says Fred how do you do, and whar have you been so long!
Says I, for the last fortnight I've been on the canal,
For it stormed all the time, and thar was the devil to pay,
When we got in Tonawandy Creek, we thar was cast away.

Now, says Fred, let me tell you how to manage wind and weather,
In a storm hug to the tow-path, and then lay feather to feather,
And when the weather is bad, and the wind it blows a gale,
Just jump ashore, knock down a horse—that's taking in the sail.

And if you wish to see both sides of the canal,
To steer your course to Buffalo, and that right true and well,
And should it be so foggy that you cannot see the track,
Just call the driver aboard and hitch a lantern on his back.

Herbert Quick recalled two stanzas of this song for his novel of the westward migration, *Vandemark's Folly* (1922):

> Come, sailors, landsmen, one and all,
> And I'll sing you the dangers of the raging canawl;
> For I've been at the mercy of the winds and the waves,
> And I'm one of the merry fellows what expects a watery grave.

> We left Albany about the break of day;
> As near as I can remember, 'twas the second day of May;
> We depended on our driver, though he was very small,
> Although we knew the dangers of the raging canawl.[17]

Different versions worked in local references with the usual abandon of folk tradition. In one of these variants, a version of verse 12 in the Union College broadside above mentions "Old Beetle," who allegedly owned most of the boats on the Erie Canal.

> I pulled into Buffalo about four o'clock,
> The first man I saw was old Beetle on the dock,
> Says he, "Young man, you're rushing your team."
> Says I, "Old Beetle, yer blowin' off steam." [18]

Another version, written in the diary of a canal captain, deals with Ezekiel Radford, a liniment manufacturer of Weedsport. Carl Carmer printed the "song" for the first time in 1952; it demonstrates clearly the way personal experiences and references become attached at will to Erie songs. One may easily conjecture that there was a verse for every significant stop along the towpath, and another for each of the local characters the canawling captains ran into frequently. One verse of Carmer's find, from *American Heritage*, follows:

> We towed into Weedsport about ten o'clock
> And the first one I saw was Ezekiel on the dock
> Says Ezekiel to me, "Who's driving this team?"
> Say I to Ezekiel, "You're blowin' off steam." [19]

(Another verse which Carmer also included is an unpoetic, unrhymed sales-pitch for Ezekiel's liniment.)

Some variations of this ballad were prodigious. A 23-verse version of "The Raging Can-all" appeared in the *Negro Forget-Me-Not Songster* (1848); that in *The American Vocalist* (1853) has twenty-four. Both of these read substantially the same, the additional verse coming at the beginning of the ballad; similar to that found in the broadside cited earlier, it goes:

> We left old Albany harbour, just at the close of day,
> If rightly I remember 'twas the second day of May;
> We trusted to our driver, although he was but small,
> Yet he knew all the windings of that raging can-all.[20]

The use of "he" in the last line of the verse (over "we" in some versions) subtly gives much more responsibility to the hoggee. Parts of this version are monstrously in the mock-heroic style, as the two verses below, excerpted from *The American Vocalist*, will show:

> The sky was rent asunder, the lightning it did flash,
> The thunder rattled above, just like eternal smash;
> The clouds were all upsot, and the rigging it did fall,
> And we scudded under bare poles on that raging can-all.
>
> A mighty sea rolled on astern, and then it swept our deck,
> And soon our gallant little craft was but a floating wreck;
> All hands sprang forward, after the main-sheet for to haul,
> When slap dash! went our chicken coop into the raging can-all.

Not all of the "Raging Erie" varieties are so blustering; although the same general idea prevails, some of the songs current at the mid-century subdue the mock-epic seriousness of the varieties presented already, and speak in more homely terms of the "muddy deep" with what one suspects to be more than tongue-in-cheek satiric intent. The following three verses come from a songbook subtitled "Choice Gems from the Operas," published probably in the 1850's.

LIFE ON THE CANAWL

A life on the raging canawl,
    A home on its muddy deep,
Where through summer, spring and fall,
    The frogs their vigils keep.
Like a fish on the hook I pine,
    On this dull unchanging shore—
Oh give me the packet line,
    And the muddy canawl's dull roar.

Once more on the deck I stand.
    Of my own swift gliding craft—
The horses trot off the land,
    And the boat follows close abaft.
We shoot through the turbid foam
    Like a bullfrog in a squall—
And, like the frogs, our home
    We'll find in the muddy canawl.

The sun is no longer in view,
    The clouds have begun to frown,
But, with a bumper or two,
    We'll say, let the storm come down.
And this song we'll sing, one and all,
    While the storm around us pelts,
A life on the muddy canawl,
    Oh, we don't want nothin' else.[21]

Another of these songs was written to be sung to a current tune that was popular in both England and America in the 1840's. "I'm Afloat," by Henry Russell and Eliza Cook, appeared in 1843, and within two years' time an Erie Canal version was also in print. Professor O'Donnell conjectures the author to be Mrs. F. M. Wicher (Frances Miriam Berry), authoress of *The Widow Bedott Papers*.[22] The text is that given by O'Donnell from the *Utica Daily Gazette* for April 17, 1845.

I'M AFLOAT

I'm afloat! I'm afloat! On the E-ri Canawl,
    Its wave is my home, and my scow beats them all—

Off! up with your hats! give three cheers! now three more!
  I'm afloat! I'm afloat! After four months on shore.
I fear not for breakers, I heed not the wave,
  I've the towpath to steer by, and a boat-hook to save;
And ne'er as a lubberly landsman I'll quail,
  When the Captain gives orders to "take in all sail."
Come, boy! Whip the mare! Keep her head to the wind,
  And I warrant we'll soon leave the snails all behind—
Up! Up! with your caps! Now give cheers three times three!
  I'm afloat! I'm afloat!

The night is pitch dark, and the rain has let loose,
  Who's afeerd! While our scow swims on like a goose;
What to her is the swash of Guv'nor Clinton's big ditch?
  She has braved it six times under Captain Saul Fitch.
The prime painted packets right past us may souse,
  They may rub, they may bunt, but they can't stave *our* bows.
With darkness around us, and the bridges so low,
  O'er the raging canawl right onward we go!
Ho! On deck here, my boys! Stand by your poles!
  There's a raft right ahead! Heaven save our poor souls!
Hard down with your helm! Make loose that line fast!
  Hurra boys! Hurra boys! The crisis is past.

Exaggeration, bravado, and spoofing came easy to the canallers and thus found expression in their songs and tall tales. In
addition to those songs just mentioned, others made less of the
storm-tossed sea imagery, but commented in various ways upon
the character of canal-boat life. In these, too, the language is
frequently nautical, for Erie canallers were proud of their
maritime mission in life.

A number of such songs have a common, although hardly
traceable, lineage. The group which follows shows the effects
of accretion and mutation in the hands of canawlers. The first
one below takes a recurrent image in Erie songs—that of the
cook, so indispensable a part of the canawler's life—and gives
it more prominence. Here the cook gets both satirized and
complimented, indicating the facility with which one verse
can supplant another in folk tradition.

Folk singer Frank Warner, of Farmingdale, Long Island,

collected the accompanying verses from "Yankee John" Galusha of Minerva, New York, around 1939.

"A Trip on the Erie" as collected by Frank Warner. Used by permission.

A second verse ran as follows:

> The cook she's a daisy, she'd dead gone on me,
> With her fiery red head, and she's twice twenty-three . . .
> She's cross-eyed and freckled, a dumpling and a pet,
> And we use her for a headlight at night on the deck.[23]

Versions of this song vary in wooing and heckling the cook; at times she is "sweet twenty-three," at other times she is "sweet *sixty*-three."

The canaller's diet included at times a commodity known as "Black Rock" pork, a canal equivalent to the western cowboy's "jerky," which provided a theme for singing Erie canallers. Usually, such a diet was spoken of in tones of lament. This single verse came from a Fort Plain resident who said the song was sung by tow-boys on the canal:

> First I went to Buffalo
>> And then I went to New York;
> And all the meat we had to eat
>> Was a slice of Black Rock pork.[24]

Other verses discuss the merits—or lack thereof—of such a diet:

BLACK ROCK PORK

> I shipped aboard of a lumber-boat,
>> Her name was *Charles O'Rourke.*
> The very first thing they rolled aboard
>> Was a barrel of Black Rock pork.
>
> They fried a chunk for breakfast
>> And a chunk for luncheon too.
> It didn't taste so goody-good,
>> And it was hard to chew.
>
> From Buffalo to old New York
>> They fed it to dear-old-me;
> They boiled the barrel and rest of the pork,
>> And we had it all for tea.[25]

This is high spoofing, in typical canalling manner. In "Canalman's Farewell," a canal lament, "Black Rock" pork took on the characteristics of something fondly remembered.

CANALMAN'S FAREWELL

> When I die, lay me on a canal boat
>> With my feet toward the bow:

> Let it be a Lockport Laker
> Or a Tonawanda scow.
> Put forty pounds of Black Rock pork
> Upon my brawny breast,
> And telephone over to the cook
> The driver's gone to rest.[26]

Influenced doubtless by various lines in versions of "The Raging Canal," the following song was presented in the *New York Folklore Quarterly* by its collector with the comment that it was "typical of the canawlers' repertoire." It opens with the beginning of a trip on the Erie Canal by a "ship" named *Danger*, again a result of that pseudo-nautical tradition in which Erie boatmen liked to think of themselves. The refrain occurs in other songs or mutations of this one. It is especially difficult with Erie song fragments to ascertain which came before what, however; and several originally separate songs may form a new amalgam in the recollections of informants. At any rate, several images which do recur frequently in Erie songs, such as that of an Erie barge ramming "a rock of Lackawanna coal," appear in "The Danger Ballad" below:

> I pulled out of Albany,
> On the good ship *Danger*
> To take a trip with the Erie boys
> I seemed most like a stranger.
>
> *Refrain:*
> For the Erie water's rising,
> For the gin is getting low,
> And I hardly think I'll get a drink,
> Till I get to Buffalo.
>
> Three days we sailed and struck a rock,
> 'Twas Lackawanna coal,
> It gave the boat a helluva shock,
> And knocked in an awful hole.
>
> I hollered to my driver
> On the towpath, treading dirt,

To come aboard and stop the leak
With his lousy undershirt.

Haul on your towline, now,
Don't stand by the sorrel mule,
Put a reef in your topsail,
Don't stand there like a fool! [27]

In other versions, the opening lines sing of a trip's completion, as in "I've just come down from Buffalo/Upon the great boat *Danger*" or "It was a long, long trip on the Erie/On the good ship called *The Danger*." Variants of this song look directly toward the popularly known version of "The E-RI-E." Most of them incorporate a cook "with a bosom like a boxcar" and vary the lines to draw in personal experiences. The nautical flavor of the previous songs, of course, remains, and some versions have the "storm-tossed sea" imagery kept alive. Here is a final variant of a canal song of which there are numerous versions.

I've travelled all around this world and Tonawanda too,
Was cast on desert islands and beaten black and blue;
I fought and bled at Bull's Run, and wandered since a boy,
But I'll never forget the trip I drove from Buffalo to Troy.

Refrain:
For it was tramp, tramp, tramp, and tighten in your lines!
And watch the playful horse flies, as o'er the mules they climb.
Whoa, back! Get up! Forget it I never shall,
When I drove a pair of spavined mules on the E-ri-e Canal.

The cook we had on board the deck stood six feet in her socks;
Her hand was like an elephant's ear, her breath would open locks.
A maid of sixty summers was she, who slept upon the floor;
And when at night she'd get to sleep, oh sufferin', how she'd
    snore! [28]

Several elements of these preceding songs (and doubtless as well numerous fragments of songs known and unknown now) appear in two well-popularized Erie items—"The E-RI-E" and "Low Bridge"—which have survived the passing of the Big Ditch and which continue in popularity. To some extent, Tin Pan Alley influence has standardized them, but folk music anthologies and recordings offer various versions of both.

Carl Sandburg considered "The E-RI-E" a song which tries for laughter at monotony and fate.[29] This song, like "Low Bridge" which follows it here, often goes by the simple title, "The Erie Canal"—a decidedly and unnecessarily confusing label. When it appears in an index or on a record jacket, one can never be sure what Erie song is meant without inspection of the song verses themselves. The text given is that which appears in *The New Song Fest* (1955):

THE E-RI-E

We were forty miles from Albany,
Forget it I never shall;
What a terrible storm we had that night
On the E-ri-e Canal.

Refrain:
Oh the E-ri-e was a-rising,
And the gin was getting low,
And I scarcely think we'll get a drink
'Till we get to Buffalo,
'Till we get to Buffalo.

We were loaded down with barley,
We were chuck up full of rye,
And the captain, he looked down at me
With his goddam wicked eye.

Our captain, he came up on deck,
With a spy glass in his hand,
And the fog, it was so darned thick
That he couldn't spy land.

Two days out from Syracuse
The vessel struck a shoal,
And we like to all been foundered
On a chunk o' Lackawanna coal.

We hollered to the captain
On the towpath, treadin' dirt;
He jumped on board and stopped the leak
With his old red flannel shirt.

Our cook, she was a grand old gal,
She had a ragged dress;
We hoisted her upon the pole
As a signal of distress.

The winds began to whistle
The waves began to roll
And we had to reef our royals
On the raging Canawl.

When we got to Syracuse,
The off-mule he was dead,
The nigh mule got blind staggers,
And we cracked him on the head.

Oh, the girls are in the Police Gazette,
The crew are all in jail;
And I'm the only living sea cook's son
That's left to tell the tale.[30]

One of Burl Ives' recordings includes verses 1, 3, and 6 of the above (with slight variation in the wording) and concludes with

The captain he got married
And the cook she went to jail;
And I'm the only son of a gun
That's left to tell the tale.[31]

Like this song, "Low Bridge, Everybody Down" has been extremely popular with recording folk singers, and it is often found in folk song collections. Its general popularity is traceable, most directly, to the words and music by Thomas S. Allen, as published in the early part of the twentieth century. Indirectly, "Low Bridge" goes back much further, if not into folk tradition, at least into an important part of American musical culture. When Edward Harrigan's comedy, *The Grip*, played the vaudeville boards in the middle 1880's, audiences heard the Harrigan-Braham show tune, "Oh! Dat Low Bridge!" picking up the Erie Canal idiom with "It's many miles to Buf-fa-lo . . ." Here are the four verses as published in 1885. See accompanying melody line.

OH! DAT LOW BRIDGE!

As sung in EDWARD HARRIGAN's New Comedy, "THE GRIP."

WORDS BY EDWARD HARRIGAN.   MUSIC BY DAVE BRAHAM.

From the original in Grosvenor Library.

It's many miles to Buffalo/Oh, dat low bridge!
Balky mule he travel slow/Oh, dat low bridge!
Dar's gravel on de towpath/Dar's hornets in de sand
Oh, pity poor canallers/Dat's far away from land.

Refrain:
Den look out dat low bridge, look out dat low bridge,
The captain, cook, and all de crew, oh, duck your head way
    down,
The fastest boat in all de fleet,
Two sisters come to town.

Dar's many locks to shut you in/Oh, dat low bridge!
Ev'ry worm must learn to swim/Oh, dat low bridge!
We're loaded down with barley,/And lumber from de west,
Oh, ev'ry poor canaller,/Now do your level best.

We're froze up in the winter time/Oh, dat low bridge!
Summer how de sun do shine/Oh, dat low bridge!
In rain or stormy weather,/De captain's on de poop,
All huddle up together,/Like chickens in de coop.

Dar's groceries in de cabin dar/Oh, dat low bridge!
Never leaks, she's full of tar/Oh, dat low bridge!
Dar's freckles on de children,/Dar's glanders on de mule,
Mosquitoes by de million/Who keep de golden rule.[32]

The *double entendre* is presumably not lost on the reader!
Finally, here is the Tin Pan Alley song which Allen wrote:

LOW BRIDGE! EVERYBODY DOWN [33]
or
Fifteen Years on The Erie Canal.

I've got an old mule and her name is Sal,
Fifteen years on the Erie Canal.
She's a good old worker and a good old pal,
Fifteen years on the Erie Canal.
We've hauled some barges in our day,
Filled with lumber, coal and hay,
And ev'ry inch of the way I know,
From Albany to Buffalo.

Chorus:
Low bridge, ev'rybody down,
Low bridge, we must be getting near a town,
You can always tell your neighbor,
You can always tell your pal,
If he's ever navigated on the Erie Canal.

Low bridge, ev'rybody down,
Low bridge, I've got the finest mule in town,
Once a man named Mike McGinty
Tried to put it over Sal,
Now he's 'way down at the bottom of the Erie Canal.

We'd better look 'round for a job old gal,
Fifteen years on the Erie Canal.
You bet your life I wouldn't part with Sal,
Fifteen years on the Erie Canal.
Giddap there gal we've passed that lock,
We'll make Rome 'fore six o'clock,
So one more trip and then we'll go,
Right straight back to Buffalo.

Extra Verses
Oh, where would I be if I lost my pal?
Fifteen years on the Erie Canal.
Oh, I'd like to see a mule as good as Sal,
Fifteen years on the Erie Canal.
A friend of mine once got her sore,
Now, he's got a broken jaw.
'Cause she let fly with her iron toe
And kicked him into Buffalo.

Chorus:
Low Bridge, everybody down,
Low Bridge, I've got the finest mule in town,
If you're looking 'round for trouble,
Better stay away from Sal,
She's the only fighting donkey on the Erie Canal.

I don't have to call when I want my Sal,
Fifteen years on the Erie Canal;
She trots from her stall like a good old gal,
Fifteen years on the Erie Canal,
I eat my meals with Sal each day
I eat beef and she eats hay,
She ain't so slow if you want to know,
She put the "Buff" in Buffalo.

Low Bridge, everybody down,
Low Bridge, I've got the finest mule in town;
Eats a bale of hay for dinner,
And on top of that, my Sal
Tries to drink up all the water in the Erie Canal.

You'll soon hear them sing all about my gal,
Fifteen years on the Erie Canal.

It's a darned fool ditty 'bout my darned fool Sal,
Fifteen years on the Erie Canal.

Oh, every band will play it soon,
Darned fool words and darned fool tune;
You'll hear it sung everywhere you go,
From Mexico to Buffalo.

Chorus:
Low Bridge, everybody down,
Low Bridge, I've got the finest mule in town,
She's a perfect, perfect lady,
And she blushes like a gal,
If she hears you sing about her and the Erie Canal.

Some amateur versions of this song substitute "fifteen *miles*" —not inappropriately, for that was a fair trick's accomplishment on the Old Erie. Whether "fifteen miles" or "fifteen years," the steady plodding of the towpath mule as the canal boat makes its slow way along seems to have been caught in the song. With "The E-RI-E" and "Low Bridge" the Clinton Ditch is left rather far behind in one sense, but their importance in keeping alive the essence of the folk traditions of the Erie should not be taken slightly. Their popularity is undeniable. It apparently extends even to the American West of Hollywood stereotype. In Republic Pictures' *Rio Grande* (1950), a colonel of cavalry (John Wayne) has his troop singing about the Erie Canal as they ride out to meet an Apache attack!

The early canallers sang for reasons easily understood— singing was a means of entertainment and a release from the monotony and hard life. Breaking into song was a trait of the pioneer, and the canawlers were a convivial, if brawling, pioneering ilk. They drank deeply, they ate heartily, they fought eagerly, and they sang lustily. That much of their material had a nautical flavor stemmed from perhaps one-tenth conscious hyperbole and nine-tenths sheer pride in boatin' on the Grand Western Canal, the finest—and longest—inland water communication in the world.

Low Bridge! - Everybody Down.

or

Fifteen Years On The Erie Canal.

Words and Music·by
THOS. S. ALLEN.

From the original in Grosvenor Library.

Tall Tales of
"The Roaring Giddap"

CANALLERS' tales stemmed from actual canalside incidents and the persons involved in them. Not infrequently, of course, the stories became exaggerated or a storyteller got hold of a real yarn and thus would begin the fabrication of a "whopper," growing into a full-fledged tall tale recognizable in variants by folklorists the world over. Sometimes the literary craftsman plays a part, too, adapting for his purposes folk material which subsequently is remembered more in the literary version than in the original of folk tradition.

One enterprising "captain," for example, made history of a highly interesting sort in the 1880's, when he conceived the idea of exhibiting a whale on the Erie Canal. A native of Sag Harbor, Oakes Anderson went into partnership with three other Long Islanders, took a whale captured off Cape Cod and had a Boston professor go to work on it with barrels of embalming fluid. Mounting the 65-foot fin-back on a barge, Oakes added a tent, hired a professional lecturer, and set off on a tour of the canal and other waterways with a $6,000 investment.

He toured across York State, over into Ohio, and up and down the Mississippi, piling up cash from curious patrons en route. Health departments and other critics found that, in comparison to Anderson's whale, the smell from Barren Island (where New York City once dumped its garbage) was like sweet attar of roses. Eventually, his partners left him, he discharged his paid hawker, and Oakes Anderson had a slightly used whale on his hands. He couldn't sell it or give it away, and one time his barge sank in the canal, whale and all. The smell finally went away, as the whale dried to mummified condition; but what finally happened to the whale no one knows. Here, at any rate, was a canaller about whom it was said his Yankee wit and power of exaggeration made him second only to P. T. Barnum as a showman.[1]

The story, somewhat modified by the years, reached Walter D. Edmonds. "Someone told me," he said, "that a canaller had stabbed a whale in the eye on his way across the Harbor and exhibited it up the Hudson and the canal . . ."[2] Edmonds went to work on the story and produced "The Cruise of the Cashalot" for *The Forum and Century* in 1932; his canawler managed also to get rid of the whale: he sold it for fertilizer for eighty cents. A 65-foot whale on the Erie Canal thus became one kind of Erie tale.

But Erie Canal stories—whether authentic, apocryphal, or invented—throw light on the nature of the canaller and of "canal culture." They keep alive, half a century after its closing, something of the spirit of what Samuel Hopkins Adams called "that vast Clintonian enterprise."

The Erie tall tale in many cases is a recognizable folk tale type transplanted, as it were, to Erie water. A variation of the culture hero motif, St. Patrick's version (A531.2),* for example, concerns snakes in and along the Erie Canal, the bane of towpath life. A packet skipper named Joe seems to have been responsible for ridding the Erie towpath of them, helped by the indomitable descendants of Erin. Going through a school of water snakes once, the canaller's boat lost an Irish greenhorn who fell overboard. According to the story, the

---

* Folklore scholarship classifies tales into types which are recognized worldwide; the numbers refer to standard classification within the motif-index or folk tale types. See Stith Thompson, *Motif-Index of Folk Literature*, rev. ed., 6 vols. (Bloomington: Univ. of Indiana Press, 1955–58). For an account of the folk tale in various cultures, see Thompson, *The Folktale* (New York: Holt, Rinehart and Winston, 1946).

Irishman hadn't washed since he left Ireland, and the snakes in the canal died of poisoning right then and there. This gave Joe an idea. Since most Irishmen carried a bowl filled with Irish field dirt, Joe took a handful of the dirt from each of the Irish passengers aboard, and scattered it liberally on the banks along the canal as he went along. Since that day, few snakes have come near the towpath.[3]

The towpath mule, being the most cussed animal in Yorker country, naturally evoked much tall-tale attention. One canal tale involves a boatsman who tried to raise bees on his canal boat, but when the hives swarmed near Pittsford, locktenders armed with whippletrees caused a near riot. Once the mules strained so hard to get away from the bees that they stretched a brand new towrope, an inch and a half thick, so much it could be used for grocery twine.

Agnes was different. A Civil War veteran turned to towpath work, she pulled barges for ten years or so, until her captain sold her for ten dollars to a young Virginian visiting Albany. Then Agnes really began to come alive. The Virginian took her to his Richmond plantation to plow peanut fields, but Agnes had other ideas. She took a liking for red coats and fox hunts, and bounded after the hounds. As a matter of fact, she put her ears up, passed the hunters, jumped fences like a kangaroo, and got to the foxes before the hounds. After that, there was no holding Agnes once she heard the dogs on the track of a fox.

Then there is the story of the giant squash (X1401, Type 1960D). One year a big drought hit the Erie, and the canal and its feeders were almost dry. A woman in Weedsport was arrested for filling her washtub from the Erie and thus stranding fifteen canal boats. Towpath walkers all that summer went along the canal cutting weeds and vines so their roots couldn't suck any water from the canal; they carried shotguns to fire at the crows and sparrows that tried to drink. One fellow from Eagle Harbor way made out all right, though. He had a squash vine that he had been nursing along by spitting on it every so often. When he finally stuck the roots into the canal to water them, the vine dragged out water like a big hose and left ten miles of the canal bottom bare. The plant swelled so fast the farmer had to run to keep from getting *squashed*. The plants swelled like rubber balloons, and one section of the vine actually passed him, going like a racer snake; he grabbed at a flower-bud, but by that time it had turned into a flower and then into a good-sized squash so fast it blew off his hand as a fistful of gunpowder would. He made a living for years selling sections of the vine's leaves—the veins made good drainage tile.

This story has appeared in other versions as the Palmyra squash, with slight variations in the telling.

Over Rome way, another story, reminiscent of Paul Bunyan legendry, concerns a giant frog (X1342.1, Type 1960B). In the early 1850's a young lad named Red McCarthy took a polliwog from the Erie Canal along Rome's South James Street. This was the canal-spawned origin of Joshua, the famous frog of Empeyville—a 100-year-old giant, with hind legs six feet long and an appetite that was said to have devoured chipmunks, squirrels, and sometimes rabbits. For a time after his polliwog days Joshua was missing, but he turned up several years later in the town pond at Empeyville. There every time he jumped the water sprayed thirty feet in the air, and the pond got six feet wider!

Yarns have sprung up around the giant frog. As an assistant sawman in Empeyville, Joshua hauled material that was too heavy for horses. He gained a fair reputation as a road-straightener, too, by hooking up a chain to the roads and pulling hard. In this way he helped straighten the Snake Hill curves. As late as the summer of 1934 the Rome *Sentinel* reported an incident involving Joshua, four of whose grandsons, owned by a man in Rome, were employed by the city as stump-pullers.[4] Other descendants still inhabit Empeyville pond.

All things seem bigger in Yorker canal country. To talk about mosquitoes and flies, especially in upstate New York, has never taken much effort. Adirondack fishing and hunting country boasts a number of sizable varieties, unfortunately not fictional. Canawlers early came to know the mosquito, especially discomforting—in both size and number—in the several marshy areas through which the Old Erie passed west of Utica. During an unnerving sleepless evening aboard a canal packet in the early 1830's, the British actor Tyrone Power came in for a little "leg-pulling" by an Erie boater. Slapping the monstrous mosquitoes, as he said, "with unwearied constancy," Power inquired of the boatman if any mosquitoes could be worse than those of the area through which they were then passing. The canawler pointed out yet another area when they came "within about forty miles of Utica."

"I guess *that* is *the place* above all for musquitoes," replied the man grinning. "Thim's the real gallinippers, emigrating north for the summer all the way from the Balize and Red River. Let a man go to sleep with his head in a cast-iron kettle among them chaps, and if their bills don't make a water-pot of it before morning, I'm d—d. They're strong enough to lift the boat out of the canal, if they could only get underneath her." [5]

The miasmal swamps frankly offended many a tourist, but canawlers who talked of "the raging E-ri-e" could speak with considerable conviction of many things, not the least of which was the weather. Storms and breaks on the canal caused much concern, but, according to one account, heavy fogs were worse. "I think it was in '73 that they had the last big fog in the Irondequoit Valley," says an old captain in one story. "We had a new driver, and when he'd passed through Bushnell Basin he missed the towpath altogether and struck off north. The steersman was too full of applejack to notice what had happened, and at daybreak, when the fog lifted, the mules was just wading into Lake Ontario water off Sea Breeze point."

This, along with some other tales, was set down by Paul MacFarland for the Society of the Erie Canal, an Albion and Rochester organization which had a vigorous if brief life of two meetings in the 1930's. Among the tall tales were three or four about a driver named McCarthy, a Paul Bunyan type who was supposed to have been the strongest man on the canal in the 1840's.

One night (so runs a story) just after his team picked up the towrope for his six-hour trick, the line broke at the whippletree. The mules, fresh and full of oats, ran away. McCarthy picked up the rope, put it over his shoulder, and hauled away for five hours, and nobody aboard the canal boat knew what had happened. Meanwhile the boat, a leaky tub filled with crushed stone, had the bottom ripped out on a sunken rock, and though she sank, McCarthy never stopped pulling. He hauled that barge along the channel for seven miles, its keel sinking deeper into the mud. Luckily, the moon came out as he approached the Genesee aqueduct in Rochester, or he would have ripped the floor of the aqueduct right out and let the canal drop smack into the river. He was pulling west, against the current, too. The State Legislature later voted him $500 for scooping the canal four feet deeper from Pittsford to Rochester.

Another McCarthy tale similarly scrapes canal bottom, but this time the canawler does it intentionally. McCarthy had been invited to a dance by the boys and girls of Knowlesville, and as he went through Spencerport he got word that the Knowlesville Village Hall had burned down and the dance was off. McCarthy loved to dance, and he couldn't see a fire spoiling his fun, so he took aboard his flat-bottomed boat enough paving blocks to weigh his boat down so it was scraping the bottom of the canal. Then he hitched his fastest mules to the boat and headed toward Knowlesville, where he heaved the boat over, bottom-side up, against the berm. The boat bottom had been so smoothed by scraping along the canal bottom that it looked like glass. McCarthy just waxed the timbers a little and the town had its dance floor on the underside of McCarthy's boat.

This McCarthy was nimble-witted, too. He owned a remarkable set of mules that he had trained. According to Erie tradition, when mules were changed the canal boat had to come into the bank and stop for five minutes or so while the "hoss-bridge" was let down for the mules to cross over from boat to towpath. McCarthy trained his mules to save time by marching single file, like tightrope walkers, along the towrope.

After that, every captain along the Erie tried to buy Mc-
Carthy-trained mules. It was a great sight, so they say, to see
two or three mules tripping along the towrope gracefully
as you please.

Fish stories form an inevitable part of Erie folklore, with
tales of both the big catch (X1150.1, Type 1960C) and the
giant fish (X1301, Type 1960B) prevalent. Giant fish—
usually sturgeon—frequented canal waters. In the spring of
the year, when the big pike and sturgeon came in from Lake
Erie, fishing on the canal (especially when the Erie was enlarged) became "big game" sport. But where there is fishing
there are also "fish stories," and fact and fancy get pretty
much intertwined. Big fish were common in Erie waters: captains had to caution their boys not to drop fishlines in the canal
unless the boat was tied up. In the 1870's, near Medina, a black-
smith made a hook out of a crowbar, placed it on a length
of old towrope, and baited it with a young pig. A Lake Erie
sturgeon grabbed the hook and hauled the canal boat—originally headed for Rochester with a boatload of barley—nearly
to Lockport before the rope could be snubbed on an abutment.
It nearly pulled three mules into the canal, and "for weeks
after that," said an old canawler, "we had to harness those
mules with their heads facing the boat, they were so used to
going backwards." On another occasion, using sturgeon-power
to get to Buffalo, the boat wound up in Detroit across the
Great Lakes! How the canal boat got through the Lockport
combines is not recorded.

One explanation is given in Carl Carmer's version of this
story, in which a Hudson River sturgeon grabbed for the
anchor of a canal boat, just down from Buffalo. Captain and
passengers felt a jerk.

> The next thing they knew they were travelling back over
> the way they had come at a much faster speed than that to
> which they were accustomed, and the mules had developed
> with startling ease the ability to run backwards.
> The *Bathsheba C. Onderdonck* flashed through Rochester

stern-first and by the time she reached Spencerport she was leaving so great a swell in her wake that the hired men working on the farms beside the canal later claimed they had seen a tidal wave.

. . . When the sturgeon reached Lockport the big locks had been filled to let a boat go through and the lockkeeper had just opened the doors to release the water. The big fish squirmed up that hill of water so fast it had no time to run out and the *Bathsheba C. Onderdonck* went right along.[6]

The captain finally cut the towrope "before they were all dragged into the depths of stormy Lake Erie."

Another time, a big Lake Erie sturgeon made its way through the canal as far as the Macedon locks, disrupting service all the way. Seen slipping through the lock into the short level to the eastward, it finally was "landed." Locktenders cleared all boats from the locks, and drained out the water to a foot-and-a-half depth. Every hunter and fisherman in Macedon was on hand to try his luck, even an Indian boy with a bow and arrow. (In Walter D. Edmonds' novel, *Erie Water*, a muskellunge gets through the first locks opened on the Buffalo section and is "worked through the locks" to the Rochester level.)

Big bass and carp seemed everywhere in the Old Erie. One story has them drunk—on hard cider which overflowed from a barge where it was being stored. The big bass and carp staggered up and down the canal, hiccoughing like leaky boilers. All the tomcats in the neighborhood thought the poor soused fish would be easy pickings, but those carp with hard-cider hangovers chased the cats so hard that, for years afterwards, the cats would not even eat canned salmon, they were so nervous about fish.

Every now and then the bank of the canal would let go and flood the country along the Erie, and one old driver reminisced that he always figured maybe it was fishermen who blew up the banks so they would have plenty of fish. According to his story, around 1857 the Old Erie broke through about two miles from Albion, between Braley's Bridge and Peck's Bridge. The farmers on the north side of the canal did not have any good wheat crops that year, because their seed was pretty well washed out, but they had a lovely lot of pike. They pitchforked them into their wagons by the ton, took them home, and salted and smoked them.

One fellow from Albion headed for the break with a gunny sack to fill up with fish. When he arrived at the scene, the good ones were about gone, but there were still thousands of bullheads around, so he filled his bag with bullheads. Then he tossed the sack over his shoulder and about forty of those sticklebacks drove their stingers into him at once. The yell he let out reportedly scared children all the way up in Barre Center, and he lit out for Albion, screaming at every jump. But he kept hold of his sack of bullheads; at every jump a new bullhead spike would jab him, and at every jab he would run faster. Up Albion way they still claim that not anybody or anything ever went as fast as John O'Brien until the New York Central's Empire State Express came along.

But Oak Orchard Creek bass are the true fisherman's fish. They have something of a reputation for jumping right into a fisherman's boat, a *fact* to which both Yorkers and visitors will readily attest.[7] John Darling's winning of the red-haired Sal by trapping the bass brings together the Catskill folk hero and the stereotype of an Erie Canal cook. At Albion he tied up his canal boat while he went to Old Orchard River to win a fishing contest and a bride. Carl Carmer, in placing Darling in Erie country, probably had in mind Oak Orchard Creek; at any rate, it happened this way:

John Darling's boat was the *Erie Queen* and his cook was Sal; and when he wanted to marry her she made a fishing contest out of her consenting. From midnight to midnight, she said, the one who caught the most fish would win her hand. That was when John Darling tied up the *Erie Queen* at Albion and headed for his favorite fishing site. Sal rather liked him, though, and when she found him after sunset without any fish, she gave him a hand. Now Sal was a fiery redhead, so John Darling figured a way to fool the bass.

"Put your head down to the water," he shouted to Sal, and when she did, the whole school of bass, forced against the bank on one side and scared out of its scales by the blinding light on the other, jumped high out of the water. John Darling swung the boat under them as they came down. After he had dug Sal out from under the pile he counted the fish that had jumped into his boat. There were two hundred and thirty-three.[8]

Redhead Sal and John Darling were married the next morning and honeymooned at Niagara Falls. When they returned, the *Erie Queen,* gaily decorated, hosted a party that lasted all night long, with twenty canal boats and twenty span of mules on or along the Erie Canal.

VIII

The Erie Canal
in Literature

FROM its inception, York State's Grand Canal seemed destined
for literary attention. A number of allusions to a canal connecting the Great Lakes and the western territories with the
Hudson River appear in early American literature and attest
to the feeling that poets and other creative writers had for the
idea of an across-the-state waterway, a feeling apparently no
less fervent than that held by the farsighted tract writers like
"Hercules" (Jesse Hawley) whose articles in the Genesee
Messenger have been credited with enlisting popular support
for an Erie canal project. Alvin F. Harlow's nostalgic *Old
Towpaths* (1926) provides considerable insight into this pre-
Erie literature, with a full chapter on "The Genesis of the
Erie." Among the more important of the items cited, Joel
Barlow's "Vision of Columbus" spoke, in terms typically
prophetic of the times, of one who

> . . . saw, as widely spread the unchannell'd plain
> Where inland realms for ages bloom'd in vain,
> Canals, long winding, ope a watery flight,
> And distant streams, and seas and lakes unite.

This vision depicted an upstate area cut by inland waterways
from east to west:

> From fair Albania, tow'rd the falling sun,
> Back through the midland lengthening channels run;
> Meet the far lakes, the beauteous towns that lave,
> And Hudson joined to broad Ohio's wave.

This was 1787; journals, diaries, reports of surveyors, accounts of travellers, and other writings voluminously recorded canal sentiment before the completion of the Erie in 1825. One of the famous wrong-guessers about the canal, William H. Seward (later Secretary of State), wrote an anti-canal essay while a member of the Literary Society at Union College, which he attended from 1816 to 1820. He later retracted, in 1822.[1] That same year, on August 8, "Stanzas on the Great Western Canal of the State of New York" appeared in the New Brunswick (N.J.) *Fredonian*. The author, signing himself merely "F," was a seventy-year-old poet well known to Americans as a commentator on the native scene.[2] In this poem on the Erie Canal, Philip Freneau reviewed at first the seemingly impossible goals:

> From *Erie's* shores to *Hudson's* stream
> The unrivalled work would endless seem;
> Would millions for the work demand,
> And half depopulate the land.
>
> To Fancy's view, what years must run,
> What ages, till the task is done!
> Even trust, severe would seem to say,
> *One hundred years must pass away:*—

But, then, the wonder of the Erie accomplishment!

> *Three years elapsed,* behold it done!
> A work from Nature's *chaos* won;
> By hearts of oak and hands of toil
> The Spade inverts the rugged soil
> A work, that may remain secure
> While suns exist and Moons endure.

With patient step I see them move
O'er many a plain, through many a grove;
Herculean strength disdains the sod
Where tigers ranged or *Mohawks* trod;
The powers that can the soil subdue
Will see the mighty project through.

Ye patrons of this bold design
Who *Erie* to the *Atlantic* join,
To you be every honour paid—
No time shall see your fame decayed:—
Through gloomy groves you traced the plan,
The rude abodes of savage man.

Ye Prompters of a work so vast
That may for years, for centuries last;
Where Nature toiled to bar the way
You mark'd her steps, but changed her way.

Ye Artists, who, with skillful hand,
Conduct such rivers' through the land,
Proceed!—and in your bold career
May every Plan as wise appear,
As *this*, which joins to *Hudson's* wave
What Nature to *St. Lawrence* gave.

In an earlier version, the poem had appeared in *True American* for June 30, 1821, with an introductory comment by the editors. "Rejoicing at the progress of Inland Navigation in the State of New York," ran the note, "and delighted at seeing the Muses directing their attention to such patriotic subjects, it may well be believed that we give a hearty welcome to the following communication from a Revolutionary Patriot and Poet." At the end of the poem in the *Fredonian* Freneau himself commented briefly upon the canal's having been completed to "an uninterrupted navigation of two hundred and twenty-eight miles." The whole Erie project obviously made an impression on him, as he added, "The whole will be completed, it is said, by October 1825.—It is calculated it will then produce an annual revenue of ten millions of dollars! A sum

almost exceeding credibility and transcending the most rea-
sonable computation—as well as sanguine expectation."

"October 1825." The gala celebration which marked the
completion of the Erie Canal produced its own literature to
a voluminous degree, albeit one would hesitate to call much
of it "literary." Everywhere—from one end of the canal to
the other—doggerel and crude verses appeared. As the *Seneca
Chief* and the *Young Lion of the West* rode on Erie water
across the state and down to New York harbor, many persons
felt the Muses must be influencing them to look upon the
noble enterprise for inspired and enthusiastic lines. Some, needless to say, were poets in name only, but their verses seemed
nonetheless stirring as they penned grandiloquent odes about
the passing entourage.

A poem by the Reverend Charles Giles is a case in point.
Digging into Erie literature sometimes uncovers strange bed-
fellows: this "ode" appeared almost as an afterthought in a
slender little volume published in the late 1830's. One would
hardly suspect that a cleric's outpourings, bearing the seemingly unclerical title of *The Convention of Drunkards*, would
be at the same time a repository for a bit of Erie lore.

True to the times, it had a rambling title three-quarters of
a page long.[3] Together with a satirical essay providing the
principal title, several clerically inspired temperance speeches,
and an Independence Day oration, the Erie verse was pref-
aced by a note on the completion of the canal and correspondence from Governor Clinton, to whom the Rev. Mr. Giles
had sent a copy of the poem:

Albany, Dec. 12, 1825.

Governor Clinton's compliments to Mr. Giles, and offers
him his sincere thanks for his communication of the 18th
ultimo. His absence in New-York has prevented an earlier
reply.

Whatever doubts there may be about the merits of the
subject, there certainly can be none about those of the
poetry.

In the clergyman's own words, the public doings attendant
on the completion of the Erie Canal occasioned the ode, written
at Utica when the Clinton party stopped "to unite with the
citizens in rejoicing on the occasion"; he entitled his ode "Celebration of the Grand Canal." The seven stanzas follow:

> Fixed as a pharos midst the flood,
>   Enwheeled by glory's noontide blaze,
>   And marked by wonder's eager gaze,
> The ruling *genius* dauntless stood!
>   Who[se] will matured the grand design
>   To change creation's ancient line;
> To prostrate mountains, rend the ground,
>   Th' opposing streams by art to guide,
> Tear up old Nature's storm-proof bound,
>   And blend proud Erie's waves with Ocean's tide!
>
> Impelled by skill and public weal,
>   Th' illustrious *sire* of state proclaimed
>   The grand emprise, which rose high famed
> O'er reasoning false and party zeal.
>   The *peers* of state, in council wise,
>   Saw in the scheme grand prospects rise.
> Forth orders went, and straight the power
>   The prompt auxiliaries obeyed,
> And seized the all-propitious hour
>   To form new wonders and give commerce aid.
>
> 'Twas said, and straight the bounding share,
>   From shore to shore, cut wound on wound,
>   Tore through dense forests, swept the ground,
> And laid Earth's hidden treasures bare!
>   The hills afrighted moved aside;
>   Deep excavations opened wide;
> Strong marble bars felt sudden shocks;
>   Huge sledges stroke their strata through;
> Impelled by flames the solid rocks
>   Leaped from their beds, and, thundering, upward flew!
>
> The levelled bed, thus urged by force
>   Through villages, and hills, and woods,
>   And rocks, and meads, and fens, and floods,

Maintained its welcome, winding course.
  O'er nether streams strong arches rose,
  On which the ponderous banks repose;
A smooth, firm way adorns the strand;
  On solid walls high o'er the road
The frequent bridges arching stand,
  And swinging gates stupendous lock the flood.

Hark! loud the signal sounds from far—
  The work's complete, the cannon roar
  Along the bank from Erie's shore:
The triumph rides in thunder's car!
  'Mid splendid trains in honor's cause,
  With martial pride and loud applause,
Throned on a pompous barge sublime
  The *patriot* comes from Erie's past,
Borne on his own invented stream,
  Bound to th' emporium on the Atlantic coast.

Now brilliant crowds convivial meet,
  With mingled music sounding high,
  And rapture sparking in each eye,
The *founder, patrons,* all to greet
  Of the grand work, and celebrate
  This novel era of the state
The festal halls with pomp abound;
  The flowing state no gift denies;
Our councils rule; our parts resound
  With commerce, learning, arts and enterprise.

Our noble *guest* awakes delight;
  From port to port loud thunders greet
  His welcome barge; the joyful treat
Sheds mimic day amid the night.
  Now all conspire in one grand cause,
  And swell the notes of just applause.
So, vassel waves, in pomp convey
  Down through the state your *charge* along!
While future years revive this day,
  And barges float let CLINTON'S name be sung!

The good clerical gentleman's central interest in this book

concerned satirizing intemperance, in the hope that he could thereby succeed where education and pulpit exhortation had so far failed. Certainly, if we read Erie literature rightly, canawlers as a lot could stand "deliquifying." But there is no evidence to tell us whether the Rev. Giles ever considered poetizing on the drinking éclat of the Erieman.

Two years after the official opening, a better-known New Yorker, James Kirke Paulding, wrote the Grand Canal into one of those delightful and charming stories which comprise *The Book of Saint Nicholas,* the first time in American literature that the Erie Canal figured as a part of the essential narrative.[4] The story, "The Ride of St. Nicholas on Newyear's Eve," depicts the good St. Nick as "exceedingly grieved," and about to abandon old Nieuw-Amsterdam's Dutch for their "incorrigible . . . backslidings" when he came upon a new canal.

> He was making his progress through the streets, to take his last farewell, in melancholy mood, when he came to the outlet of the Grand Canal, just then completed. "Is het mogelyk?"—which means, is it possible—exclaimed St. Nicholas; and thereupon he was so delighted with this proof that his beloved people had not altogether degenerated from their ancestors, that he determined not to leave them to strange saints, outlandish tongues, and modern innovations. He took a sail on the canal, and returned in such measureless content, that he blessed the good city of Fort Orange, as he evermore called it, and resolved to distribute a more than usual store of his Newyear cookies, at the Christmas holydays.[5]

Jolly Old Santa Claus thus became the first to ride the Erie Canal—in literature—and Paulding's working the canal into the story indicates, even this early, how the Erie would figure in the folklore and literature of the State.

The earliest use of the Erie Canal in the American drama— and, for that matter, one of the earliest instances of the canal's appearance in literature in general—was William Dunlap's three-act farce, *A Trip to Niagara,* written for the Bowery Theatre, New York, in 1828. First staged at the Bowery Theatre, November 28, 1828, this was Dunlap's last published play.[6]

The play concerns several tourists to America, chief among them Mr. Wentworth, who appears quite misanthropic toward everything he encounters in America; and his sister Amelia, who, finding the travels both pleasurable and interesting, seeks to cure her brother of his prejudices against anything not English so that he, too, may enjoy himself. Mr. Jonathan Bull, a fellow Englishman and cousin, with a sense of humor and a more tolerant attitude, accepts the challenge of curing Wentworth of his prejudices. Among the secondary characters, Dennis Dougherty, a quaking Irishman who cannot return to his native land soon enough (he is rather worse than Wentworth!), provides comic commentary on the Erie trip. Most of the characters are recognizable stereotypes, and the whole play is delightfully typical of early nineteenth-century American stage fare. Much punning and other confusion of words, resulting from the interplay of the speech of Americans, English, Irish, Germans, and Frenchmen, make this Dunlap drama engaging armchair reading.

The itinerary of the travellers includes a trip to Niagara Falls, and as the play opens Wentworth discloses that he has secured berths on a Hudson River line to Albany. For most of the trip he remains disagreeably aggravated at everything he sees and does. The party meets the Erie Canal en route, of course. They apparently take a canal boat from Albany, and one scene (III, iv) at "the little falls of the Mohawk" (Little Falls) has the canal and the aqueduct crossing the Mohawk River as its setting. As the scene opens, Wentworth and Amelia have just stepped off the canal boat for a moment with the other travellers, to view the local falls.

> AME. This is delightful, brother.
> WENT. Is it?
> AME. The opportunity we so frequently have, of stepping from the canal boat, and thus walking on the bank,

adds to the pleasure derived from the ever changing scenery that is presented to us.

WENT. Pleasure! To be dragged along upon a muddy ditch, hour after hour, in constant dread of lifting your head above your knees for fear of having it knock'd off your shoulders by a bridge!

AME. But your head is safe, now, notwithstanding . . . the canal bridges, and you must admire this great patriotic work—this union of the inland seas with the Atlantic Ocean.

WENT. What is this, to the work of the Duke of Bridgewater.

AME. Let praise be given, where praise is due. There are two names, which will live in the memories of Americans, as long as they can appreciate the blessings that flow in a rapid interchange of every good from one extreme of their republic to the other. Fulton and Clinton. And I hope that the gratitude of their countrymen, will not only be shown to their names and memories, but to their children, and their children's children.

At this point Jonathan Bull enters; he has apparently been talking to one of the Palatinate Germans.

BULL. What do you think that tarnation Mohawk Dutchman says?

WENT. Praises the great canal, I suppose.

BULL. No. He says, "Effer dince Glinton gut de pig canawl, de peef ant putter of de Sharman-flats ave falt fifty bur sent; ant dey pring all de tam dings to New-York, all de vay from Puffalo, and de tuyvil knows vere."

AME. Ha, ha, ha! Fault finding every where . . .

WENT. I dare say he is right. But . . . when shall we get to the wilderness!

BULL. Ah, that's what every body says. But these curst creatures have spoilt all that. What with their turnpike roads, and canals, they have gone, like tarnal fools as they are, and put down towns and villages, gardens and orchards, churches and schools, and sich common things, where the woods and wild beasts and Indians and rattlesnakes ought to have ben.

The latter remark of John Bull's satirizes the typical English attitude toward American progress, an attitude reflected in many of the journals and travel diaries of the times.

Wentworth spies someone waving a hat at them from a passing canal boat. Dennis Dougherty, who joins the group, is found to have had to work his passage when he saw his "dollars grow light," as he put it: he wound up as a hoggee. "When the boat started," he complained, "they put me ashore to lade the horses." Later, when Bull asks him, "Pat, how do you like sailing on a canal boat?" the disgruntled Irishman, still confused, could only say, "Fait . . . if it was not for the name of the thing, I'm thinking I might as well be walking a fut." Poor Dennis had learned the hard way what *walking passage* meant!

At this juncture Jonathan reminds the travellers that their boat is crossing the river on "that unnatural thingumbob they call an aqueduct" and that if they don't hurry a bit, they will be left stranded. Everyone agrees that this would be a catastrophe—to be marooned on the bank in this American "wilderness"!—and so, the party boards the canal boat and *exeunt*, while the boat is seen crossing the aqueduct. Meanwhile, *A Trip to Niagara* has been the setting and the occasion for much spoofing of both American and foreign attitudes toward York State's Grand Erie Canal.

The first "Erie novel" came out in 1844; it bore the intriguing (and lengthy) title of *Marco Paul's Travels and Adventures in the Pursuit of Knowledge on the Erie Canal.* The story concerns a young lad, Marco Paul, and his guardian-tutor, Forester. The novel, a juvenile of some 140 pages, opens on the Hudson River boat to Albany.

As Forester was sitting upon a settee, by the side of one of the great doors leading into the ladies' cabin, on board the North America, coming up to Albany, thinking of future plans, he said to himself, "How shall I begin to interest Marco Paul in the acquisition of knowledge?" [7]

As a way to achieve this end, Forester decides to let Marco Paul learn firsthand about the Erie Canal. This very pragmatic motivational technique works well on the youth, who finds much of interest about the canal, which they travel on from Albany. He soon learns, by the dialectic of question-and-answer, about packets and line-boats, feeders, waste weirs, runners, the "Battleground," and weighlocks. He also becomes acutely aware of the sleeping problems aboard a canal packet —and of their highly distressing but withal humorous resolution.[8]

Beyond these preliminary instances of the use of the Erie Canal in poetry, drama, and the novel, nineteenth-century writers (if we exclude the tourists) did not prove exceptionally canal-conscious once the fever-pitch enthusiasm over having a canal had subsided. Herman Melville included in *Moby-Dick* (1851) a brief but thoroughly engaging digression on the Erie and its canallers in Chapter LIV; and some time later William Dean Howells had his honeymooners, Basil and Isobel March, tour Erie country in *Their Wedding Journey* (1872). The canal commentary that Howells worked into that novel formed no essential part of the narrative (the Marches rode the trains) but appeared rather as reflections of the narrator; with typical Howellsian charm, however, they epitomize the nostalgic feeling which thoughts about the Old Erie seem to evoke. Speaking of the Marches passing through the Mohawk area, Howells wrote,

It is a landscape that I greatly love for its mild beauty and tranquil picturesqueness, and it is in honor of our friends that I say they enjoyed it. There are nowhere any considerable hills, but everywhere generous slopes and pleasant hollows and the wide meadows of a grazing country, with the pretty brown Mohawk River rippling down through all, and at frequent intervals the life of the canal, now near, now far away with the lazy boats that seem not to stir, and the horses that the train passes with a whirl, and leaves slowly stepping forward and swiftly slipping backward.

The narrator's mind lingers for a moment longer on the canal; he imagines himself once more on the towpath of the Erie, "beside that wonderfully lean horse, whose bones you cannot count only because there are so many."

He never wakes up, but, with a faltering under-lip and half-shut eyes, hobbles stiffly on, unconscious of his anatomical interest. The captain hospitably asks me on board, with a twist of the rudder swinging the stern of the boat up to the path, so that I can step on. She is laden with flour from the valley of the Genesee, and may have started on her voyage shortly after the canal was made. She is succinctly manned by the captain, the driver, and the cook, a fiery-haired lady of imperfect temper; and the cabin, which I explore, is plainly furnished with a cook-stove and a flask of whiskey. Nothing but profane language is allowed on board; and so, in a life of wicked jollity and ease, we glide imperceptibly down the canal, unvexed by the far-off future of arrival.[9]

In 1872, also, Mark Twain's *Roughing It* included a poem, "The Aged Pilot Man," which had its setting on the Erie Canal. Twain thought the poem was suggested "by an old song, 'The Raging Canal,'" and reminisced that his own doggerel, at the time he wrote it, he felt to be "one of the ablest poems of the age." [10] A few lines should give an adequate idea of the whole:

THE AGED PILOT MAN

On the Erie Canal, it was,
    All on a summer's day,
I sailed forth with my parents
    Far away to Albany.

From out the clouds at noon that day
    There came a dreadful storm,
That piled the billows high about,
    And filled us with alarm.

A man came rushing from a house,
Saying, "Snub up your boat, I pray,
Snub up your boat, snub up, alas,
Snub up while yet you may."

Our captain cast one glance astern,
Then forward glanced he,
And said, "My wife and little ones
I never more shall see."

Said Dollinger, the pilot man,
In noble words, but few—
"Fear not, but lean on Dollinger,
And he will fetch you through."

Subsequent stanzas follow the mock-epic mode of the "Raging Erie" varieties, as discussed in a preceding chapter. The stanza containing the lines "Fear not, but lean on Dollinger,/And he will fetch you through" is repeated several times as a kind of reprise.

Of all the early works discussed here, Edward Noyes Westcott's *David Harum* (1899) probably needs the least introduction to New Yorkers. The Yorker character David Harum endeared himself immediately to Westcott's readers.[11] The plot of the novel involves homespun shenanigans—banking and horsetrading—in Homeville, "near Syrchester" in upstate New York, where Harum as a conservative but eccentric banker lived with his maiden sister, Polly. John Lenox, a young man recruited from New York City, joins the bank and begins to learn about human nature as well as about financial matters. He finds his employer to be somewhat more kindly than the complete scoundrel he first appeared to be. Mary Blake, who seems to flit between New York and the Continent in higher social circles than John provides the romantic situations; she becomes, of course, Mrs. John Lenox at the close of the novel.

One of the opening comments in the 1934 motion picture version of the novel epitomizes the philosophy of *David Harum:* "I go a long way on a man's character and a longer way on collateral. I let him have about half what he wants. Most people can get along on about half what they think they can." His admission (in the novel) that he was "apt to speak in par'bles sometimes" is more than adequately demonstrated, for one of the things which contributes to making *David Harum* valuable to the literary historian interested in regionalism is its Yorker speech, much of which contains nuggets of homespun wisdom. David was glad to have John replace a former, rather worthless clerk. "It haint rained wisdom and knowlidge in his part of the country for a consid'able spell," observed David about the departing figure.[12]

Living as he had all his life in central New York State, David Harum recalled the Erie Canal as a part of the experience of his adolescent years. "By the time I was about twenty-one," he remarked, "I had got ahead enough to quit the canal an' all its works fer good, an' go into other things." He then had taken a job as lock-keep, but added that before "the job of lock-tendin' I had made the trip to Albany an' back twice— walkin' my passage, as they used to call it, an' I made one trip helpin' steer." He concluded that his "canal experience was putty thorough, taken it all 'round."

On the subject of canallers and canal life, he held to his usual conservative judgement of things. "Most things go by comparin'," he said.

> I s'pose if at that same age you'd had to tackle the life you'd a' found it hard, an' the' was hard things about it—trampin' all night in the rain, for instance; sleepin' in barns at times, an' all that; an' once the cap'n o' the boat got mad at somethin' an' pitched me head over heels into the canal. . . . The canalers was a rough set in gen'ral, but they averaged fer disposition 'bout like the ord'nary run o' folk; the' was mean ones and clever ones; them that would put upon ye, an' them that would treat ye decent.

Reminiscing at a society function in Newport, Rhode Island, to which he found himself invited and placed at table rather against his preferences, Harum grew expansive as he realized, as he put it, that "a good many better men 'n I be walked the ole towpath when they was young." As a matter of fact, he was (to use his idiom) willing to bet two dollars to a last year's bird nest that if all the respectable society gentlemen "that air over fifty" were to hear the cry of "Low bridge!" an appreciable number of them would duck their heads instinctively. (The only person at the dinner party who failed to be amused was a bewildered Englishman; he didn't know what "Low bridge!" meant.) [13]

Twentieth-Century Fox filmed *David Harum* in 1934 with Will Rogers in the title role. The screen play, by Walter Woods, further romanticized, but hardly improved upon, Westcott's novel, and with the usual Hollywood urge to change things for no apparent reason, made Homeville "Homedale" and metamorphosed Mary Blake into "Ann," a rather different young lady who proved to be a horse trader equal to David. The Erie Canal was not mentioned in the screen version, which is memorable chiefly because of Rogers' characterization of the Yorker Harum and Stepin Fetchit's Sylvester (another Hollywood addition to the story).[14]

Following *David Harum* the history of Erie literature up to the appearance in 1929 of Walter D. Edmonds' *Rome Haul* is a sparse study, only Alvin Harlow and Herbert Quick deserving mention. As has been cited, Harlow called his nonfiction account of the canal days *Old Towpaths*. Quick's work was a semi-autobiographical novel. Interestingly enough, it was a book which Edmonds credits as having influenced his thinking about writing a "canal novel," [15] a genre which, with the exception of the already cited juvenile *Marco Paul*, he may be said to have invented.

Herbert Quick's *Vandemark's Folly* (1922) touches upon canal boating in the early chapters of this story of a Dutch-American youth who migrated westward to Iowa in the mid-nineteenth century. The novel is, partly at least, autobiographical; the author's ancestry is similar to that of his character, and his expressed feelings about the frontier, the West, and the Erie Canal, are similar to those in the novel.[16] In *One Man's Life* (1925), Quick's autobiography, a painting by the famous illustrator N. C. Wyeth is captioned, "The boy Vandemark returns to his home near the Erie Canal."

Jacobus Teunis Vandemark, the narrator and protagonist of *Vandemark's Folly*, moved at a young age with his mother and stepfather to Tempe, which he placed as "near the Erie Canal somewhere between Rome and Syracuse" and "farther west than Canastota." [17] There he marvelled, albeit half fearfully, at the canallers.

I used to go down by the canal and watch the boats go back and forth. Sometimes the captains of the boats would ask me if I didn't want a job driving; but I scarcely knew what they meant. . . . I used to sit on a stump by the towpath, and so close to it that the boys driving the mules or horses drawing the boats could almost strike me with their whips, which they often tried to do as they went by. . . . There just below was a lock, but I seldom went to it because all the drivers were egged on to fight each other during the delay at the locks, and the canallers would have been sure to set them on me for the fun of seeing a fight.

When he was thirteen, as a result of his stepfather's cruelty and the opportune intervention by a canal boat captain who fought off an assault on the boy, Vandemark ran away from home and went to work as hoggee for Captain Eben Sproule. For the next several years he saw all aspects of canal life, both good and bad, from Albany to Buffalo. But "the West was on the road," he found; and, as Vandemark himself declared in introducing his narrative, "I was caught in the current. Nobody could live along the Erie Canal in those days without feeling the suck of the forests, and catching a breath now and then of the prairie winds."

In addition to Quick's work, two other pieces of full-length fiction, both of them after Edmonds and possibly influenced by him, are of interest to the literary historian of the Erie; only one is fully set in Erie country.

Clyde Davis's *Nebraska Coast* (1939), a novel dealing with a Yorker family's emigration to "Nebrasky" in 1861, contains some authentic scenes of canawling, as experienced by a 10-year-old boy.[18] When Clint Mcdougall's father wanted to buy a canal boat as "just an excuse to make some money" hauling, Clint's mother saw little good in the plan—or in the Erie, for that matter. "Pastor Rucker said," she told them, "that canal-boating can't last much longer. All the rotten characters in the country are being gathered right on the Erie Canal, he said, and the Lord will be fixing to do something." Father was unperturbed and went ahead with buying the *Samuel W. Read*. Father repainted the boat brilliant red and yellow, with the hull "a flaming scarlet and the cabin yellower than a lemon." He brought the *Samuel W. Read* down to Palmyra. "It was all very exciting," concluded Clint, who became towpath driver, with his older brother, Alan, assigned as steersman. The boy's feeling about this new experience makes it easy for the reader to understand the appeal the Erie Canal must have had for youth.

Spring frogs were creaking in the marshy spots and birds were twittering in the thickets. Bonnie and Alex kept yalking to each other with blubbery sighs. Their hoofs thump-thumped in rhythm on the hard-packed towpath, and in my nostrils was the strong smell of horses and the wet, fishy smell of the canal. I was very happy, for I was bound for new places and I was filling an important niche in the world. I was practically a man now, and only ten years old.

The Ring Buster (1940), by James Monroe Fitch, has as its protagonist a young lad who is forever canal-conscious. Somewhat more a biographical novel of young Grover Cleveland than a story of Erie canallers, *The Ring Buster* nonetheless differs from most of the other novels already mentioned in that the canal provides the background throughout the entire length of the story. Tim Brady, "born on the wrong side of the Canal," and a towpath hoggee as the novel opens, rises rapidly through opportune circumstances—but not, of course, without the trials and tribulations a good hero must encounter. The plot itself is rather typically "rags to riches," a kind of Horatio Alger story set canalside.

The story opens on the canal in November of 1873—incidentally one of the latest periods of the Erie to be treated in full-length fiction—with Brady's hometown, Gasport, and Buffalo the principal locales. Having discovered, at the hands of a cruel canal boat captain, that there "was no morality and no conscience on the towpath," Tim jumped ship, as it were, striking off at a time Gasport was in sight. In the manner of melodramatic romance, he manages to save a maiden's virtue from the assaults of a bully and thereby ingratiate himself at the outset with her brother, her father, and of course her trembling self. By happy coincidence, these first-met turn out to be old chums, the girl—from the *right side* of the canal— loved but hitherto unapproachable. This is the beginning; the ending is never in doubt. Bill Wade, a rising young engineer, gullible but honest, is a foil for Tim Brady, the 18-year-old canal boy. Mary Wade, Bill's sister, is obviously in love with the protagonist from the moment he saves her from the clutches of the bully. Ann Brady, Tim's sister, first a canal boat cook, then a bookkeeper in Buffalo, rounds out the two-couple pattern as the girl in love with Wade.

While the story is rather maudlin, *The Ring Buster* does contain some excellent Erie material. The times are depicted appropriately; the characterizations, for the most part, are extremely well handled. Typical canalside personalities fill the pages of the story. Bill Wade, as the enterprising canal engineer who finally joins the forces of right and later inspects the canal for evidence against the "Canal Ring" is credible if wooden. Of the seamier kind of canal character, however, ample examples abound. Ezra Baldwin and Silas Latham represent the subcontractors who try to sustain themselves and their cohorts by skulduggery in maintaining and repairing their sections of the Erie waterway; Jerry Sykes is an appropriately drawn town drunkard, who is finally redeemed; and Red Moll, his wife who ran off to become a tavernkeep, provides human interest and some down-to-earth warmth. George Goss, a typical foreman of the day, would doublecross both sides if he could do so undetected. Bud Haynes, a "recon-

structed" canalside bully, throws his good right arm in with
the do-gooders, and marries a Wild West circus gal with the
improbable name of Lotta Tubbs.

In addition to Tim Brady, Grover Cleveland—then a Buffalo lawyer—plays the most prominent part. Essentially, the
story is Cleveland's. "Big Steve's" morality, his conscience, his
sense of rightmindedness in government, pervade the book;
this aspect is authentically depicted.

The "ring buster" of the title is Samuel J. Tilden, governor
of the state. "I am proud of the Erie Canal," he said. "It has
made New York an empire within an empire." But perhaps
more far-reaching than this pride was the significance of his
reminiscences about the Old Erie. With eyes and mind aglow,
Tilden continued, "There is something about the canal that
appeals to the hearts of the people. What small boy will ever
forget the fascination of the cheering crowds, the brass bands,
the torchlight processions from the near-by towns, the huge
bonfires made with barrels stacked fifty feet high?" [19]

The Ring Buster, despite its faults as a novel, helps people
to remember.

These relatively few novels incorporate something of the
Erie story, and a formidable array of Erie-inspired fiction was
produced by two upstate writers who made a special province
out of Erie country—Walter D. Edmonds and Samuel Hopkins Adams. Except for these, juveniles account for a majority
of the more recent novels dealing with Erie life and lore. Such
works, of course, have a natural appeal for youth, just as the
canal itself had; they serve to recreate something of the magic
of another time, going back beyond Tom Swift's (and often
even beyond Horatio Alger's) era to a time which, if one reads
correctly, saw every youngling in the Empire State aspire to
be captain of a proud Erie packet. In these books, a number of
authors have tried to recapture, for a new generation all too
frequently weaned on television and comics full of spacemen,
a sense of a more romantic era. While all do not succeed, some
of them are perhaps worth noting, for they represent a
flourishing if minor aspect of our literary history.

Helen Fuller Orton's *The Treasure in the Little Trunk*

came out in the early 1930's when regional writing was just catching on in Yorker country. It is the story of a family's moving from the Green Mountains of Vermont to the Genesee country of New York in 1823. This was before the completion of Governor Clinton's Big Ditch, and the trek of the Armstrong family westward was made in their own lumber wagon converted for turnpike travelling. The events of the story cover the period 1823–25, culminating with the opening-of-the-Erie celebration at Lockport in October of 1825. Other than this, the Erie does not play a part, except that Father Armstrong and his family note from time to time the condition of travel and commerce and the prosperity anticipated by those pioneers living in Holland Patent of western York State. The "embellishments by Robert Hall" are interesting to the juvenile reader; one depicts Lockport on the day of the opening celebration.

Four chapters of *Boy with a Pack* (1939) by Stephen Meader deal with the Erie Canal, in a story concerning a New England lad who sets out as a peddler with $40 worth of merchandise on his back to tour the western lands. Seventeen-year-old Bill Crawford meets the Old Erie at Troy and hires out as driver boy on the *Mohawk Tiger*, meeting thereon pretty Mary Ann Bennet, who has been forced to take a job as cook, and Buck Hoyle, the freighter's fighting captain.

The 1940's proved fruitful for Erie juveniles, and several works were published which dealt in their entirety with the canal experience. *Along the Erie Towpath* (1940), while hardly stirring of plot, does live up to its title. As this juvenile novel opens, Stephen and Emeline David, orphaned when their parents fell to the New York City yellow fever epidemic, go to live with Aunt Polly Burns in Albany. The "Widow Burns" has six children of her own, with only the eldest, Joel, working; he, as the children soon learn, helped build the canal. David, one of the 11-year-old twins, answers Stephen's query about "What canal?" by making a rough drawing for his newly-discovered cousin. According to David, the Erie Canal was a "jiggly line running from Lake Erie to Albany." He added, "They've been digging on it for six years

and it isn't all finished yet. But it will be some day and then
boats can go all the way from Lake Erie to the Hudson River."

David, in particular, plays an important role in this story,
at least as far as the canal is concerned. Like countless other
Erie novels, this one has its runaway. David, unhappy at school
and desperately wanting to help alleviate the financial plight
of the family, runs away one night, hitching a ride on an out-
ward-bound Pennsylvania wagon, which takes him to Utica.
There, at the age of twelve, he finds his first canal job, on the
Flying Cloud out of Utica, at 35 cents a trip. Meanwhile, his
oldest brother Joel and Stephen have set out for Buffalo,
where the latter is determined to use the money left him by his
father to buy property for his kindly aunt and the family.
Simon Swig, a canaller of sorts, gladly promises Mrs. Burns he
will search the canal for news of David, who by this time has
gone to work on the book-boat, *Encyclopaedia*. It all naturally
comes out well, the family moving to Buffalo where David
joins them. At the close, they all watch the *Seneca Chief* begin its historic trip as the Erie Canal celebration of 1825 opens.

The plot follows the formula of numerous other such
stories; they might all, perhaps, be described as "Tom Swift
on the Erie Canal." The pace in this one is quite leisurely; but
its characterizations are interesting, and some of the descriptions—on and off the towpath—are historically edifying to
young readers. And although seen but slightly in these pages,
DeWitt Clinton, who offers two small and shivering skaters a
ride home in his carriage, seems a very warm and human personage. "Is he such a great man?" asked Debbie, the 11-year-
old.

> "Great? Why Debbie, it's his canal I'm working on! It's
> his canal that's changing all our part of the country, mak-
> ing cities out of little towns and making villages grow up
> in what was a wilderness, making farmers richer and food
> cheaper for the city people. But you can't know what all
> that means because you're still only a little girl and—"
>
> "I'm not little," Debbie declared warmly, "and I want to
> know. Is it Mr. Clinton's canal—all of it—really?"

Joel laughed, more at himself because of his absurd statement than at Debbie.

"No, of course it isn't really his canal," he explained. "It belongs to the people of New York State. But there might not have been a canal if it hadn't been for Mr. Clinton." [20]

Erick Berry's *Lock Her Through* (1940) involves a 15-year-old girl, Sabrina, and an immigrant driver boy, Gideon, in a novel set along the canal. *Dick and the Canal Boat* (1943), a junior book by Sanford Tousey, tells of a small boy's first trip on the Erie, helping out on the *Ella E.* from Albany to Buffalo and return one summer. Zillah Macdonald's *Two on a Towpath* (1942) tells the story of twin orphan boys, Jarvis and Jerry, who go to live with grandparents on a barge boat; the scene is the State Barge Canal after the turn of the century, and only at the very close does the Old Erie get mentioned, as the boys hear "the friendly song," "Low Bridge." Despite its suggestive title, *Jon of the Albany Belle* (1943), by Hazel Raybold Langdale, contains little Erie lore. It is the story of a young boy seeking treasure buried by his late grandfather at Whitesford, on the right bank of the Mohawk up Utica way. Most of the action takes place not on the canal but overland as Jon runs into Abolitionists who suspect him of trying to interrupt Underground Railroad activities. At the close of the story he does have the *Belle* for himself, however, bought with the treasure he found.

A year earlier, in 1942, Miss Langdale published *Mark of Seneca Basin*, a juvenile which can rightly be called an Erie novel, for it deals with, and is set along, the Erie Canal. The plot of the book concerns Mark Kingsbury's search for his maternal grandfather, a search which takes him from his foster parents' home at Seneca Basin in Wayne County ("Around Twelve Miles east of Watson Landing, which is nearer to Rochester Village than any other Place but not near to that either," as Mark put it), to New York City at the time of the grand celebration of 1825, when he discovers that his old friend, Trapper Luke, is really the grandparent he seeks. Much Erie lore and the history of the building of the Big Ditch finds reflection in the pages of this book, as Mark goes through a series of Erie-connected adventures, first as a member of Mr. Hawley's construction crews, then as mule-driver for an early canal boatman, and finally as guest aboard the *Seneca Chief* in the celebration cavalcade.

The Erie continued to inspire juveniles in the 1950's. The subtitle of Herbert Best's *Watergate* (1951), "A Story of the Irish on the Erie Canal," aptly describes this contribution to Winston's "Land of the Free" series. At times an awkwardly written work, much of it striving for creative effect over the heads of young readers, *Watergate* does present in an interesting way the adventures and misadventures of Sean Kildare along the Big Ditch which his own father helped cut through the Montezuma swamp. A junior book, *Molly's Hannibal* (1957) capitalizes on canal enthusiasm also with its subtitle, "A Story of the Erie Canal." Written by Robert Wallis, who had spent his childhood in upstate New York and remembered the canal yarns he had heard during winter evenings, this charming little story of Molly Flynn ("the only girl driver on the Erie") and her towpath mule Hannibal moves in a leisurely way along the Erie and Black River canals, as Molly wishes desperately for a china doll she saw in a Watertown store. In 1958, Grosset and Dunlap added to its "We Were There" series Enid LaMonte Meadowcroft's *We Were There at the Opening of the Erie Canal.*

Few juveniles command attention of critics for literary (or other) values, but occasionally one written by a master story-teller proves an exception. With a protagonist who is heroic in the best sense of the word, Samuel Hopkins Adams' *Chingo Smith of the Erie Canal* (1958) is a juvenile epic. Chingo's "rise" from nondescript beginnings as a higgler's boy to a wondrous position as captain of his own Erie Canal packet (the "youngest shipmaster on Erie water") follows inevitably the rags-to-riches formula; but the story is more than that. Much more, as a matter of fact: *Chingo Smith* is chock full of Erie lore and of York State history, as one might expect from the author of *Canal Town, Grandfather Stories,* and the numerous other York-set novels and stories. "It's reassuring to know," one reviewer commented, "that what we used to call rather proudly 'The American Dream'—the old, pristine vision of pre-Civil War days, that is, rather than the later, Golden Age version—still comes alive occasionally *somewhere* in contemporary fiction, even if we do have to look for it in a book that is ostensibly for juvenile readers." [21]

The story begins in 1816—Eighteen-Hundred-and-Frozen-to-Death, as Yorkers recalled that year of no summer—when the waif Chingo, "either an overgrown seven or a wizened-up ten," arrived in Rochesterville, or "Rochester," as most of the inhabitants already preferred to call it. (His first name had been bartered from a Seneca Indian lad for a broken-bladed knife and a turtle; the "Smith" came from the gypsies who took him in.) From ort-boy (odd-jobs boy) at a local inn, Chingo went on to adventures ranging across the state, with one winter as far south as Washington, D.C. For a time he ran reluctantly with the runagates, boys who roamed the towpath and byways, too shiftless to work or too ornery to be hired. He had a taste of digging the canal, too. His first meeting with the canal project, when it was yet a mass of mire and mud, brought him only disillusion, and for some time thereafter Chingo Smith was dead-set against the Erie. Remembering a kindly cinder-wench's advice that "education's the biggest thing in the world," he searched out the Learned Tinker, a knowledgeable mender-of-pots who taught him to read and write, as they went from hamlet to hamlet. Chingo learned the art of "fistiana" and self-defense from the prizefighter, Terrible Tigg: it was a skill which more than once paid dividends along the towpath when Chingo eventually returned to following Erie water. This time (the Erie was now nearing completion) as he caught something of the glorious Grand Canal-to-be the "shining ribbon of water" alone held his interest.

Chingo Smith of the Erie Canal is rich in incident, as it is rich in social history; each episode is an authentic vignette. For the reader—regardless of age—here is the American

Dream as it must have been in the 1820's, when the tall stove-pipe hat of an Erie captain was the greatest thing to which youth aspired.

Adams also wrote, for the Landmark series, *The Erie Canal* (1953), widely acclaimed as "the best juvenile of them all." It doubtless is. In simple language, with an easy, informal style, *The Erie Canal* traces the building of the Grand Western from inception to completion, here and there interspersing the objectiveness of the "documentary" with just enough of the inimitable Adams' personal reminiscences to give the book flavor as well as authenticity.

It is not surprising that Samuel Hopkins Adams should write these works, nor that his name and that of Walter D. Edmonds should appear again and again in any tracing of the literary history of the Erie Canal. For each of them canalism formed a part of his experience. Edmonds, hailing from Boonville and the Black River Canal, an important feeder of the Erie, put his experience into themes at Harvard and then into numerous novels and short stories, with titles like *Rome Haul, Erie Water,* and *Mostly Canallers.* At the same time, Hamilton-educated Adams began channeling his already wide-ranging talents and literary experience into such books as *Canal Town* and *Banner by the Wayside.* These writers brought Yorker regionalism into full flower, and they drew significantly upon Erie canal folklore and history for the largest part of their work.

IX

Edmonds
Sounding a Brand New Note

WHEN *Rome Haul* was published in 1929 critics remarked favorably upon the achievement of the recent Harvard graduate who had dipped his pen into canal water. A reviewer for the New York *Herald Tribune* commented that " 'Rome Haul' would be a notable book in any season. As the first novel of a man born in 1903 it is extraordinary." [1] Walter D. Edmonds' book was the first novel to deal in its entirety with canal setting and Erie Canal life; for this it stands as a pioneer. At the same time, the novel evidenced all the archetypical characteristics of the Erie novel. This pioneer representative of Erie-inspired upstate regionalism became, furthermore, an influence of considerable importance, as other writers turned their attention to New York themes.

Even to the casual reader, *Rome Haul* seemed a rich treasure-house of Erie Canal life and lore, with full descriptions of York State's Erie country and apt characterizations of canallers. For Edmonds to write convincingly of such subjects was not surprising; this first novel seemed only the natural product of a young man who had grown up around canallers and who had written as his initial theme for Professor Copeland at Harvard a canal story which promptly proved marketable.

He wrote his first canal story, however, for the *Harvard Advocate*. This story, "The Last of the Black Dwarfs," he reflects, was "a kind of fantastic development from Dickensonian scenes of the marshes in *Great Expectations* combined with the Black River Canal." [2] Some time later the *Advocate* published three more of Edmonds' canal stories—"The Death of Jotham Klore," "Solomon Tinkle's Christmas Eve," and "The Hanging of Kruscome Shanks." [3] It was important that the fledgling writer came, at this particular time, under the critical eye of Harvard's Charles Townsend Copeland, who helped so many on the road to authorship. Edmonds submitted as his first contribution in Copeland's class a story which he hoped would be "a truer picture of upstate canallers." [4] It was "The End of the Towpath," which Edmonds' friend, David McCord, claimed "won the coveted Copeland praise of sounding a brand new note." [5] *Scribner's Magazine* bought the story at once. Later Edmonds included it in a collection of tales he called *Mostly Canallers* (1934).

Edmonds really wanted to write a *novel* about the canal and to make his living by writing. With this in mind, he spent the winter after Harvard at the Edmonds' farm in Boonville on the Black River Canal, where he managed to produce several short stories. Three of these he sold to the *Atlantic Monthly* and *The Dial*.[6] When he applied to the *Atlantic* for a job, he was, he said, "persuaded instead by Ellery Sedgwick to come to Cambridge, hole up, and write *Rome Haul*." [7] He did just that. "By the first of November," he said, "I was installed in a room, with a typewriter, and the second morning I wrote 'Rome Haul' at the top of the sheet, 'I' under it, and under that 'The Road and the Peddler.' 'In 1850, the road to Boonville wound out of the Tug Hill country . . .' No fresh start, no hesitation: I finished the first chapter by lunch time. That morning at breakfast I had thought of a peddler describing the Erie, saying of it, 'It's the bowels of the nation, it's the whole shebang of life.' I thought it was good for an opening chapter, and it turned out to be good for the whole book." [8] The manuscript, which he had promised for March, was delivered in February and became an Atlantic Monthly Press book for 1929.

The Big Barn, published a year after *Rome Haul*, also dealt with Erie Canal country. As the title suggests, however, its theme is primarily concerned with traditions rooted in the soil, in this case the family of Ralph Wilder, a Boonville farmer. This book did not sell well, and Edmonds admits to having "thrown away" another book. But luck has been largely with him; the reputation begun by *Rome Haul* was furthered when Marc Connelly made that novel into a play—*The Farmer Takes a Wife,* which subsequently appeared as a movie starring Henry Fonda and Janet Gaynor. In 1940 *Chad Hanna,* Edmonds' very popular novel about circus life, secured his reputation by presenting authentic characters and capturing again a period of the American past, this time the Mohawk Valley in the 1830's. His most enduring book, *Drums Along the Mohawk* (1936), depicts the same area in the Revolutionary War era of 1776–77. Both of these novels quickly found markets in Hollywood. In addition, Edmonds ventured successfully into the realm of children's literature, winning the Newberry Medal in 1941 for *The Matchlock Gun.*

Union College, at Schenectady, New York, awarded Edmonds an honorary Doctor of Letters degree in 1936. In conferring the degree, Union's president, Dixon Ryan Fox, cited the writer for his "affection for the State and its people" and for his power of "summoning their ancestors to live again." Edmonds was, said the degree citation, a "second builder of our Grand Canal."

It seems obvious from the start that canallers and the Black River Canal influenced Edmonds. *Rome Haul,* he confesses, "was written out of three sources—first, the old canallers I had talked to in my winters in Boonville; second, two scrapbooks of newspaper clippings from upstate papers kept by my grandfather through the fifties and sixties; third, by Alvin Harlow's *Old Towpaths.*" [9] In addition, his boyhood had been "canal," when he had, as he adds, "watched the canal boats going by, loading sand and potatoes and lumber."

Rome Haul is an *Erie* Canal story, however, which draws much from history and canal lore. Basically, the novel concerns the coming of age of the orphaned Dan Harrow, who through

numerous opportune circumstances rises very quickly from an
initial job as towpath hoggee to that of captain of his own
canal boat hauling cargo on the Erie. The canal is that of the
1850's, with the day of the sleek packets gone and passenger
trade almost entirely eclipsed by the rising New York Central
and other railroads, and when freight operations provided the
chief traffic for canawlers.

At the outset, as Dan Harrow plods his way toward the
Black River Canal for an eventual job on the Erie, an old peddler fills him in on the significance of Clinton's Ditch:

> "Well, I hope you'll like it. The Erie is a swarming hive.
> Boats coming and going, passing you all the while. You can
> hear their horns blowing all day long. As like as not there's
> a fight at every lock. There's all kind of people there, and
> they're all going all the while. It aint got the finish and
> style as when the packet boats was running, but you'll find
> fancy folks in the big ports. It's better without the packet
> boats; let the railroads take the passengers. It leaves the pace
> steady for growing. There's freight going west and raw food
> east, all on the canal; there's people going west, New Eng-
> landers, Germans, all them furrin folk, and there's people
> coming east that've quit. But the canawlers keep a-moving.
>
> "Water-Level trade route, they call it, and it is. By grab,
> it's the bowels of the nation! It's the whole shebang of
> life!" [10]

Dan's first contact with the canal itself and with Erie canallers
brought these last words of the peddler back to his mind. He
found the Erie Canal awe-inspiring, complex, earthy.

> "The bowels of the nation . . . the whole shebang of
> life." He could see it in the hurry and a certain breathless-
> ness above the easy noise; he could smell it in the boats com-
> ing from the West, the raw foods, the suffocating odor of
> grain, the scent of meat, of pork, the homely smell of po-
> tatoes, to be digested in the East and produce growth. It
> mystified him, though he seemed to understand it, and it

stirred a great affection in him for living, for the people round him, and the clean light of the sun.

Edmonds knew his materials and how to use them to produce a story both authentically regional and artistically sound. In *Rome Haul* he created a novel deeper in significance than a simple romance; he not only captures the flavor of a past era but also presents basic human issues in a way that transcends any narrow regionalism. Dan Harrow, starting out as a hoggee, comes into possession of the canal boat of a captain who befriended him and who died from the cholera. The girl, Molly, provides the incentive to Dan's coming into his own, for he literally rescues her from a life as a canal-boat cook, a situation often tantamount to being mistress to captains of a highly unsavory ilk. He hires her himself from Mrs. Cashdollar's Cooks' Agency (for Bachelor Boaters), as soon as he is certain the late Samson Weaver's boat is really his own and he can continue to haul freight with it for the contractor. The love which develops between Dan and Molly fills out much of the rest of the story, which is replete with canalside characters and canal lore, including the songs of the Erie canawlers. That Molly is mistress and wife *de facto* is not condemnable, for this was the way of the canal. As Mrs. Gurget tells Dan,

> "Mostly, there ain't anything wrong in not being married on the canal. As long as you're honest there ain't any real sense in it. It's different if you're going to get off the canal. Then you've got to act like other folks. But here living's just a working agreement, and if you want you can get a minister to lick the revenue stamp to seal it with; but it don't add a lot. And a gal's free to back out. Sometimes it makes it hard for her, but if she wants it that way, it ain't any bother of yours. Unless you want to take her off'n the canal."

In terms of plot, the question of taking Molly "off'n the canal" and whether Dan Harrow will stick to boating becomes the crux upon which the novel finally focuses. Harrow, in choosing to leave the canal for a farming position, loses the girl; at the end of the novel he leaves the canal, its people, and its associations. Molly has, in the meantime, served as a catalyst in his maturing. Part of the plot involves Dan's fear of fighting—over Molly—the acknowledged "bully of the Erie Canal," Jotham Klore. This fear is present from the time Molly and Dan first meet. That he and Klore will eventually "have it out" is anticipated by the reader, for the situation forms an essential part of the plot structure of the novel. The knowledge of the fight's inevitability and the eventual occurrence of the match also form a part of Harrow's maturing.

Even had Dan Harrow remained on the canal, it is problematical whether he would not have lost Molly anyway. In the fashion of the Twenties, she might be seen as representing the love that is both easily attainable and needed, yet at the same time a love which offers only a temporary warmth and security for Dan. One gets a feeling of considerable negation in the novel—perhaps it was something of the "Waste Land" or "Lost Generation" contagion in the literary air during the 1920's. Analogies to Hemingway's *A Farewell to Arms*, also published in 1929, are intriguing to consider, for the situation of Lieutenant Henry and Nurse Barclay is much the same as that of Edmonds' Molly and Dan Harrow—the girls' fear of marriage and their philosophies (largely pragmatic and expedient), the men, Frederick and Dan, caught in the times. Nobody really wins, in either novel, at least not in the central environment of the works.[11]

Rome Haul does contain elements characteristic of other works of the Twenties—the stretches of the canal, for example, with their marshes and rising vapors, are reminiscent of Scott Fitzgerald's Long Island as seen from the commuter train in *The Great Gatsby*—and in some respects the novel may be viewed as a product of the times.[12] Were it only this, *Rome Haul* would still be a worthwhile novel; but it is much more than something only reflective of other literary currents of the American Twenties. It contains the essentials of regionalism at its best—realistic depiction of setting, credible colloquial dialogue, and honest portrayal of the folkways and mores of the people.[13]

To read *Rome Haul* is to take a rewarding trip on the Erie.

With the auspicious beginning represented by the success of *Rome Haul*, Edmonds was thoroughly launched on Erie water. It was inevitable that he would turn his talents to the inspiring times of the earlier canal and to the men who built it. After *The Big Barn*, a definite "side trip," he returned to his first love, canallers.

An historically accurate treatment of a romantic subject, *Erie Water* (1933) follows the history of the state closely in the period from 1817 to 1825. Edmonds unifies his novel, as indeed all New York's history seemed unified, around the digging of the Big Ditch. The principals in Edmonds' case are Jerry Fowler, a Lebanon Valley youth determined to make his own way in the world, and Marry Goodhill, an English redemptioner whose paper Jerry buys at the outset. Their love and the domestic crises occasioned by Jerry's having to travel frequently far from home provide the necessary plot for making the novel popularly palatable. Fowler, like Dan Harrow in *Rome Haul*, has some growing up to do. In a real sense, he matures as the Erie Canal grows: Jerry comes of age only when water finally flows from Lake Erie to the Hudson River.

Meanwhile, a period rich in history and inspiration has been presented in authentic, colorful fashion. Caleb Hammil, typical of the pioneering contractors, didn't even know what a lock looked like when he bid on—and won—a $17,000 contract for laying foundations for the locks and aqueducts. With Yorker good humor and common sense, he turned aside a query about the locks. "Well," he said, "I'm a contractor and no mechanic. I've never see none. But they've got them down in Massachusetts, so I guess we can build them. Anyway, I've got a book about it." [14] Caleb hires Jerry on the spot to help him build the first of the locks of the Erie Canal. *Erie Water* relates, via these and other characters, the story of the building of the Erie, from the initial toilsome but enterprising coping with the problems of locks, aqueducts, swamp drainage, and the myriad other aspects of cutting a waterway through central New York State, to the completion of the job with the famous Lockport combines. Edmonds' hero is drawn into this final activity, too: "You and I started the first lock," his old friend told him. "In 1817—six years ago. . . . It would be fun to build the last on the line."

Lake Erie water at last flows into the final locks and throughout the forty-foot-wide ditch, snaking and extending its long length from Buffalo to Albany. The Irishman O'Mory and the Negro Jay-Jay, who contributed with countless others as "sons of toil" to the making of transportation history, symbolically unite in Edmonds' narrative to view the task completed.

> They walked down to the Deep Cut, and they saw that the canal was more than half full. Coming slowly for the new banks, the water had some small impression till the lock gates dammed it. Then it had risen quickly. It made a dark, straight track along the towpath wall, stretching back into the still blackness of the stone. But even in that blackness, it held reflections of the stars.

For such poetic treatment as this, combined with an essentially epical theme, *Erie Water* is a rewarding novel to read. What is equally important about *Erie Water*, of course, is that authenticity in dealing with York State's history which characterized *Rome Haul* and for which Edmonds has since become so well known.

The year following *Erie Water* Edmonds gathered together a potpourri of short stories under the title of *Mostly Canallers* (1934). To be sure, most of the twenty-four stories deal, in some way or other, with the canal and its people; and whether they treat of the Erie Canal, the Black River country, or the Lansing Kill Gorge, canalism fills the pages, as Edmonds faithfully depicts the times. Much of *Mostly Canallers* might better be termed episodes than stories, since they present for plots little more than the rather ordinary events which characterized

living on or near the canal. These episodes are like reminiscences, anecdotal depictions which here and there manage to
catch something of the true comedy or tragedy of life.
Edmonds can present authentic detail even when romanticiz-
ing. Tales like "At Schoharie Crossing" depict the times and
the tribulations of canawlers expertly and authentically, as
boats queue up, waiting for the raging Schoharie Creek waters
to abate, so the Erie traffic can make the crossing. "There were
plenty of such crossings on the old Erie," explains Edmonds,
"and the Schoharie was the worst of the lot." The waiting led
to the inevitable fight, brought about in this case by Herman
Peters, "bully of Utica," who insisted that no one pass ahead
of his boat. ("Since she come on the Erie, the *Pretty Fashion*
ain't never been second on any lock she come to.") The Irishman O'Mory—probably the same O'Mory met in the final
chapters of *Erie Water*—rejoined with a challenge from the
Dublin Queen; but it was young Dan Wagner, impatient with
anything or anyone who stood in his way of getting in Ohio
in time for the planting season, who took on the bully. Both
obstacles—the bully and the crossing—were overcome, the
latter causing by far the greater comment. "You're a stranger
on this canal," he was told, "or you'd know it couldn't be
did. . . . The last four boats that tried crossing on high
water went over the dam. One took three mules with it, and
the rope broke on the others." But Dan, after besting Peters,
crossed with his team. His boat's name, incidentally, was the
Sure Arrival.

As might be expected, bullies and brawling provide the setting and incident for other tales as well. "Water Never Hurt
A Man" leans heavily on the fighting tradition of canawlers,
although the story concerns the Black River people rather
than men of the Erie. Jotham Klore, already beaten by Dan
Harrow in *Rome Haul*, re-appears fleetingly in "Who Killed
Rutherford?" a somewhat macabre and provocative little tale
concerning a canaller whose death provided something of a
mystery for his friends to gossip about. In "Citizens for Ohio"
a teamster fears that the new Erie Canal may ruin team-haul-
ing; he runs into a redemptioner and after an incident of brawl-

ing decides to move on; like the Wagners who crossed at Schoharie, he heads for Ohio.

By contrast to these, mild-mannered men have their day. In "Mr. Dennit's Adventure" a warehouse clerk finds himself for the first time in his life in the midst of a life-and-death situation on one of the numerous setbacks in the Blacksnake region of the Long Level. Since this uncommon escapade involves his being saved by a nude girl on her wedding eve, the glamour of this Erie Canal adventure needs no elaborating!

Mostly Canallers presents a seemingly endless array of people in an equally endless variety of situations. Some of the characters are new to Edmonds' readers; a fair number of them, like Jotham Klore, Lucy Cashdollar, Mrs. Gurget, and "the Old Jew," recur in Edmonds' writings from time to time. In subject, the tales range from the naive "romance" between Eve Winslow and Perry Hoslin, "the craziest lock-tender on the Kill Gorge" and "queerest coot on the whole canal" (in "Blind Eve") to the awesome times of the cholera epidemic (in "The Old Jew's Tale"); in time, they range from the beginnings of the canal to "The End of the Towpath," in which two oldtimers wreak vengeance of a sort on one another or on themselves.

Certainly a memorable character of Erie legendry is rounded out by Edmonds in "Big-Foot Sal," inspired perhaps by the cook in the many-versioned ballad:

> The cook we had upon the deck
> Stood six feet in her socks;
> Her hand was like an elephant's ear,
> Her breath would open the locks.[15]

Edmonds' Sal is drawn with much sympathy. The story concerns the anxiety on the freight-hauler *Ohio*, on the Long Level just before the winter closing of the canal, as Opal's "time" is due, unexpectedly early for George, who thought they would have time to make Utica and Lucy Cashdollar's. ("Lucy took care of her girls that way.") The last locktender's house has been passed, and no lights disclose a habitation beyond the towpath. Like a miracle in that Erie wilderness the boat of Cooney and Sal appears coming toward them.

A broad, squat figure was stumping along the towpath. As Edmonds describes her, George saw "a middle-aged woman with hair of indeterminate color straggling from under her shawl, and the biggest feet he had ever seen. Her eyes were bleary and her breath whistled; but she looked like an angel. . . ."

"I'll do the whole thing," Sal says to George.

In the interval that follows, Cooney fills George in on Sal. "Sal don't look so good," he said, "but she's the best damned cook on the Erie Canal." This gin-drinking, awkward chunk of a woman with a Samaritan sensibility always wanted a baby and never had one; her midwifing to George's Opal (and doubtless to countless others before) would "play billy-bubs with Sal's works" (as Cooney put it).

Along with the near pathos of such human-interest episodes as "Sal," much tongue-in-cheek tale-telling comes from Edmonds' pen. Both as entertainments and as literary accomplishments, the tall tales are perhaps the better part of Edmonds' book. Of these, "An Honest Deal" and "The Cruise of the Cashalot" are stories in the best camp-fire tradition, to be retold and savored, but only one of them rightly belongs to a discussion of Erie literature. The former deals with an inimitable horsetrader, who could probably out-Harum Harum: he not only sold off a dead horse for a $100 profit, but he kept his honor doing it. The other tale, "The Cruise of the Cashalot," which takes a monstrous whale the full length of the Erie Canal, makes a genuine contribution to York State legendry. Edmonds based his tale on an actual account which had already become a folk tale by the time it reached him.[16]

As Edmonds tells the tale, Aunt Em made Uncle Ben's life a pretty henpecked existence. When Em had to leave to visit her diabetic Ma, leaving Uncle Ben to freight down to New York City, she never dreamed what a turning point in their life the ensuing events would cause.

Uncle Ben and his driver rammed a whale in New York harbor. That is, the canal boat *Louisa* did. "What," says the

driver, "are you going to do with a whale?" and he reminded
him that Em would "squeak" him when she found out. "Em,"
retorted Ben, "hasn't got anything to say about this whale.
. . . I'm going to load that whale aboard the *Louisa* and take
her up the Erie." And that's just what he did. They hoisted
the whale on the *Louisa* with her nose on the cabin roof and
her tail hanging over the front end. They dug out the inwards,
so Ben could put in a bar and a refreshment parlor. ("I'd ought
to get the ladies and children, too.") At Troy, he showed the
outside for fifteen cents, but when he had it full-rigged, the
Louisa-and-whale made quite a spectacle going up the Canal.

> They had kind of washed her outside but she looked a little
> greasy; but, as Uncle Ben said, everybody had seen a bull-
> head boat anyway. It was the whale they'd look at. And
> sure enough, there was the whale stretched out on the boat,
> looking Uncle Ben right in the eye where he stood steering.
> She had a door in her side opposite the gang, and a flag
> stuck into her nose hole saying CASHALOT in green let-
> ters. And over the door was a sign saying, "Be a Jonah for
> fifty cents." And underneath it said, "Complete equipment."

Uncle Ben even added a pair of glasses he had gotten from an
oculist in Albany. Before he reached Rome, he'd made over a
thousand dollars. Farmers came from fifty miles away to look
at the whale. Difficulties arose, however, especially with the
hot weather, for the whale began to swell, forcing Ben to trim
it to get under the Erie's low bridges. As Ben trimmed, the
price of admission came down. But when Aunt Em returned
the worm had turned. The money Ben had made impressed
her: even she could see that Uncle Ben was an heroic whale-
killer who wasn't scared of a woman any more. He asserted
himself, sold the whale for fertilizer in Rochester, for eighty
cents, and told Em to clean up the boat. And she did.

In 1947 Edmonds published *The Wedding Journey*, a novelette which *The New Yorker* appropriately called "a slight
but altogether graceful and amusing story." [17] The scene is a

wedding trip on an Erie packet; the time, August 18, 1835. In this story, Edmonds again captured the times, the places; but the characters, except for the realistic Captain Harrow and the rude but kindly Mrs. Cashdollar (by now an old friend to Edmonds' readers), seem more ethereal than real. Touring on the packet boat *Western Lion* seems quaintly sedative in Edmonds' depiction:

> There was a pleasant coolness, and a faint fresh smell of grass under dew in the air fluttering the curtains. But the lamp slung over the table burned without flickering. There was no sound of travel, no rattle of trace links, no squeak of springs, no rumble of wheels. There was no sound at all but the roar of bullfrogs among the lily pads in the set-backs, and since sunset that had been continual. Only when the driver boy's voice came back to them shrilly crying, "Bridge!" and the steersman answered, "Low bridge!" were the passengers aware that every minute saw them further west.[18]

Nothing seems to mar the utter tranquility, not even gambling and minor encounters with an occasional passenger of the less desirable sort. It all seems rather Howellsian.[19]

In the meantime, Edmonds' *Rome Haul*, which as a novel seems to have been largely responsible for the upsurge of interest in Yorker regionalism, appropriately enough had become one of the more popular plays during the 1930's. The book, when first dramatized by F. B. Elser, was called *Low Bridge;* it had a rather desultory stage history with little-theatre stock groups. Elser, despairing after numerous unsatisfactory rewritings of his play, consulted Marc Connelly, and the collaboration resulted finally in *The Farmer Takes a Wife* (1934). Cast and directed by Connelly and produced by Max Gordon, it opened in New York's 46th Street Theatre October 30, 1934, for a run of 104 performances.[20]

The Connelly-Elser drama changed the original Edmonds story into one which had a more insistent nostalgic twinge; by playing up the rivalry between the Erie Canal and the railroads, the canawlers were given a chance to make numerous remarks of a highly evocative sort, and this approach made, in general, for a unifying theme. But somehow everyone in the drama seemed to have already decided that the Old Erie was passé. Fortune Friendly, *Rome Haul*'s renegade preacher now appearing as a dentist, summed up their basic philosophy. "Time is flying!" he said. "Not only time, but everything else. We don't stay satisfied with what's wonderful. We've always got to make *perfection* better. The railroads will give us more speed, all right, but they'll make people forget how fine the world could go at *four miles an hour*." [21]

Connelly's choice of Henry Fonda for the role of the young canaller Dan Harrow was fortunate, and typed Fonda for subsequent Erie-inspired productions. He played the same role in the motion picture version, in what turned out to be a further reworking of *Rome Haul*, by now hardly recognizable. Then when the next Edmonds novel went Hollywood, Fonda again was cast as a young canaller, Chad Hanna, who left the canal to join the circus and begin a tremulous love affair with two equestriennes.

With the concurrence of Connelly, at least one major post-Broadway production of *The Farmer Takes a Wife* returned closer to the original novel in respect to utilizing a natural outdoor setting and something of the atmosphere of a canal town, geographically at least if not in time. This was the Charles Coburn offering during the 1937 season of the Mohawk Drama Festival at Schenectady, New York; Wylie Adams, understudy to Fonda in the Broadway production, had the lead. Directed by Percival Vivian, the Drama Festival production ran from July 13 through July 17, 1937.[22] It seemed fitting that this popular play should be in the repertory of the Mohawk Drama Festival, held on the grounds of Union College, which the year before had granted Edmonds an honorary degree. It was fitting in another regard also. As one headline put it: "Festival Play Reverses Erie Tradition." [23] The Old Erie literally brought drama to Schenectady in the days when travelling troupes of actors used the canal and played their stands in canal towns—and with *The Farmer Takes a Wife,* drama was bringing the Erie Canal back to Schenectady.

It is not hard to see why the Modern Library called Edmonds "the laureate of the Erie Canal." [24] Nor is it hard, with his attention to Yorker material and locales, and his singular emphasis on the life and lore of Erie Canallers, to surmise Edmonds' influence on subsequent writers. In no small degree he made Yorkers aware of themselves and of their regional characteristics. Along with Carmer and Thompson, who worked largely in the area of nonfiction, Edmonds opened up New York State to literary prospectors. Like the first "Forty-Niner," he struck a rich vein, and the rush was on. His first novel, *Rome Haul,* stands as a milestone in the history of Yorker literature. It was an important instrument in influencing more recent writers toward the use of upstate materials and, doubtless too, in tempting some to travel Erie water. How direct or far-reaching this influence is would be difficult to determine quantitatively, but the evident increase in Yorker regional literature might well be attributed to Edmonds' influence. Before *Rome Haul* few novels treated the upstate region. After Edmonds' success, however, a veritable flood of words set in Yorker country were produced, continuing up to the present time.[25]

One might say Edmonds invented the "Erie novel"; certainly he was the first to write full length about Erie life in adult fiction. He set the pattern, providing most of the framework—in *Rome Haul* and *Erie Water*—which other writers adopted. Furthermore, it was in *Rome Haul,* his first novel, that Edmonds began the tradition that all Erie-inspired fiction should have a fight-scene between the hero and a canal bully (or *the* canal bully) for a climax, similar to the typical western's conventional gun-duel between hero and gunfighter.[26]

Whether he is writing a slight novelette, a canalside tall tale, or a novel of major proportions, Walter D. Edmonds strikes literary historians as important essentially for his regional flavor. But he is never too narrowly regional, and his best work, like *Rome Haul* and *Drums Along the Mohawk,* captures a sense of the epic of America. "I was lucky," he said, "to be born in New York State, which is almost in miniature a cross-section of the entire United States." [27] In the final analysis, Edmonds' significance lies in his authenticity in detailing for us his feelings for that epical and microcosmic quality which is inherent in his home state's history. His authenticity, of course, always remains of the romantic sort. As one reviewer summed up *Erie Water*, "Edmonds can recreate the people and the folkways of an era; he is rich in odd lovable characters; he tells of the wind and the waters, horses and crops, the humors and passings of plain people, of child-bearing and the patience of women. I suppose he is romantic, neglecting labor and health and political problems, but he registers a moment in history, and some human beings." [28] It is precisely for this kind of "romantic realism" that Edmonds and the Erie Canal make such a happy combination in our literary history.

Adams
Rhapsodist of the Old Erie

SAMUEL HOPKINS ADAMS (1871–1958) had, if not a typical canalside upbringing, at least one in which he was thoroughly immersed in Erie water. His great-grandfather, Deacon Abner Adams, was a canal contractor, and his grandfather, Squire Myron Adams, whose stories about canal life and lore form the basis for *Grandfather Stories* (1955), never left off loving the great Clinton Ditch, nor reminiscing about it, if what Samuel related is true. There is no reason to doubt it. Literally, as well as literarily, the Erie Canal was home to him. From Wide Waters, the old Hopkins residence outside Auburn, not far from the Erie towpath, came many of his novels, stories, and articles. As one might suspect, the Adams name became even more surely linked with Erie history, a village along the canal having been named in honor of an Adams' contribution to the digging of the Big Ditch.[1]

In a number of novels and stories Adams demonstrated his personal loyalty to the Old Erie. It echoes in the words he heard from Grandfather Myron in the 1870's, when that nautical-minded gentleman rhapsodized about the times when "the Grand Western Canal was the pride and glory of the nation, vaunted as the eighth wonder of the world." The canal had been, he said, wrought with our hands and filled with our sweat.[2]

Hamilton College, at Clinton, New York, knew Sam Adams as a most loyal alumnus. As a matter of fact, Adams' grandfather, father and five uncles were also Hamilton men. To be sure, it seems easy for an Adams or a Hopkins to be famous, ran a tribute in the *Hamilton Alumni Review;*[3] but Sam had a unique versatility. In college he wrote for *Lit* and the college newspaper; he won the college's Scollard Prize more than once; and he liked especially to recall—with nonliterary satisfaction—that he started football at the college, importing it from that rival institution, Union College, farther down the Erie at Schenectady. His first job came from Chester Lord, managing editor of the *New York Sun*, Adams having been preceded there by such literary talents as David Graham Phillips, Arthur Brisbane, and James Huneker. From 1900 to 1905 he worked for the McClure interests, as managing editor of their newspaper syndicate and as staff member of *McClure's Magazine*, in which a number of his early short stories appeared. Adams free-lanced after 1905, and by 1911 he had published an impressive array of short stories and one collection, *Average Jones*, containing a story which has appeared in several anthologies of great detective stories. His first full-length fiction, *Flying Death*, appeared serially in *McClure's* in 1903 and was published by Doubleday in 1908.

His initial fame, however, came when he published in the now defunct *Collier's* two series of articles later collected in book form for the American Medical Association. *The Great American Fraud* (1906), documented with chemical analyses and other clinical proofs, deserves major credit for the passage of the Pure Food and Drug Act. In recognition of such results produced by Adams' articles, the American Medical Association created for him the unique honor of an Associate Fellowship, and Adams continued for some time to publish wide-ranging articles on public health and hygiene.

He wrote biographies of Webster, Harding, and the Broadway raconteur, Alexander Woollcott, his fellow alumnus. Hamilton College awarded Adams an honorary L.H.D. degree in 1926. In the realm of fiction he has much to his credit. Sixteen of his novels and stories reached Hollywood, among them *The Gorgeous Hussy* and the highly successful "It Happened One Night," which became the Clark Gable–Claudette Colbert Academy Award winner. But the thing about Samuel Hopkins Adams most germane to a literary history of his native state concerns his emphasis on regionalism which began at a time when most men would be retiring. At 73 he wrote his first "Erie novel" which launched him on an entirely new and quite successful career as a regional writer. He titled the book, appropriately enough, *Canal Town.*

"The plot," wrote Walter D. Edmonds in reviewing *Canal Town* (1944) for the *Atlantic*, "is the least important element of the novel. What counts is the elaborate, colorful, and affectionate portrait of a canal town in its growing pains. Obviously, Mr. Adams has not only gone back to the sources but has lived with them for a long time." [4] The "canal town" is Palmyra, the time about 1820, when (as Adams put it) the digging of "that vast, Clintonian enterprise, the Erie Canal, brought with it to western New York not only progress and prosperity but unforeseen upheavals." [5] With marvelously authentic detail, Adams recaptured the spirit of the times, the upheavals and the struggles on the new frontiers—the engineering frontier which the building of the Erie represented, the medical frontier which the swamp fever and cholera epidemics of the Erie project disclosed, and the social and economic frontier manifested in the very expansion which "progress" denoted. Skepticism, as well as unbounded enthusiasm, ran rampant: "The canawl! The canawl!" jeered one character. "I'll spit you all the canawl you'll get." Ejecting a welter of tobacco juice over the rail, he continued, Adams tells us, in his "hoarse basso":

> "Clinton, the federal son-of-a-bitch,
> Taxes our dollars to build him a ditch."

Canal Town, with its rich background of the building of the

Big Ditch, is skillfully plotted romance. Arranged as two books, the novel presents, first, a thorough and quaintly sympathetic introduction to the times and to Palmyra, the town that forms the focal point of the novel; and, second, a swiftly paced narrative involving chiefly the state of medical science and medical practice in the 1830's. Written with all the intensity of a mystery story, this latter section draws the reader into close sympathy with the principal character, Dr. Horace Amlie.

From the day he first enters Palmyra and decides to take up practice there, Dr. Amlie, Hamilton College, class of 1818,[6] finds he has much on his hands. Aramintha ("Dinty") Jerrold is not the least of these problems, for she falls in love with him immediately, although, to be sure, she is much too young to recognize or perhaps even to feel the love that one day finds her as the doctor's wife. At first, she is content to find in the young medico a person with a humane interest in his fellow man, and one capable of understanding her and her friends as well.

The novel is rich in characters of the times—some good, some bad, most of them caught up in one way or another in the effects of what Adams calls the "alien irruption" which the coming of the Erie represented. Genter Latham and his daughter Wealthia stand for the prevailing social order of the times; Silverhorn Ramsey, "canaller by trade," represents the adventurous spirit rampant as a result of the canal's coming. If one were looking for further symbolism in *Canal Town,* an easy case could be made for the Silverhorn-Wealthia love affair (and her pregnancy and death) as an allegory of the effect of the coming of the canal on the old social structure. By the end of the novel, Genter Latham (and his pinnacle-of-society position) is completely shaken, and the more democratic social order of Dr. Amlie, on the one hand, and of the canallers, on the other, is a *fait accompli.*

Other characters are folk types from America's past. T. Lay, the archetype of the frontier merchandiser, advertised that he "trafficked in anything and everything vendible." Ephraim Upcraft ("Uncurrent notes bought") appears as an honest lawyer (his own admission) who tries to know which side his bread is buttered on. The Reverend Theron Strang is Palmyra's respectable clergyman; and the Reverend Philo Stickel, "the Exhorter," known also as "the Scythe of Salvation," arrives on the Palmyra scene with his favorite discourse on the Seven Plagues of the Erie. These he listed as Harlotry, Blasphemy, Bastardy, Drunkenness, Rioting, and Chills-and-Fever. The last, a common Erie ailment, he said, "counts as two." In addition to the cast mentioned, various others parade through the novel, giving it fullness and perspective; and the use of the jargon and idiom of the day—terms like *cheapjack, pillslingers, ninnyhammers, didoes, cockshy, Miss Bettsy Uppish, kine-box matter, clappermaws*, and *spilled the nosebag*—make for authenticity and flavor.

These qualities, Adams' authenticity and flavor, along with the author's deep sensibilities regarding the Old Erie, are nowhere better illustrated in Adams' writings than in a scene in *Canal Town* where Dr. Amlie, as a young man recently arrived in the bustling canal area, rides out to see for himself the building of the Ditch. Adams spoke of the great cut as it pushed slowly east and west, and of Amlie's seeing a hundred men and a score of horses sweating and straining in the cut, "dragging dredges, plucking out recalcitrant stumps as a dentist plucks out a broken root." With pick and shovel the canal workers dug out the obstructive boulders, fashioned the towpath on one side, the berm on the other, "toilfully embodying the dream of DeWitt Clinton, the pride of the Empire State, the longest, broadest, deepest, mightiest canal in all history."

Horace Amlie felt his pulse stirred at the sight. He knew already that the Erie Canal was a classic of American achievement, that it represented a new artery for the life blood of a new commerce and a stronger nation.

A gang of barrowmen, trundling the new Brainard or "canal" wheelbarrows back to the sheds, lifted rough voices in the song of the ditch.

We are digging the Ditch through the gravel;
Through the gravel and mud and slime, by God!
So the people and freight can travel,
And the packets can move on time, by God!

Horace hummed the dogged refrain under his breath. "So the people and freight can travel." A saying of his old mentor, the wise, robust, irascible Dr. John Vought, merged with the measure. "The mainspring of human progress is the itch of the restless man to be otherwise than where he is." There beneath him was the surge and pressure of that invincible desire. It was a vision of expanding America.

In *Canal Town* Samuel Hopkins Adams has given us a deeper insight into that vision.

The Thalia Dramatic Company, with its emblem of a great "T" against a white background, travelled York State in the 1830's, "bearing illusion and delight," as Adams put it, "to the dark fringes of civilization." Their story, and that of two young aspirants to the Thespian art, Adams related in *Banner by the Wayside* (1947), a novel teeming with the life of the period. It is not rightly an Erie Canal story, for the Thalia performers could doubtless have existed apart from towpath and berm. Yet, perhaps significantly, Erie water permeates the book: the pungent, spicy, canalside chatter of York State in its expansive days of the Canal Era overflows each line, and many of the characters and incidents belong to Erie legendry —factual or fictional in origin—of which they have become an inevitable part.

The relatively simple plot of *Banner by the Wayside* revolves about the two protagonists, Endurance ("Durie") Andrews and Jans Quintard, as they weave their lives and at times their fortunes among those of a roving theatrical troupe. Durie, a foundling, was raised by a New York bookseller, Adams P. Andrews, whose *magnum opus* (and the sole creation of his life) he titled *The Maze of Marriage: a Diatribe.*

Durie's upbringing was a decidedly masculine one, culminating in her unmaidenly but not unnatural desire to matriculate at her foster-father's alma mater on the banks of the Charles. There at Harvard she encountered for the first time Jans Quintard, who twice had his connections with the venerable institution severed by administrative decree. Quintard thus found himself in continuous "hot water" with an uncle who supported him, a would-be roué who appreciated nothing of the situation save the motto of Jans' Corinthian brotherhood— *Caveat puella* ("Let the maiden beware"). Both Durie Andrews and Jans Quintard play their roles before the Thalia backdrop for most of the rest of the novel.

Whatever else may be said of it, *Banner by the Wayside* is not slender of plot. As a novel, it perhaps suffers from its very exuberance of setting and characters: it is as stuffed with incident as a Thanksgiving turkey with dressing. As one reviewer put it, the novel "has the same relation to reading that ice cream has to eating—rich, healthful, tasty and appropriate at any time for anybody." [7] Adams' recurrent representation of the Erie Canal as an "immense current of human traffic" is perhaps nowhere better exemplified than in the pages of this novel. From the time the innocent Durie and her worldly-wise friend Gypsy Vilas set out on the towpath, *Banner by the Wayside* sprawls over the countryside, usually along the canal, occasionally in hamlets elsewhere in Yorker country. Gypsy's ribald toast, at the *Sign of the Hungry Pike*, sets the pace: "Here's to path and berm and free passage west," she said, "and may our roads never spread wider than a spinster's knees."

As she travels the towpath for the first time, Durie meets canal life face-to-face. The traffic includes Looby, a 20-year-old hoggee who desperately needs a friend, and Captain Bully Suggs of the *Water Witch*, who turns Looby out with his ten dollars season's pay withheld; there is Deacon Gildersleeve and the *Peace-on-Earth*, a canal craft handled by a hoggee so comfortably clad, said Adams, and so sleek-bellied with good food that "he was a phenomenon in that ill-used calling." (The good Deacon freighted rum, whiskey, pickled eels, and pork.) Also riding the Erie is the party-boat, the *Merry Mount*, "the

dandiest Durham on the Erie," with its crew of Harvard roister-
ers who, later, after Durie had adopted the more theatrical
name of *Le Jeune Amour*, proved an almost ever-present audi-
ence wherever the Thalia banner signified the troupe's performances in a canalside village or town.

During the course of the novel the reader meets such other
figures as Mr. Gospel, the keeper of Auburn's famed state
prison; Lucky Seven Smith, as unethical a manhunter as ever
claimed a bounty; Pig Baker, Albany's municipal swineherd;
and Four-skate Pilkington. The latter is the least unsavory.
When Mr. Baseford Pilkington, in eluding a Pennsylvania
sheriff, borrowed two pairs of skates, ostensibly to demon-
strate quadrupedal skating, and proceeded up the Susquehanna
to the York State line, he entered Yorker country with a new
tag as a result. "Four-skate" returned the blades (by leaving
them at an inn on the Yorker side of the state line) and kept
out of sight at logging for a while. His adventure on the
Susquehanna made him a legendary figure in the area; and, as
Adams says, this gratified his vanity, but complicated his career.[8]

Pilkington ran up against the carcagne once, too, and regret-
ted it, as he and Jans Quintard rode out a terrific storm con-
jured up by the batwinged hag of sinister legend. When the
storm abated, he took a long drink, and shook his fist at the
clearing sky:

> "Fooled yeh!" he crowed.
> "Lookout," warned Jans with a grin. "You'll make the
> carcagne mad again."
> "She'll never get another crack at me," declared the other.
> "What sailin' I do from now on'll be on the Ee-rye-ee
> Canal." [9]

Pig Baker, too, becomes in Adams' hands something of a
legendary figure. Having been appointed by the Albany city
council to the "honorable if not over-remunerative post" of
swine warden, Pig Baker made the job pay. At one point in
the novel he asks a shilling to call off the half-wild pigs so

Durie can get down from a tree whence she climbed in some desperation. Baker's career was not very long; he died in the cholera epidemic of 1832.

York State's great cholera epidemic provides much of the substance of the final chapters. The plague created hysteria all along the canal. Many persons superstitiously feared that it followed the Erie; others, with the uncertain state of medical science in the 1830's, sent the price of camphor up to five dollars a pound, and burned tar and other nauseating vapor-producing substances to ward off the evil vapors of the cholera. Many persons suspected that canal boats carried and spread the contagion. (A burned-in letter "C" often served to brand canal boats which had cholera patients or which were thought to be carriers.) The cholera epidemic much interested Adams, and in a factual account written the year in which *Banner* was published, he documented his story. In this article written for *New York Folklore Quarterly* he provided the historic detail upon which the events in his novel are based.[10] Later, in *Grandfather Stories*, he included a short story "The Monster of Epidemy," which contains much lore connected with the plague.

In the closing chapters of *Banner by the Wayside*, Jans and Four-skate, running supplies doggedly up and down the canal for the Commissioners, found their entrance into the Syracuse basin blocked by the frightened town's guardian officials. Neither a governor's warrant, granting them priority of passage through all the locks, nor the great need for the supplies could move the Syracusans. Quintard marshalled the crews of a dozen or so canal boats, lined up for lockage, to help get the medicines to the Syracuse docks whether the Syracusans wanted them or not. Erie boatmen, loyal to the tradition of the canal and always ready to join in a good scrap, responded willingly and, in due time, the boat was snugged up in Salinas Basin, the Syracusans were provided with the anti-cholera drugs, and *Banner by the Wayside* was provided at last with the Erie novel's traditional brawl.

Adams also provided this novel with a foreword and an afterword, each devoted to comments regarding his great-aunt

Sarah Hopkins Bradford. She knew the Thalians and witnessed their final curtain; she knew, too, the Quintards, who in later years became the proprietors of a "book-boat," until that trade passed, even as did the travelling troupes who brought their entertainment and culture to the canal towns.

"Only a memory of them remains," concludes the author nostalgically via Mrs. Bradford. "But what a memory! For it springs from the roots of mirth and happiness, of contempt for all things mean, of fervor for all things joyous and sane and kind, and its flowering is imperishable."

In 1950 Random House published *Sunrise to Sunset*, which the dust-jacket preview termed "another of Samuel Hopkins Adams' romantic novels, richly documented with obscure and fascinating regional lore, language and customs." Properly considered, the novel has nothing or little to do with the Erie Canal; over a hundred pages go by before *canawlers* are mentioned, and a good deal farther on one meets *Erie* for the first time. Yet this story is, in many ways, more the story of a representative town in the early Canal Era than its predecessor with a Palmyra locale. For Troy, directly across the Hudson River from the notorious Side-cut, was in the 1830's a hurly-burly of activity, representative of, in Adams' words, an essential character of early industrial America. Inevitably, Erie canallers play their vigorous if minor parts.

The plot concerns the love of Becky Webb, a young factory worker, for Guy Roy, rising Troy manufacturer of the first detachable collars.[11] As with Adams' first Erie novel, *Sunrise to Sunset* provides an interest on two levels. The first gives the reader a tremendously panoramic and authentic view of the civilization of the times; the second offers a swiftly paced and skillfully woven narrative which evidences Adams' surety of touch as a novelist. Obedience (Becky) Webb, when yet a child, is hired as a bobbin-doffer in the Eureka Mills, owned by Gurdon Stockwell, "the most influential mill owner in Troy"; Stockwell, a pillar of the church, magistrate, and holder of various other titles of honor and social distinction, is, as his epitaph later so aptly phrased it, "a man of principle." The central male character of the novel, Guy Roy, maintains other principles which include a greater feeling for his fellow man.

An interesting parallel exists between *Canal Town* and *Sunrise to Sunset* as far as the central characters are concerned, for Becky and Guy Roy appear in many ways to be Dinty Jerrold and Dr. Amlie set in another locale and situation. Although Becky's marriage to Gurdon Stockwell destroys the complete parallelism, both Becky and Dinty are children when they first meet their beloveds, and both all but worship their men. In their respective novels, Guy Roy and Horace Amlie are morally high-principled individuals who are unappreciated by the townspeople for being so; both are innovators who bring about enduring social reform; and both are humanists.

An engaging novel, *Sunrise to Sunset*—the title arises from the sunrise-to-sunset working hours of the early mills, the labor day felt by many to be ordained by God—is in many respects reminiscent of Theodore Dreiser's *An American Tragedy* (1925), for the situation which provides the main element of plot structure in the second half of the novel is not unlike that in Dreiser's work. The pregnancy of the factory girl, the surreptitious disclosure to her lover, the attempted abortion, and her final death—accidentally, ironically, yet at the hand of her paramour—are much the same ingredients; only the locale changes, from Chester Gillette's Adirondack lake to Sadler's Island at Troy.[12] Furthermore, in a quite real sense, Gurdon Stockwell's story *is* an American tragedy of the 1830's, for Adams provides authentic detailing of a doubtless representative and tragic situation in early American milltowns.

The Erie canallers' principal role in the novel, except for an occasional drifting in here and there, comes in a scene which contains one of the most vividly detailed accounts of canallers' participation in mob violence to be found in Erie literature. A mob of townspeople, bent on lynching an innocent man whom they assume to be a murderer, is reinforced by canallers, fresh in and eager for scrapping. The townspeople can be shouted down, cowed by the oratory of Mr. Stockwell, who is their pillar of the community, but Erie men are not so malleable. As one onlooker put it: "Those are only the townsfolk. It's the wharfers and canallers and high-kettles that won't be scared so easily." At this point, "a gangling, hardwood lath of a man," pushing his way to the front, shouted "Come on lads! . . . What the hell's a magistrate! Judge Lynch is good enough for us." An immediate melee is frustrated only by an interruptor whom Adams describes as arrayed in the full splendor of an Erie packet captain's regalia. In typical sporting fashion, the canawling captain had a proposition for Stockwell and a small group who stood with him. The ensuing dialogue shows clearly the kind of situation which canallers relished and evidences at the same time the skill of the author in depicting the times.

"Avast, my hearty," the captain protested. "Hold your broadside." No deep-sea mariner could be quite as nautical as a seasoned canaller. This one took off his caster and swept Stockwell a mock bow. "Captain Trigg of the *Western Wave*, at your service."

"Trigg! Bull Trigg!" The words passed through the crowd accented with respect.

The man was built like a bull: vast chest, bulky shoulders, neck like a tree-bole supporting a craggy head. He stood above Stockwell's six feet by a good three inches and looked to outweigh him two stone or more. Solid and uncompromising, the man with the gun said, "What do you do on my premises, Captain Trigg?"

"Will you put down that gun and run me off?"

"No, I am no brawler."

"I'll lay you a test."

"State it."

"You have the murderer, Barlow, secreted."

"I hear you say so."

"Will you fight me for him?"

A hush spread over the assemblage.

Gurdon Stockwell said coldly, "Let me be sure I understand you. If I fight and best you, will this mob disperse peacefully to their homes?"

The answer came in a roar from the crowd.

"No." "Not without Barlow." "Give us the murderer and we'll go." "We'll get him and we'll get you, too, if you meddle with us." "Hemp for both of 'em."

"You see," Stockwell said contemptuously to his challenger.

Trigg, somewhat discomfited, rubbed his nose. "Tell you what, brother; I'll make a bargain with you just the same."

"Speak up."

"I can't warranty this crowd of blacklegs and guttermuck. But we got thirty-forty rough-and-tumble Erie men here."

"Well?"

"You best me, and they're yours. That kee-rect, boys?"

The responses came from all sides "Right-o, Cap!" "We're with you, Bully." "The Ee-rye-ee forever!" Little did the canallers care on which side they fought, just so the battle was a good one.

The ensuing fight between the wealthy mill owner and Bull Trigg provides *Sunrise to Sunset* with a semblance of that convention of the Erie novel, the big fight. In this case, it comes not between hero and bully, but the situation is analogous: Stockwell, whatever his faults of self-righteousness, must be considered, in the framework of the novel, a secondary "hero," if rather a despicable one on a number of counts. The fight between the two men is short and violent. When Stockwell does indeed best Trigg, the canallers join forces with the Stockwell men: "We're your men," they said, "you're the boss."

The code of the Erie was rigid.

Doubtless the best expression of Erie sentiment and the most engaging use of Erie materials by Samuel Hopkins Adams—if we except his classic juvenile, *The Erie Canal*—is to be found in a collection of short stories based on the hearthside story-telling of his paternal grandfather, Squire Myron Adams of East Bloomfield, New York. Adams called the volume, simply enough, *Grandfather Stories* (1955).

Admittedly half-fact, half-fiction, *Grandfather Stories* offers the reader a rich serving of Erie lore. Much of the book concerns the Erie; what does not, at least concerns New York State. Written largely as anecdotal reminiscences, the tales range from the accounts of such hearty and imperative canal-side activity as staying "The Big Breach," to whimsical studies in the lore of the early canal days, like the pie-eating contest in "Piety and Pie," or the old caisson used by the canal town of Cayuga as its unique jailhouse ("Grandfather's Criminal Career"). The perilous times are recalled in the cholera epidemic of 1832 ("The Monster of Epidemy") and the inventiveness of Canal Era York Staters probed in such tales as "The Camera and the Chimera," "Mr. Stumpy's Preview," and "Mrs. Montague's Collar." The final story in the volume, "Canal Bride," presents an authentic picture of the impressions of a young girl, wed to an Erie packet captain, in the late 1820's.

Grandfather Adams, who modestly called himself a "plain, everyday American," operated a stump-puller with eight-foot wheels in the construction of the canal and later worked on the canal itself. (Adams points out that his maternal grandfather, the Rev. Samuel Miles Hopkins, D.D., was actually more companionable, but that "the difference in appeal to youthful imagination needs no emphasizing." Among other things, the Squire had been a member of the Wayne County Horse-Thief Society, the very name of which awed young minds.) Grandfather loved the Erie with an enduring love, so great that he never quite forgave the railroads for encroaching upon hallowed ground, progress or no. All he asked, according to an account in "The Parlous Trip," was a good, reliable, four-mile-an-hour Erie packet behind a tandem of stout horses. When passenger accommodations no longer were provided on the canal boats, his turn to rail travel came only with the greatest of resignation. "No one ever got a cinder in his eye on the Grand Canal!" he snorted. The Squire could not restrain his indignation the time a railroader prodded him too far, by insulting the Old Erie:

"He said, 'Ho, you cheap canawler!' but, being a peaceful man, I let it pass. Then he said something that I'd take from no railroader. He said he could spit a better canawl than ever Old Clinton built with all the poxy Adamses from Adams Basin to Lock Seventeen helping him. Then, . . . I punched his eye."

On one particular occasion the Squire's towpath travelling proved opportune. This was 1829 or 1830, when five-day August rains filled every tributary stream to flooding and Erie water rose a foot an hour. Pathmaster Tom Culver ("no better canaller could be found between Hudson's River and the Long Level") had sounded his silver whistle to summon help. Under the rules of the Canal Commissioners, a pathmaster could commandeer help and the order must be obeyed. With a broken leg and ribs stove in, Culver feebly struggled to plug holes in the breaching berm. Taking Culver's orders, the elder Adams, now a deputy pathmaster, rode to rouse the countryside. "Once a canaller, always a canaller," Tom had reminded him: Erie loyalty was unfailing and unflinching, duty a responsibility willingly taken. How the Squire saved the canal—and the energetic way he contrived it—makes "The Big Breach" one of the best of the Erie-laden tales in *Grandfather Stories*.

The reader of an Adams book will most certainly feel himself a part of the history which unfolds before him, for Samuel Hopkins Adams has few peers in contemporary fiction in the area of historical romance. In many of the works in Adams' wide repertoire, one may find a deep sense, especially, of the grandeur and the greatness which the Erie Canal represented to nineteenth-century America. Almost any novel taken at random seems to have, as a review of one of them suggested, "a way, as it rolls along, of throwing an oblique and penetrating light on one of the surging periods of American expansion and development." [13] Certainly, more than any other writer, he has been able to capture the meaning of the Old Erie in its heyday. With such competent and absorbing fiction vivifying New York State's notable history, it is easy to realize how Sam Adams could recall that as a boy he "had nothing but pity . . . for those unfortunate children who lived in canal-less regions." [14]

Culture and Canawlers

THE ERIE CANAL has been called "an expression of man's courage, vision and determination." [1] Like all monumental human experiences, it proved to be an influence of no minor importance upon the life, literature, and culture of the people. Its inspiration lay quite obviously in the achievement of men working largely by rule of thumb to build an inland waterway some 360 miles long, and with eighty-two locks and a feeder system properly arranged for, to connect the tidewater of Hendrick Hudson's River with the Great Lake, Erie. At several points solid rock had to be assaulted by blasting crews of "powder monkeys," directed by self-made engineers who were little more experienced in canal-building than those they directed. The Great Cayuga Marsh alone provided a story as stirring—and as similar, in climate if not in setting —as that of the Panama Canal almost a century later. And the refusal of help by the Federal Government made the whole Erie project the more remarkable. The Erie Canal was the work of the State, and as one writer put it, when proud Yorkers used *State* they meant "the plural noun referring to people, not singular, referring to government." [2]

It is no small wonder then that the Erie affected folklore and literature, for it was, during a considerable part of the nineteenth century, one of the principal social and economic factors in the daily lives of a great many people. And the canal, of course, affected still others who had no direct experience with it.

The stream of travellers from Europe who visited America during the first half of the nineteenth century found, after 1825, an attraction which had to be seen and experienced. Until the Civil War, when the tourist mania finally abated, foreign travellers came to York State to see the falls at Niagara and Trenton, and, in the earlier period especially, the marvel of the Lockport flight of locks and other feats of engineering which the Erie Canal had to offer. Many of these persons, as have been noted earlier in this book, were literary personages, and actors, actresses, and statesmen—persons who contributed, in diaries, journals and travel-books, to creating very early a body of Erie literature.

Native American writers, among them notables like Hawthorne, William Dunlap, Melville, and Howells, found in the Erie something interesting and usable, but their contributions provided quality rather than quantity for the literary history of the canal. Not until Yorker regionalism itself reached out for mature expression did writers see in the canal a fruitful area for exploitation. *David Harum* began the process; *Rome Haul* put the capstone on it. For this latter achievement, Edmonds might rightly enough be called "the father of the Erie novel." Samuel Hopkins Adams, starting later, proved more sustaining, but Edmonds' highly productive Erie years, from *Rome Haul* (1929) to *Chad Hanna* (1940), are an enviable record.

The canal's influence on other areas of literature has been significant, too. Juvenile fiction, for obvious reasons, found the Erie story useful; and non-fiction juveniles like *Through the Locks* (1954) are perhaps inspired largely by the popularity which the Erie Canal has had with young and adult readers alike. Where the canal figures in other literature, it is usually tangential, contributing to authenticity of setting and mood. Often it rides along, so to speak, as a part of necessary regionalism. A "gang from the Erie canawl," for example, join a veritable multitude of other Yorker characters in viewing the central figure in *The Cardiff Giant*, a regional play by A. M.

Drummond and Robert E. Gard. The canallers ("We're—the —best—damn—singers—on—the—damn—canal . . . !") enter chorusing "The E-ri-e." [3] This drama, subtitled "New York State Show," and based upon the famous hoax of 1869, catches much of the authentic flavor of the human comedy at work to prove the truth in the statement of P. T. Barnum (who, incidentally, wanted to buy the giant) that "there's a sucker born every minute."

The giant and canallers also figure, along with York State's David Hannum, in *The Cardiff Giant Affair*, a Clarence Buddington Kelland novel serialized in the *Saturday Evening Post* early in 1959. Set largely in and near Syracuse, this novel draws upon the showing of the giant as a principal framework for mysterious events to take place. One canal couple, Ma and Zacharias Wheelwright, are both charmingly and authentically drawn, and canawlers run generally through the story.[4]

Canal lore and an interest in regional literature combined to influence the writing of a one-act play, *A Dam for Delta*, by Thomas F. O'Donnell. The action takes place in April 1905 when the villagers of Delta were faced with eviction by the State when the new dam went through. Capt'n Snyder, described as "a retired—involuntarily retired—canawl captain, a vigorous and peppery old man," recapitulates the canawler's experience in New York State: "First we build the Erie, then we build the Black River Canawl, then we build railroads. Now we build a whole lake. Tell you, always somethin' doin' around here." [5]

Drama and the Erie Canal seem always to have gone hand in hand. When Edmonds' *Rome Haul* reached Broadway as *The Farmer Takes a Wife*, national interest in the Erie story was rekindled. When the motion picture version appeared, as Harold Thompson pointed out, the Middle West welcomed it warmly, for there were sons and grandsons of the hardy emigrants who knew firsthand the full worth of the Erie Canal.[6] Through the medium of the novel, Samuel Hopkins Adams' *Banner by the Wayside* added further insights into York State's dramatic history; as already noted, the Thalia "T," like most touring troupes, rode the canal boats from "port" to "port." The Erie greatly influenced the dramatic-arts aspect of culture in New York State. "The old 'canawl' literally," said one writer, "brought the drama to Schenectady, and every other town and hamlet between Albany and Buffalo which could boast of a local 'opera house' or even a good sized hall. Travelling troupes of thespians rode the canal packets from village to village, pausing to present their dramatic wares to a populace which found romance and release from the humdrum existence of small town life." [7] The most important theatrical companies always tried to make Buffalo before the annual freeze-up of the canal, an important factor in Buffalo's rise to metropolitan stature. (Any town could temporarily become the center of drama if a boatload of actors became froze-in there.) Famous names like Joseph Jefferson and Junius Booth "played the boards" in York State, joining the many other thespians, known and unknown, who travelled the Erie Canal.

The Erie has, of course, been of greater influence on fiction than on any other single genre. For a time it was the subject of intensely patriotic, if not too profound, verse. In the drama its influence, as has been noted, served more to affect culture in the main than to provide inspiration for playwrights. Biographical works include the Erie only insofar as the canal touched the lives of the principals,[8] and no biographies exist of the famed "Erie engineers" whose stories in themselves ought to be romantic and rewarding tasks for the biographer. In the area of children's literature, the Erie story has provided a number of creditable juveniles, the vast majority within the last two decades.

Certain conventions and motifs are noticeable to the critic of Erie fiction. Many of the novels, whether juvenile or adult, present a version of the "rags-to-riches" theme, or "the country boy makes good." Dan Harrow, Chingo Smith, and others, such as Dr. Horace Amlie in *Canal Town*, could probably be considered a variation on this theme. Most of these stories involve, perhaps more importantly, the concept of the maturing hero. Edmonds' Dan Harrow and Jerry Fowler fall into this category. What might be called the "standard" Erie novel ought to contain a fight—a convention begun by Edmonds in *Rome Haul* and adopted by Adams, Fitch, and other novelists. A depiction of the "fighting canawler" reflects the times and adds to the authenticity of the novel's setting; a fight scene between a central character, especially the hero, and the canal bully becomes furthermore a structural literary device, contrived by the author for purposes of plot and tension. When Dan Harrow and Jotham Klore meet in *Rome Haul* it is as much a "showdown" as that occurring in the climax of any western novel. The "runaway befriended" seems to be another tried-and-true convention for the Erie novelist. Thus, Jacob Vandemark, befriended by Captain Sproule (*Vandemark's Folly*); Tim Brady, befriended by the Wades (*The Ring Buster*); and juvenile heroes like David Burns (*Along the Erie Towpath*) and Chingo Smith (*Chingo Smith of the Erie Canal*) show the popular appeal of the Samaritan approach. Even Obedience (Becky) Webb (*Sunrise to Sunset*), lured by promises of grand living at a Troy mill, fits into this pattern; Guy Roy—the knight-errant, as it were—plays the role of protector throughout the novel.

Carl Carmer has said that "York State is a country," and certainly the Erie Canal contributed to making it so in the popular imagination. Nothing in modern history quite matches the Erie story in its influence on the memory of a state, and in capturing the imaginations of writers who look for inspiration in the state's past. A centennial celebration, held in 1926, looked back over the intervening years from the first waterway improvement in New York—a lock at Little Falls, built by private capital in 1791—to the growth of the Erie from a narrow ditch carrying what in retrospect seem almost minuscule packets and freighters to a system handling barges of upward of 300 tons. "The world," noted the Centennial Commission, "has moved a long way since the first canal was opened, but the wonderful advancement seen in the engineering and construction field, the discoveries made in scientific research and our modern inventions, can in no way dim the

glories of the 'Grand Canal' . . . nor can the canal's benefi-
cent influence on the State and Nation be overrated." [9]

Progress. Here and there along the route of the Old Erie
one can still see a fragment of an aqueduct, a part of an old
lock; and if he is sentimental and perhaps a bit sympathetic
toward the Canal Era, a vision of the old-time grandeur can
be gleaned. At Waterford, a progress-created anachronism
graphically lets a tourist look at the old and the new, as an
original Erie lock stands diminutively but proudly like a
smaller brother, beside the New York State Barge Canal's
Erie Division Lock No. 2. A similar scene meets the visitor to
Lockport, where one side of the old Erie's famous combines
remain, quaint historical monuments alongside the present-day
Barge Canal's massive locks. The more persistent "canal-lorist"
can search more thoroughly across the State and still discover
traces of the "ribbon of water" youth found so appealing and
canawlers sang about so heartily. But all of the scenes are
moss-covered. Something of the nostalgia has been caught by
one Yorker, a resident of Frankfort who comes from a family
who have lived along the canal since it "was a glint in DeWitt
Clinton's eye":

> Choked with rushes and cattails, partly filled with water
> that is green-scummed and stagnant, the few remaining
> stretches of the Erie Canal are lonely relics of an era long
> since passed away. In some places the outlines of the old
> towpaths remain, grass-grown, and trodden by complacent
> cows grazing there. Here and there one can still find a
> crumbling lock, or sometimes an old stone bridge, by-passed
> by the years. Bullfrogs and peepers call across the stretches
> where once resounded the bawling of the captains and the
> teamsters. The packet boats, barges, mule teams, the lusty
> two-fisted canawlers, all have vanished from the scene to be
> remembered by succeeding generations in song and story. [10]

The Erie Canal has not only profoundly influenced the
course of American history, it has also had a significant effect

upon our folklore and culture. The Erie story has its moss-covered, nostalgic side, but there is also recapturable at times the jubilance of Yorkers who, in 1825, were "running across the fields, climbing on trees, and crowding the banks . . . to gaze upon the welcome sight." [11] The Grand Erie Canal continues to draw crowds. It may even give us a sense of perspective, for, like Fortune Friendly in *The Farmer Takes a Wife*, we may find it good to recall how wonderful the world could go at *four miles an hour*.

Notes

In the notes which follow, an abbreviated form is used to indicate these sources appearing frequently in the citations:

Buff. Hist. Soc. Pubs.: Buffalo Historical Society Publications.

Folklore Archives: New York State Historical Association, Folklore Archives at Cooperstown. This material consists of unpublished miscellany of canal lore and other folklore of New York State. Where known, collectors and informants are indicated within parentheses below.

NYFQ: *New York Folklore Quarterly.*

NYH: *New York History.*

NOTES TO CHAPTER I

1. Quoted in Henry Wayland Hill, "An Historical Review of Waterways and Canal Construction in New York State," Buff. Hist. Soc. Pubs., XII (1908), 98.

2. William L. Stone, "Narrative of the festivities . . . in honor of the completion of the Grand Erie Canal," in Cadwallader D. Colden, *Memoir, prepared . . . at the celebration of the completion of the New York canals* (New York: W. A. Davis, 1825), p. 331.

3. New Brunswick *Fredonian*, Aug. 8, 1822; repr. in Lewis Leary, "Philip Freneau at Seventy," *The Journal of the Rutgers University Library*, I:2 (June, 1938), 2ff.

4. For the general history of the Erie Canal project, several sources are recommended. Whitford's *History* (Albany: Brandow Printing Company, 1906) remains the best general work available.

A. Barton Hepburn offers a brief but adequate account in his chapter, "The Period of Inception," in *Artificial Waterways of the World* (New York: The Macmillan Company, 1914), pp. 34–53. For documentary readings see especially the appendix to David Hosack, *Memoir of DeWitt Clinton* (New York: J. Seymour, 1829), for reprints of proposals, letters and other documents. Colden, *op. cit.*, gives a contemporary's review of events leading up to the building of the canal; see also Hill, *op. cit.* Alvin F. Harlow, *Old Towpaths* (New York and London: D. Appleton and Company, 1926), is recommended among the popularly written studies as an introduction to canals, including the Erie.

5. Quoted in *Report of the Joint Legislative Committee on Preservation and Restoration of Historic Sites,* [N.Y.] Legislative Document No. 82 (1958), p. 42.

6. Cited in Hill, p. 44, and Whitford, p. 25.

7. The letter appears in Hosack, p. 257.

8. *Ibid.*, p. 261.

9. A contemporary pamphlet, *Facts and Observations in relation to the origin and completion of the Erie Canal,* which credits Morris with originating the idea, is cited by Hosack, p. 259. See also *ibid.*, pp. 245ff., for further discussion of the Morris claim; and Whitford, pp. 50ff. The question of the "originator" remains, as Whitford points out, a "mooted question" and perhaps only of academic interest. James Geddes inclined toward Morris; canals between various sections of the route, he said, "must have been contemplated by the first navigators on these waters . . . but the idea of the Erie Canal is of very modern origin." (Hosack, p. 260.)

10. Letter from Col. Robert Troup to David Hosack, *ibid.*, p. 291. Watson delivered his journal to Schuyler in January 1792. Watson, a merchant, banker, and agriculturist, was an early advocate of public support for canals and turnpikes. In 1820 he published abstracts of his journals of trips to Fort Stanwix (1788) and to Seneca Lake (1797), in an effort to support his claim of having pioneered the canal idea. Watson manuscripts are in the New York State Library at Albany.

11. Merwin S. Hawley, *Origin of the Erie Canal* . . . A paper read before the Buffalo Historical Club, Feb. 21, 1866 (printed for private circulation, n.d.), p. 19. Italics are mine.

12. "Atticus, to the Citizens of the State of New York," in Edward Paine and others, *Remarks on the importance of the contemplated grand canal, between Lake Erie and the Hudson River* (1814), p. 15.

13. *Ibid.*, p. 25.

14. See Charles G. Haines, *Considerations on the Great Western Canal* . . . (Sec. ed., Brooklyn: Spooner & Worthington, 1818).

15. Quoted in *Report of the Joint Leg. Comm.*, p. 43.

16. As Whitford points out, however, the war demonstrated clearly the practicality of a canal. "The hardships and disastrous delays, caused by the breaking down of wagons and the wearing out of horses, were potent arguments in favor of canals. The debts that the Nation had incurred for the mere transportation of war materials would have gone far toward constructing the canal." (p. 72.)

17. *Ibid.*, pp. 74–75.

18. Francis P. Kimball, *New York—The Canal State* (Albany: The Argus Press, 1937), p. xiii.

19. It has been suggested that the Rensselaer Polytechnic Institute, founded by one of the canal commissioners as the first school of engineering in the English-speaking world, "came about largely as a school for educating engineers for the canals of New York State." (*Report of the Joint Leg. Comm.*, p. 45.)

20. *Ibid.*

21. Quoted in Harlow, p. 300.

22. Colden, p. 122.

23. Quoted in Hepburn, p. 51.

24. (New York: The Macmillan Company, 1902), I, 303.

25. Theodore Dwight, *The Northern Traveller* (3rd ed., New-York: G. & C. Carvill, 1828), p. 38.

26. J. H. French, *Gazetteer of the State of New York* (Syracuse: R. Pearsall Smith, 1860), p. 58, noted that "the day for traveling upon the canals may be considered as virtually passed, unless steam canal boats—now being introduced into use—prove successful competitors in speed upon the railroads." For the decline of the Erie, see Hepburn, pp. 70–87; and David M. Ellis, "Rivalry Between the New York Central and the Erie Canal," NYH, XXIX:3 (July 1948), 268–300. Professor Ellis points out that the "extraordinary success of the Erie Canal," on the other hand, "tended to retard the development of the railroads within the state." (*Ibid.*, p. 270.) Edward Everett Hale indicated the irony of history that saw the canal opened at the time the steam engine came into being. "In 1825 —about the time when, with firing of cannons and ringing of bells, New York celebrated the marriage of the Hudson with Lake Erie —George Stephenson built a special engine factory at Newcastle-upon-Tyne in England, that he might create a school of men. I

count this enterprise as the date when modern civilization begins."
(Hale, I, 308.)

27. Hill, pp. 82–83.

28. The boat company—*The Six-Day Line*—formed by Jerry Fowler in Walter D. Edmonds' novel, *Erie Water* (Boston: Little, Brown, and Company, 1933), shows something of the canal's significance in this respect. "That's a good name," Jerry's friend told him, "six days to the 'Hio country, I expect." (p. 461.) Even travellers between New York City and New Orleans used the Erie, transferring to an overland stage to Pittsburgh to connect with the Ohio River steamers; see John A. Krout and Dixon Ryan Fox, *The Completion of Independence* (New York: The Macmillan Company, 1944), pp. 226–27. The greatest influence was that of transporting emigrants to settle the West, however. See Lois Kimball Mathews, "The Erie Canal and the Settlement of the West," Buff. Hist. Soc. Pubs., XIV (1910), 189–203.

29. Kimball, p. 1.

NOTES TO CHAPTER II

1. Informant: Neil B. Reynolds, New York City, formerly of Scotia.

2. Edward Noyes Wescott, *David Harum* (New York: D. Appleton and Company, 1899), p. 250.

3. The term is used by Samuel Hopkins Adams, *The Erie Canal* (New York: Random House, 1953), p. 145.

4. Theodore Dwight, *The Northern Traveller* (4th ed., New-York: J. & J. Harper, 1831), p. 48.

5. *A New English Dictionary on Historical Principles*, ed. by James A. H. Murray (Oxford: Clarendon Press, 1888–1928).

6. Informant: Richard N. Wright, Syracuse. See also Clifton Johnson, *Highways and Byways of the Great Lakes* (New York: The Macmillan Company, 1911), p. 30.

7. Informant: Walter D. Edmonds, Boonville.

8. Informant: Richard N. Wright. The original Long Level ran from Lock 53 at Frankfort to Lock 54, three-quarters of a mile east of Syracuse in the town of Salina. This Long, or Utica, Level was cited as "the longest canal level in the world"; see Thomas F. Gordon, *Gazetteer of the State of New York* (Philadelphia: printed for the author, 1836), p. 77.

9. Professor Harold W. Thompson, *Body, Boots & Britches* (Phil-

adelphia: J. B. Lippincott Company, 1940), says "It is generally assumed that we got the pronunciation *canawl* from the Irish. Mr. Joel Munsell, the antiquary-printer, maintained that it was of Dutch origin." (p. 224fn.)

10. Eric Partridge, *A Dictionary of Slang and Unconventional English* (Rev. and enl., New York: The Macmillan Company, 1950).

11. *A New English Dictionary.*

12. Johnson, p. 25.

13. Folklore Archives (Olive E. Desnoyers, Hugh Graham); see also Arch Merrill, *The Towpath* (Rochester: The Democrat and Chronicle, 1945), p. 166.

14. *Grandfather Stories* (New York: Random House, 1955), p. 186.

15. *Slang and its Analogues Past and Present,* comp. and ed. by John S. Farmer and W. E. Henley (1890–1904), III, 52. See also *A Dictionary of Americanisms on Historical Principles,* ed. by Mitford M. Mathews (Chicago: University of Chicago Press, 1951). Most authorities agree that "foofoo" was a term of contempt.

16. Adams, *Grandfather Stories,* p. 146. The terms "wild cat" and "red dog" were given to monies whose credit was nil; the most worthless were called "red dog." See *A Dict. of Americanisms.*

17. Nathaniel Hawthorne, "The Canal Boat," *Mosses from an Old Manse* (Boston: Houghton, Mifflin and Company, 1882), p. 486.

18. Walter D. Edmonds, *Mostly Canallers* (Boston: Little, Brown and Company, 1934), p. 3.

19. Walter D. Edmonds, *The Wedding Journey* (Boston: Little, Brown and Company, 1947), p. 105.

20. A ballad of the D and H Canal contains lines about a "squeezer" (informant: Barbara Moncure, Woodstock). See also Leon Sciaky, "The Rondout and its Canal," NYH, XXII:3 (July, 1941), 285fn. For "hoodledasher," see Adams, *Grandfather Stories,* p. 282, and Thompson, p. 236.

21. Informant: Larry Hart, Schenectady.

22. Elizur Wright, *Myron Holley* (Boston: Printed for the author, 1882), p. 84.

NOTES TO CHAPTER III

1. As a matter of fact, a York State tour was being referred to as "the fashionable tour" as early as 1822; see, e.g., the guide-book, *The Fashionable Tour* (Saratoga Springs: G. M. Davison, 1822). Con-

taining much information for travellers, Davison's was typical of many such publications in the years 1825–50. *The Fashionable Tour* was revised and re-issued in succeeding editions in 1825, 1828, and 1830; sections on "Erie Canal" and "Canal Passage" appeared in the later editions.

2. T. L. McKenny; quoted in Madelaine S. Waggoner, *The Long Haul West* (New York: G. P. Putnam's Sons, 1958), p. 113.

3. *The Fashionable Tour, in 1825* (Saratoga Springs: G. M. Davison, 1825), pp. 116–17.

4. William L. Stone, "From New York to Niagara. Journal of a Tour, in part by Canal, in 1829," Buff. Hist. Soc. Pubs., XIV (1910), 220.

5. John Fowler, *Journal of a tour in the State of New York, in the year 1830* (London: Whittaker, Treacher, and Arnot, 1831), p. 66fn.

6. *Notes of a tour through the western part of the state of New York in 1829;* repr. from *The Ariel* (Philadelphia: 1829–30) for George P. Humphrey (Rochester: 1916), pp. 16–17. The author remained anonymous, but a prefatory statement in *The Ariel* called the *Notes* a "journal of a very intelligent traveller."

7. In July, 1830, naturalist Asa Fitch rode the *Surprise* out of Troy, but when they reached the Cohoes locks he left the canal boat and walked cross-country with his "bug-net" in hand, rejoining his boat farther on—a procedure he repeated frequently during the trip; see Samuel Rezneck, "Diary of a New York Doctor in Illinois—1830–1831," *Journal of the Illinois Historical Society*, LIV:1 (Spring, 1961), 29. One prominent tourist did, however, take a packet boat to Schenectady. A German duke, Bernhard of Saxe-Weimar Eisenbach, found it a "slow trip," which averaged three miles per hour, four minutes per lock, for the total of twenty-seven locks; see *Travels through North America, during the years 1825 and 1826* (Philadelphia: Carey, Lea & Carey, 1828), p. 63. For a further account of the duke and the Erie Canal, see below, this chapter.

8. "Everybody who makes the passage of the Erie Canal," wrote newspaperman N. P. Willis, "stops at the half-way town of Utica, to visit Trenton Falls"; see *Life, Here and There* (New York: Baker and Scribner, 1850), p. 82. Trenton Falls provides the setting for Catherine Maria Sedgewick's popular contemporary novel, *Clarence; or, A Tale of Our Own Time* (1830).

9. Tyrone Power, *Impressions of America, during the years 1833,*

1834, and 1835 (London: Richard Bentley, 1836), I, 412–13, 415.

10. Patrick Shirreff, *Tour through North America* (Edinburgh, 1835), reprinted in Clayton Man, *The Development of Central and Western New York,* rev. ed. (Danville: printed for the author, 1958), p. 299.

11. Entry for July 21, 1835; see *The Diary of Philip Hone,* ed. by Bayard Tuckerman (New York: Dodd, Mead and Co., 1899), I, 149. When Hone travelled on one of the Pennsylvania Canals he was less charitable; sleepers were, he said in an entry for June 13, 1847, "packed on narrow shelves fastened to the sides of the boat like dead pigs in a Cincinnati pork warehouse." (*Ibid.,* II, 312.)

12. *Mosses from an Old Manse;* vol. II of *Works* (Boston and New York: Houghton, Mifflin and Co., 1882), 490–91.

13. Frederick Gerstaecker, *Wild Sports in the Far West* (Boston: Crosby, Nichols and Co., 1859), pp. 47–48.

14. He found the sleeping conditions on an American canal boat like "hanging bookshelves, designed apparently for the volumes of the small octavo size." His berth was "just the width of an ordinary sheet of Bath post letter-paper"; the way in which he got into it is an enjoyable bit of Dickensian prose. See *American Notes* (1842), in, e.g., *The Works of Charles Dickens* (National Library Ed., New York: Bigelow, Brown and Co., n.d.), XIV, 192–93.

15. For a slightly expanded version of this section, see my article, "Mrs. Gilman and the Erie Canal," NYFQ, XIV:4 (Winter, 1958), 265–68. All quotations are taken from Caroline Gilman, *The Poetry of Travelling in the United States* (New York: S. Colman, 1838), pp. 89–93.

16. For this and succeeding quotations, see Frances Anne Butler, *Journal* (Philadelphia: Carey, Lea & Blanchard, 1835), II, 183–84. The *Journal* was published under Miss Kemble's married name, although she met her husband—an American—and married after the tour of 1832–33.

17. Frances Trollope, *Domestic Manners of the Americans,* ed., with a history of Mrs. Trollope's Adventures in America, by Donald Smalley (New York: Alfred A. Knopf, 1949), p. 369. The original appeared in 1832 and in several editions immediately thereafter, in London and New York. Quotations are made from the Smalley ed., pp. 369–76 *passim.*

18. Capt. [Frederick] Marryat, *A diary in America, with remarks on its institutions* (New-York: Wm. H. Colyer, 1839), p. 39. Subsequent quotations are taken from this ed., pp. 43–45.

19. *Reise Sr. Hoheit des Herzogs Bernhard zu Sachzen-Weimar-Eisenbach durch Nord-Amerika in den Jahren 1825 und 1826* (Weimar:Heinrich Luden, 1828); pp. 115–35 of Ch. VI deal with the Erie Canal. For convenience, quotations are taken from an American ed.: *Travels through North America* (Philadelphia: Carey, Lea & Carey, 1828), pp. 61–78 *passim*, covering his Erie Canal journey on 14 and 15 Aug. 1825.

20. She added that "the vibration it occasioned through the nerves of the republic, from one corner of the Union to the other, was by no means over when I left the country in July, 1831, a couple of years after the shock." See Trollope, Ch. XXXI ("Reception of Captain Basil Hall's Book in the United States").

21. Hall in a preface to his work stated, however, that "although I dare scarcely hope that my account will be very popular in America, I shall deeply lament having written on the subject at all, if these pages shall be thought to contain a single expression inconsistent with the gratitude . . . I must ever feel [for] the attention and hospitality we received from the Americans, or with the hearty good-will we bear to every individual whom we met in their widely extended country." See *Travels in North America in the years 1827 and 1828* (3rd ed., Edinburgh: Robert Cadell, and London: Simpkin and Marshall, 1830), I, vii–viii. Quotations which follow are taken from this ed.

22. Probably A. T. Goodrich's *Northern Traveller* (sec. ed., New York: 1826), a standard guide to points of interest for the tourist.

23. It is this kind of candid appraisal apparently that American readers did not find palatable, especially when the remarks came from an Englishman and an aristocrat. "You can imagine what steady, sturdy champions we are for England," wrote his wife, "and how Basil battles the watch on every point where he is attacked." See *The Aristocratic Journey*, being the outspoken letters of Mrs. Basil Hall written during a fourteen months' sojourn in America, 1827–28, ed. by Una Pope-Hennessy (New York: G. P. Putnam's Sons, 1931), p. 75. The editor's analysis of the inflexible aristocratic code of Mr. and Mrs. Hall shows how a clash in views with the' fundamentally democratic Americans—including their indifference —was an inevitable thing.

24. Hamilton College, on the periphery of Utica at Clinton, New York, figures as background in some of the fiction of Samuel Hopkins Adams; e.g., Dr. Horace Amlie, the hero of *Canal Town*, studied

there (see below, Ch. X). It is one of the half-dozen oldest liberal arts colleges in the United States.

25. See John Shaw, *A Ramble through the United States, Canada, and the West Indies* (London: Hope and Co., 1856), p. 31. He travelled from Syracuse to Oswego by canal boat.

26. See A. Levasseur, *Lafayette in America in 1824 and 1825*, tr. by John D. Godman (Philadelphia: 1829); repr. in Clayton Mau, *The Development of Central and Western New York* (Rev. ed., Danville: privately printed for the author, 1958), pp. 224–25. Mau reprints in full that part of Levasseur's journal (pp. 185–95) treating the New York State phase of Lafayette's visit.

27. Michael Chevalier, *Society, Manners and Politics in the United States*, tr. from the third Paris ed. (Boston: Weeks, Jordan and Co., 1839), p. 376.

28. See James Stuart, *Three Years in North America* (from the sec. London ed., New York: J. & J. Harper, 1833), I, 55ff.

29. Allan Nevins, *America Through British Eyes* (New York: Oxford University Press, 1948), titles a chapter on British travellers of 1825 to 1845 "Tory Condescension." See also the interpretive study of Jane L. Mesick, *The English Traveller in America 1785–1835* (New York: Columbia University Press, 1922), esp. Ch. I, "Motives and Geography."

30. *Pathway to Empire* (New York: Robert M. McBride & Co., 1935), p. 81.

NOTES TO CHAPTER IV

Background material on the lore of the upstate area can be found in a number of works, but the material relative to the Erie Canal is widely scattered. Codman Hislop, *The Mohawk* (New York: Rinehart & Company, 1948), and Carl Carmer, *The Hudson* (New York: Rinehart & Company, 1939), present historical data in readable fashion. For early legends and tales, see appropriate tales in Charles M. Skinner, *Myths and Legends of Our Own Land* (2 vols., Philadelphia: J. B. Lippincott Co., 1896), and *American Myths and Legends* (2 vols., Philadelphia: J. B. Lippincott Co., 1903). Doubtless the most valuable book and the most complete survey of Yorker folklore is Harold W. Thompson, *Body, Boots & Britches* (Philadelphia: J. B. Lippincott Co., 1940). This pioneer study contains a chapter on "Canawlers."

1. Skinner, I, 31. (Hereinafter cited as Skinner 1896.)

2. Tyrone Power, *Impressions of America, during the years 1833, 1834, and 1835* (London: Richard Bentley, 1836), I, 420.

3. Samuel Hopkins Adams tells a story of the carcagne in *Grandfather Stories* (New York: Random House, 1955), pp. 126ff. The word *owler* derived from late seventeenth-century England as a term for "those who privately in the Night carry Wool to the Sea-Coasts . . . and ship it off for France against the Law"; see *Slang and its Analogues Past and Present. A Dictionary, Historical and Comparative . . .* , comp. and ed. by John S. Farmer and W. E. Henley (printed for subscribers only, 1890–1904).

4. Skinner 1896, I, 61–63, and Skinner, *American Myths and Legends* (hereinafter cited as Skinner 1903), I, 214–218.

5. Frederick Gerstaecker, *Wild Sports in the Far West* (Boston: Crosby, Nichols and Company, 1859), p. 48.

6. Caroline Gilman, *The Poetry of Travelling in the United States* (New York: S. Colman, 1838), p. 103. Some, inevitably, were not impressed; Fanny Trollope in the 1830's called Lockport "a most hideous place"; see her *Domestic Manners of the Americans*, ed. by Donald Smalley (New York: Alfred A. Knopf, 1949), p. 378.

7. James Monroe Fitch, *The Ring Buster* (New York: Fleming H. Revell Company, 1940), p. 18. Although fictionalized, Fitch's description is that of a typical Yorker community of the nineteenth century. See also Edward Noyes Westcott's novel, *David Harum* (New York: D. Appleton and Company, 1899), which presents another typical upstate town in "Homeville."

8. This and other Medina lore appears in Arch Merrill, *The Towpath* (Rochester: The Democrat and Chronicle, 1945), pp. 22–31. The Eagle Tavern burned down in 1841.

9. *Ibid.*, p. 78.

10. For a useful history of Spiritualism, see Charles A. Huguenin, "The Amazing Fox Sisters," NYFQ, XIII:4 (Winter, 1957), 241–76; see also Carl Carmer, *Listen for a Lonesome Drum* (New York: Farrar & Rinehart, 1936), Ch. VII.

11. Samuel Hopkins Adams, *Banner by the Wayside* (New York: Random House, 1947), p. 167.

12. See, e.g., Joseph H. Murphey, "The Salt Industry of Syracuse —a Brief Review," NYH, XXX:3 (July, 1949), 304–315; and W. Freeman Galpin, "The Genesis of Syracuse," *ibid.*, XXX:1 (Jan., 1949), 19–32.

13. William Cullen Bryant (ed.), *Picturesque America* (New York: D. Appleton and Company, 1874), II, 458. It should be noted,

of course, that Utica was also a terminus, after 1836, of the Chenango Canal.

14. Folklore Archives. See also T. Wood Clarke, *Utica for a Century and a Half* (Utica: The Widtman Press, 1952), p. 108.

15. Bryant, II, 460.

16. See *Mostly Canallers* (Boston: Little, Brown, and Company, 1934), pp. 30–47.

17. Skinner 1903, I, 195–97.

18. Adams' story of the first school outhouse appears in his novel, *Banner by the Wayside*, pp. 286–87. In a footnote, Adams states: "My Great-aunt Sarah recalls that, as late as the middle of the century this type of architecture was known in the northern counties as an 'Andy,' whence the juvenile euphemism, 'Going to the Andes.' This she surmises to have been a belated recognition of Endurance Andrews' missionary work in hygiene." (*Ibid.*, p. 287; Endurance Andrews, a schoolteacher in the Palatinate at this point in the novel, is the heroine of *Banner*.)

19. The wooden suspension bridge at Schenectady was erected in 1808 and replaced by an iron structure in 1874; see Nelson Greene, *The Old Mohawk Turnpike Book* (Fort Plain: Nelson Greene, 1924), pp. 64–65. Schenectady lore is the subject of Jeanette Neisuler, "When Schenectady and the Erie Canal Were Young Together," NYH, XXXV:2 (April, 1954), 139–58; and city history is fully reflected in a special issue of the Schenectady *Union-Star*, Aug. 22, 1959, for the sesquicentennial celebration. Larry Hart did two articles on the Erie for a weekly historical series in the *Union-Star* (Dec. 15, Dec. 22, 1959).

20. See Noble E. Whitford, *History of the Canal System of the State of New York* (Albany: Brandow Printing Company, 1906), pp. 125–26. A group of handsomely uniformed Union College students, calling themselves the "College Guards," did, however, welcome the canal boats by musket salutes.

21. Rutherford Hayner, *Troy and Rensselaer County, New York. A History* (New York and Chicago: Lewis Historical Pub. Co., 1925), II, 560, 567.

22. For the story of the Troy collar, see Arthur James Weise, *Troy's One Hundred Years* (Troy: William H. Young, 1891), p. 174. A fictionalized account appears as "Mrs. Montague's Collar," in Samuel Hopkins Adams, *Grandfather Stories*, pp. 104–115.

23. Weise, pp. 165–66.

24. George W. Clinton, "Journal of a Tour from Albany to

Lake Erie by the Erie Canal in 1826," Buff. Hist. Soc. Pubs., XIV (1910), 273–308. See also Samuel Rezneck, "A Travelling School of Science on the Erie Canal in 1826," NYH, XL:3 (July, 1959), 255–69. For a note about Rensselaer's having been founded to supply canal engineers, see note 19 to Chapter I.

25. For the Legend of the Baker's Dozen, see Skinner 1896, I, 29–31; and Moritz Jagendorf, *Upstate Downstate* (New York: The Vanguard Press, 1949), pp. 28–33. For the Dutch influence on Albany, see Dorothy V. Bennit, "Albany Preserves Its Dutch Lore," NYFQ, XI:4 (Winter, 1955), 245–55.

26. A. M. Maxwell, *A Run through the United States, during the autumn of 1840* (London: Henry Colburn, 1841), I, 149–50.

27. Theodore Dwight, *The Northern Traveller* (New-York: J. & J. Harper, 1831), p. 28. Many local fortunes were said to have been made there; see Albany *Knickerbocker News* (Dec. 13, 1958), p. B9.

28. Marvin A. Rapp, "Old Beales and Coffee Beans," NYFQ, XII:2 (Summer, 1956), 96, 98.

29. Hazel A. McCombs, "Erie Canal Lore," NYFQ, III:3 (Autumn, 1947), 206–207.

30. Philetus Bumpus is the central character in a story in Carmer's *America Sings* (New York: Alfred A. Knopf, 1942). Carmer said Bumpus was a real person but "I chose him because I liked the name." (Notes to writer, April, 1959.)

31. The names of canallers frequenting "The Side-cut" and the story of "The Jumper": Folklore Archives (Mary Brierton, Cyrus B. Dingham).

32. Thompson, p. 234.

33. P. 53.

34. *Grandfather Stories*, p. 124.

35. Georgianna Pritchard, "On the Erie Canal," NYFQ, X:1 (Spring, 1954), 45.

36. Marvin A. Rapp, "The Ghost of Lock Herkimer," *Museum Service*, 31:1 (Jan., 1958), 12.

37. Louis C. Jones, *Things That Go Bump in the Night* (New York: Hill and Wang, 1959), pp. 146–48.

38. Rapp, "The Ghost of Lock Herkimer," pp. 14, 17. The Black River canal version: Folklore Archives.

39. For Yorker witch lore, see Wheaton P. Webb, "Witches in the Cooper Country," NYFQ, I:1 (Feb., 1945), 5–20. Evelyn E. Gardiner, *Folklore from the Schoharie Hills New York* (Ann Ar-

bor: Univ. of Mich. Press, 1937), includes a chapter on "Witchcraft" (Ch. III).

40. Rapp, "The Ghost of Lock Herkimer," p. 13.

41. Folklore Archives (Geraldine Merhoff, Mary Jane Gass).

42. Marvin A. Rapp, "Canawl Water and Whiskey," NYFQ, XI:4 (Winter, 1955), 297.

43. Informant: Paul MacFarland, Binghamton.

44. Thompson, p. 232.

45. Philip D. Jordan, *Uncle Sam of America* (St. Paul: The Webb Pub. Co., 1953), pp. 19–20.

46. Adams, *Grandfather Stories*, p. 266. The most complete account of Patch lore is Richard M. Dorson's "Sam Patch, Jumpin' Hero," NYFQ, I:3 (Aug., 1945), 133–151. A week earlier Patch had successfully jumped the Falls; ironically, the advertisement for his next leap proclaimed "Higher Yet! Sam's Last Jump. Some things can be done as well as others. . . ." (*Ibid.*, 137–38.) For a contemporary account, see F. A. Ferrall, *A Ramble of Six Thousand Miles Through the United States of America* (London: Effingham Wilson, 1832), p. 27. Patch is also the subject of Arch Merrill, "Old Legends Never Die," NYFQ, XIII:1 (Spring, 1957), 59–61.

47. Julia Hull Winner, "The Rattlesnake Hunter," NYFQ, XIV:4 (Winter, 1958), 274.

48. *Ibid.*, p. 275. Dean Ronald A. H. Mueller, Rensselaer Polytechnic Institute, recalls a "Rattlesnake Pete," a tavern-keeper in Rochester whose establishment was "practically wallpapered in snake skins."

49. Carl Carmer, *The Hurricane's Children* (New York and Toronto: Farrar & Rinehart, 1937), pp. 131ff. For further notes on John Darling, see Carmer, *Listen for a Lonesome Drum* (New York: Farrar & Rinehart, 1936), pp. 379–80.

50. Moritz Jagendorf, "Catskill Darling: Facts about a Folk Hero," NYFQ, I:2 (May, 1945), 69–82. Herbert Halpert, "John Darling, a New York Munchausen," *Journal of American Folklore*, 57:224 (April–June, 1944), 97–106, publishes 21 tales and variants; none, however, are concerned with the Erie Canal.

NOTES TO CHAPTER V

Several of the items in this chapter came from the Folklore Archives at Cooperstown. These include, in order of their appearance in the chapter: story of Leonard's saloon (Sue Crandall Davis, William G. Crandall), bulldog fighting (Mary Brierton, Cyrus B. Dingham), story of the *Damfino* (Dorothy Cox, William Cox II), story of Oneida Lake field day with greased pole and greased pig contests (Mildred K. Empie, Wendall Conrad of Fort Plain), lore of the Side-cut and Troy (Mary Brierton, Cyrus B. Dingham), story of the "riproaringest fight" at Macedon (Ralph Weaver of Macedon).

1. Samuel Hopkins Adams' paternal grandfather, Myron Adams; see *Grandfather Stories* (New York: Random House, 1955), p. 96.

2. *Mostly Canallers* (Boston: Little, Brown and Co., 1934), p. 48.

3. Informant: Larry Hart, Schenectady.

4. Informant: Mrs. E. G. Smith, Ticonderoga, the canaller's granddaughter. Mrs. Smith also furnished other items of correspondence from her grandfather, Captain John Thompson, including the cited letter of November, 1879.

5. Unidentified newspaper clipping furnished by Mrs. E. G. Smith, Ticonderoga.

6. The interview with Cap'n Hanks was taken from a newspaper account (originally in the *New York Sun* but otherwise unidentified). Informant: Mrs. E. G. Smith, Ticonderoga.

7. *Bottoming Out*, III:1 (Oct., 1958), 7.

8. Arch Merrill, *The Towpath* (Rochester: The Democrat and Chronicle, 1945), p. 94.

9. See "Piety and Pie," in Adams, pp. 116-25.

10. *Wild Sports in the Far West* (Boston: Crosby, Nichols and Co., 1859), p. 44.

11. *Travels through North America, during the years 1825 and 1826* (Philadelphia: Carey, Lea & Carey, 1828), p. 65.

12. Adams, p. 305.

13. See, e.g., such Edmonds stories as "At Schoharie Crossing," "Citizens for Ohio," and "Water Never Hurt a Man," in *Mostly Canallers;* and his *Rome Haul* (Boston: Little, Brown and Co., 1929), pp. 323-28, which presents the fight scene between Dan Harrow and Jotham Klore which set the pattern. See also Samuel Hopkins Adams, *Canal Town* (New York: Random House, 1944), pp. 236ff.; and *Sunrise to Sunset* (New York: Random House, 1950), pp. 241-44.

14. George Denniston, Waterloo; quoted by Harold W. Thompson, *Body, Boots & Britches* (Philadelphia: J. B. Lippincott Co., 1940), p. 224.

15. *Old Towpaths* (New York and London: D. Appleton and Co., 1926), p. 139. Harlow adds, "The police, we are told, 'dared not interfere.'"

16. In addition to the items in the Folklore Archives noted above, see the Troy *Times Record* (Oct. 19 and Oct. 26, 1935), for articles dealing with the lore of the Sidecut and Troy.

17. Deacon M. Eaton, *Five Years on the Erie Canal* (Utica: Bennett, Backus, & Hawley, 1845), pp. 114–15.

NOTES TO CHAPTER VI

1. For a note on Yorker interest in "Johnny Troy," see Hazel A. McCombs, "Erie Canal Lore," NYFQ, III:3 (Autumn, 1947), 208ff. The ballad, sung by Ellen Steckert, appears in *Songs of a New York Lumberjack* (Folkways FA 2345), with textual notes by Kenneth S. Goldstein and Miss Steckert.

2. Thomas F. O'Donnell, "'I'm Afloat!' on the Raging Erie," NYFQ, XIII:3 (Autumn, 1957), 176.

3. John A. and Alan Lomax, *American Ballads and Folk Songs* (New York: The Macmillan Co., 1934), p. 459.

4. "Dark-Eyed Canaller" appears in Lomax, *Our Singing Country* (New York: The Macmillan Co., 1941), pp. 218–19. A ballad, "The Dark-Eyed Sailor," was found in western New York after the 1830's; see Harold W. Thompson (ed.), *A Pioneer Songster* (Ithaca: Cornell University Press, 1958), pp. 49–51.

5. "This group of stanzas," said Lomax, "I put together without changes as one song, *The Ballad of the Erie Canal*, in the form of a continuous narrative." See *Adventures of a Ballad Hunter* (New York: The Macmillan Co., 1947), p. 245; texts of the nine verses appear in *ibid.*, pp. 245–46. G. Malcolm Laws, *Native American Balladry* (Philadelphia: The American Folklore Society, 1950), pp. 263–64, lists this as a peripheral folk song, "weak or disunified in narrative action." Another "peripheral" type in the Lomax collection has "Sandy Dan the Clam-Peddler" on Erie water in a verse which goes:

> Sunday night he went
> To see red-headed Sal,
> And took her to his clam-boat
> 'Way down on the Erie Canal.

(from Mrs. G. W. Tillapough, Mexico, N.Y.; see *American Ballads and Folk Songs*, p. 458.) This type of artless modern invention is of little interest to the field of traditional Erie folk songs, but it is a curiosity.

6. Walter D. Edmonds, *Rome Haul* (Boston: Little, Brown and Co., 1929), p. 92. An Edmonds short story, "Big-Foot Sal," appears in *Mostly Canallers* (Boston: Little, Brown and Co., 1934), pp. 89–204. It is interesting to note that, largely through the influence of Edmonds, "Sal" has become for most people the stereotype of the Erie Canal woman.

7. First stanza: Samuel Hopkins Adams, *Canal Town* (New York: Random House, 1944), p. 118; second and third variants: Adams, *Chingo Smith of the Erie Canal* (New York: Random House, 1958), pp. 114–15.

8. *The American Vocalist* (New York: Huestis & Cozans, 1853), pp. 137–38.

9. Silas Farmer, *The History of Detroit and Michigan* (Detroit: Silas Farmer & Co., 1884), pp. 335–36.

10. (Philadelphia: J. B. Lippincott Co., 1940), p. 238: Mrs. A. H. Shearer, Buffalo; Mrs. Broadbeck, Tonawanda.

11. Informant: Richard N. Wright, Syracuse.

12. First version: Folklore Archives (Helen MacGreivey, from her father); second version: Folklore Archives (Shirley Wurz, John O'Brien of Herkimer).

13. Thompson, *Body, Boots & Britches*, pp. 241–43: A. M. Walsh, Buffalo; Alex Stearns, Syracuse.

14. McCombs, pp. 206–207. The site was Jacksonburg Lock, near Little Falls.

15. Thompson, pp. 248–49; Mrs. W. W. Gay, South Glens Falls, as recited by W. Roselle, Ft. Edward; the canaller in the song "is supposed to be a Dan Smith, canal grocer at Smith's Basin, who may have been at some time captain of a packet."

16. Sigmund Spaeth, *Read 'em and Weep* (New York: Arco Publishing Co., 1945), p. 45.

17. *Vandemark's Folly* (Indianapolis: The Bobbs-Merrill Co., 1922), p. 30. Copyright 1922 by Herbert Quick, 1949 by Ella Corey Quick; reproduced by special permission of the publishers. For an account of Quick's book as it bears on the Erie story, see below, Ch. VIII.

18. McCombs, pp. 202, fn. 2, 208.

19. Carl Carmer, " 'O the Ee-rye-ee Was Risin',' " *American Heritage*, 3:3 (Spring, 1952), 11.

20. *The American Vocalist*, p. 150.

21. *The Boquet Melodist, or Choice Gems from the Operas* (New-York: Wm. H. Murphy, 1850?), p. 87. The song also appears in *The American Vocalist*, p. 26.

22. O'Donnell, " 'I'm Afloat!' on the Raging Erie," pp. 178–80.

23. Informant: Frank Warner, letter to writer (May 28, 1959). Song used by permission of Mr. Warner and NYFQ.

24. Folklore Archives (Raymond Lowell, Fort Plain).

25. Thompson, pp. 243–44: Capt. W. Thomas. Included are four other verses not concerned with Black Rock pork.

26. Folklore Archives (Mildred K. Empie, Raymond Lowell).

27. McCombs, p. 207. Miss McCombs included another verse which more properly belongs with the original "Raging Erie" varieties.

28. Laws, p. 220, cites what seems to be a variant of the first verse as "An Arkansas Traveller"; interestingly enough, this song begins with the mention of "Buffalo Town."

29. *American Songbag* (New York: Harcourt, Brace & Co., 1927), p. 180.

30. (*The New*) *Song Fest*, ed. by Dick and Beth Best (New York: Crown Publishers, Inc., 1955), p. 20.

31. Decca DL 5080. This song is listed on the jacket as "The Erie Canal."

32. From the original sheet music (copy in the Grosvenor Library, Buffalo).

33. From the original sheet music c. 1913 by F. B. Haviland Pub. Co., Inc. (copy in the Grosvenor Library, Buffalo).

NOTES TO CHAPTER VII

Several of the stories included in this chapter came from Paul MacFarland, Binghamton; the source of them lay, in turn, in Albion canal yarns, drawn upon for a meeting of the Society of the Erie Canal. Credits for all stories not otherwise cited include, in order of their appearance in the chapter: the towpath mule stories and the Weedsport squash tale: Paul MacFarland; another version (Palmyra): Nancy A. Logan; the giant frog: Joan Littler, Oswego, who heard the tale from people in Empeyville, including Charles Beacraft, who claimed to have seen the frog (letter to writer, Oct. 16, 1958; see also her article as noted below); Mc-Carthy tales: Paul MacFarland; the Medina fish story: Nancy A. Logan and Paul MacFarland; Macedon Locks tale: Folklore Archives (Edythe Weaver, Ralph Weaver); the drunken fish who chased the cats, and the two tales of the Albion break: Paul Mac-Farland.

1. Nathaniel R. Howell, "A Long Island Whale Story," NYFQ, X:1 (Spring, 1954), 42–44.

2. Quoted in "Editor's Note" to *ibid.*, p. 44. Edmonds' story appeared in *The Forum and Century*, LXXXVII:1 (Jan., 1932), 24–31, with illustrations by Donald McKay. It was later included in *Mostly Canallers* (Boston: Little, Brown and Co., 1934).

3. See Nancy A. Logan, "Look for a Post!" NYFQ, XII:4 (Winter, 1956), 285.

4. Cited by Joan Littler, "The Empeyville Frog," NYFQ, XIV:2 (Summer, 1958), 147.

5. *Impressions of America, during the years 1833, 1834, and 1835* (London: Richard Bentley, 1836), I, 416–17.

6. *America Sings* (New York: Alfred A. Knopf, 1942), pp. 55–56.

7. Oak Orchard bass are the subject of Helen E. Allen, "The Jumping Bass of Oak Orchard Creek," NYFQ, VI:2 (Summer, 1950), 90–95.

8. The story appears in Carmer, "How Johnny Darling Went Fishing and Caught a Bride," *The Hurricane's Children* (New York and Toronto: Farrar & Rinehart, 1937), pp. 131–38.

NOTES TO CHAPTER VIII

1. Cited in *Report of the Joint Legislative Committee on Preservation and Restoration of Historic Sites*, [N.Y.] Legislative Document No. 82 (1958), p. 20.

2. See Lewis Leary, "Philip Freneau at Seventy," *The Journal of the Rutgers University Library*, I:2 (June, 1938), 2–6. Leary states that this "was probably one of the last poems that Philip Freneau composed." The poem also appears in Leary (ed.), *The Last Poems of Philip Freneau* (New Brunswick: Rutgers University Press, 1945), pp. 21–24.

3. The full title ran: *The Convention of Drunkards:* a satirical essay on intemperance. To which are added, three speeches on the same subject; an oration on the anniversary of American in-

dependence; and an ode on the completion of the Erie Canal. Quotations are taken from the sec. ed., New-York: Scofield and Voorhees, 1840, pp. 124–26.

4. This story is cited as "the first significant mention of the Erie Canal in American literature"; see Thomas O'Donnell, "Note for a Bibliography of the Canals of New York State," *Bottoming Out*, II:2 (Jan., 1958), 13.

5. James Kirke Paulding, *The Book of Saint Nicholas* (New-York: Harper & Brothers, 1836), p. 209.

6. William Dunlap, *A Trip to Niagara; or, Travellers in America*. A farce in three acts (New-York: E. B. Clayton, 1830). See also my article, "A Farce on Erie Water," NYFQ, XVII:1 (Spring, 1961), wherein this discussion of Dunlap first appeared.

7. Jacob Abbott, *Marco Paul's Travels and Adventures in the Pursuit of Knowledge on the Erie Canal* (Boston: T. H. Carter & Co., and New York: A. V. Blake, 1844), p. 1.

8. See *ibid.*, pp. 56–57.

9. Quotations from Howells, *Their Wedding Journey* (Boston and New York: Houghton Mifflin Co., 1872), pp. 83, 85.

10. S. L. Clemens [Mark Twain], *Roughing It* (New York and London: Harper & Brothers, n.d.), II, Ch. 10.

11. "In his title character," observes one critic, "Westcott gave America one of its favorite stereotypes dressed in upstate New York costume." See Thomas F. O'Donnell, "The Regional Fiction of Upstate New York" (unpublished doctoral dissertation, Syracuse University, 1957), p. 16. According to a contemporary critic, *David Harum* presented "a masterly delineation of an American type." (Adv. in Westcott, *David Harum. A Story of American Life* [New York: D. Appleton and Co., 1899], p. 400.) For two tales of David Hannum, the original upon which Westcott based his character, see Shirley J. Williams, "David Hannum of Homer," NYFQ, VIII:3 (Autumn, 1952), 215–16. All quotations, unless otherwise noted, are taken from the 1899 ed. as cited.

12. *David Harum* (20th Century-Fox, 1934).

13. For the complete scene, in which Harum's spilling breakfast eggs on his shirt front leads to his telling the assembled guests an amusing Yorker tale of Elder Maybee's powder, see Chs. XXVI and XXVII.

14. *David Harum* also was staged as a three-act comedy; adapted by R. and M. W. Hitchcock and produced by Charles

Froham, it opened at New York's Garrick Theatre, October 1, 1900, for a run of 148 performances. It was revived in 1902 and 1904. See Burns Mantle and Garrison P. Sherwood (eds.), *The Best Plays of 1899–1909* (New York: Dodd, Mead and Co., 1944), pp. 372–73.

15. Letter to writer (Feb. 4, 1959).

16. See Herbert Quick, *One Man's Life. An Autobiography* (Indianapolis: The Bobbs-Merrill Co., 1925), p. 16.

17. Quotations are taken from *Vandemark's Folly* (Indianapolis: The Bobbs-Merrill Co., 1922), Introd. and Chs. 1–4. Copyright 1922 by Herbert Quick, 1949 by Ella Corey Quick, reproduced by special permission of the publishers.

18. (New York: Farrar & Rinehart, 1939), Part One ("York State").

19. James Monroe Fitch, *The Ring Buster. A Story of the Erie Canal* (New York, London and Edinburgh: Fleming H. Revell Co., 1940), p. 170.

20. Enid LaMonte Meadowcroft, *Along the Erie Towpath* (New York: Thomas Y. Crowell Co., 1940), p. 65.

21. Thomas F. O'Donnell, review of *Chingo Smith of the Erie Canal, Hamilton Review* (July, 1958), p. 209.

NOTES TO CHAPTER IX

1. New York *Herald Tribune Books* (Feb. 17, 1929), p. 5.

2. Edmonds, letter to writer (Feb. 4, 1959). The story appeared in *Harvard Advocate*, CVII:6 (March, 1922), 157–63.

3. These appeared in the *Advocate* issues for Sept., Dec., and Jan., 1925, respectively. Although characterizations changed, the names were to be found later in *Rome Haul*.

4. Letter to writer.

5. "Edmonds Country," *Saturday Review of Literature*, XVII:7 (Dec. 11, 1937), 11. When the story was published in *Scribner's Magazine* for July 1926, it appeared with Robert E. Sherwood's first published short story, "Extra! Extra!"

6. "The Voice of the Archangel" and "An Honest Deal" appeared in *The Atlantic Monthly* for Jan., 1928, and March, 1929, respectively; "The Swamper" was published in *The Dial* for March, 1928.

7. Letter to writer.

8. Edmonds, Introd. to *Rome Haul* (New York: The Modern Library, 1938), pp. viii–ix.

9. Letter to writer.

10. Quotations are taken from *Rome Haul* (Boston: Little, Brown and Co., 1929).

11. One is reminded of Robert Spiller's calling *A Farewell to Arms* "a farewell to everything"; see *The Cycle of American Literature* (New York: The Macmillan Co., 1955), p. 205. Professor Douglas Washburn, Rensselaer Polytechnic Institute, has pointed out to me that perhaps the "uncommittedness" of the central characters of both novels provides further analogy. Like Frederick Henry of the Hemingway novel, *Rome Haul*'s Dan Harrow is essentially an "outsider" and remains so. Edmonds' use of the dairyland and its appeal to Dan seems analogous to Hemingway's Switzerland, doubtless to Lieutenant Henry's mind the manifestation of the priest's hometown, as a symbol of the ordered and the secure.

12. An intriguing analogy might be made between a closing scene in Edmonds' novel and T. S. Eliot's *The Waste Land*. After the Harrow-Klore fight, Molly leaves Dan and Fortune Friendly, a renegade Yale minister, jumps from the canal boat.

> "It don't seem right," Fortune said to the rumps of the horses. "Each one thought he was fighting for her. And neither one won."
>
> Down the old Sarsey Sal sank in the walls of the locks. It grew colder. An old man sat on the dock at Han Yerry's fishing for sunfish.
>
> "Frost tonight," he prophesied to Fortune.

It is too tantalizing not to suggest Eliot's *The Waste Land* itself; cf. ll. 424–25: "I sat upon the shore/Fishing . . ." and note also Eliot's earlier use of "fishing in the dull canal" (l. 189). (However intriguing such analogies are, one should not assume that Edmonds' work is other than regional romance; it commands attention largely on its own terms.)

13. Edmonds himself said that writing *Rome Haul* made him stop seeing characters only as "characters" and the Erie as something quaint: it became "a serious panorama of a real phase of life and of the people who lived it." (Introd. Modern Library ed., p. ix.)

14. *Erie Water* (Boston: Little, Brown and Co., 1933), p. 108. This situation offers some interesting punning on the word *locks*.
15. A verse sung about 1877 in Buffalo's Bonny's Theatre; see John A. and Alan Lomax, *American Ballads and Folk Songs* (New York: The Macmillan Co., 1934), p. 463. For the story of "Big-Foot Sal," see Edmonds, *Mostly Canallers* (Boston: Little, Brown and Co., 1934), from which quotations are taken.
16. For the background of Edmonds' tale, see Nathaniel R. Howell, "A Long Island Whale Story," NYFQ, X:1 (Spring, 1954), 42–44, including Edmonds' note as epilogue. Quotations which follow are taken from *Mostly Canallers*, pp. 205–18 *passim*.
17. (Oct. 11, 1947), p. 126.
18. *The Wedding Journey* (Boston: Little, Brown and Co., 1947), p. 23.
19. One is struck, as a matter of fact, by the obvious similarities. The title, of course, corresponds to that of an early Howells novel which, interestingly enough, saw the Basil Marches on the route of the Erie Canal during *their* wedding journey. Edmonds' Bella seems an obvious steal from Howells' Irene Lapham; and, like her counterpart in *The Rise of Silas Lapham*, Bella—plain in contrast to her more attractive sister—surprised the family by her marriage to a man who everyone thought came wooing her sister. (It should be added, however, that in Edmonds' story the situation is revealed only by Bella reflecting upon past events and forms no essential part of the narrative structure.)
20. Burns Mantle (ed.), *The Best Plays of 1934–1935* (New York: Dodd, Mead and Co., 1935), p. 262. Mantle chose *The Farmer Takes a Wife* as one of the year's ten best. Elser's *Low Bridge* appears in *Plays for the College Theatre*, ed. by G. H. Leverton (New York: Samuel French, 1932).
21. Mantle, p. 278.
22. The master prompt-book for this production, together with other material concerning the performance, is in the Library of Union College, Schenectady.
23. *The 1937 Drama Festival Magazine*, III:2 (July 13, 1937), 6.
24. *Rome Haul* (Modern Library ed.), p. v.
25. Thomas F. O'Donnell, "The Regional Fiction of Upstate New York" (unpublished doctoral dissertation, Syracuse University, 1957), pp. 5–6, states that "whereas the decade before *Rome Haul* had produced a scant half-dozen novels in which the great upstate area provides an identifiable, significant background, the decade

that followed . . . produced at least three dozen. The next decade, the 1940's, saw the publication of at least sixty more. And during the first half of the present decade, the 1950's, there have been at least fifty." O'Donnell has also prepared "A Bibliography of the Fiction of Upstate New York, 1929–1955" (Utica College, mimeo, 16 pp.).

26. For the Harrow-Klore fight scene, see *Rome Haul*, pp. 323–28.

27. Quoted in *Twentieth Century Authors*, ed. by Stanley J. Kunitz and Howard Haycroft (New York: 1942), p. 415.

28. Leon Whipple in *Survey Graphic*, XXII (May, 1933), 274.

NOTES TO CHAPTER X

1. Adams Basin, three miles west of Spencerport. Abner Adams had a contract for digging the canal in that sector; see Arch Merrill, *The Towpath* (Rochester: The Democrat and Chronicle, 1945), pp. 74–75.

2. Adams, *Grandfather Stories* (New York: Random House, 1955), p. 39.

3. Harold W. Thompson, "Samuel Hopkins Adams, '91," *Hamilton Alumni Review* (Jan., 1937), p. 53.

4. *Atlantic Monthly* (June, 1944), p. 125.

5. Adams, *Canal Town* (New York: Random House, 1944), p. vii. Other quotations from the novel follow without further reference.

6. Adams' loyalty to his alma mater is seen in many of his novels and stories which contain men with Hamilton backgrounds. In Dr. Amlie's case, the College is a particularly appropriate choice, for the College has always had an enviable pre-med record. At one time it did have a law department—it has always been a small liberal arts college—and "in 1812 it would have become a medical college had not an obstetrician declined to join its first faculty." See "Hamilton College," in David H. Beetle, *Along the Oriskany* (Utica: Utica Observer-Dispatch, 1947), pp. 126–46.

7. New York *Herald Tribune Weekly Book Review* (March 16, 1947), p. 8.

8. See Adams, *Banner by the Wayside* (New York: Random House, 1947), p. 100; the episode also appears as "The Saga of Four-Skate Pilkington," in *Grandfather Stories*, pp. 171–82.

9. *Banner by the Wayside*, p. 110. The carcagne is described as "a storm-hag with bat wings and a borrowed wolf's head, generally held accountable for such ships as put forth on Ontario and Erie never again to be reported." For another account of the carcagne, see "Munk Birgo and the Carcagne," in *Grandfather Stories*, pp. 126–35.

10. "Our Forefathers Tackle an Epidemy—the Cholera of 1832," NYFQ, III:2 (Summer, 1947), 93–101.

11. See *Sunrise to Sunset* (New York: Random House, 1950), to which references are made. The story of the invention of the collar appears as Ch. 8 of the novel and also in *Grandfather Stories* ("Mrs. Montague's Collar"), pp. 104–15.

12. Whether or not Adams had Dreiser in mind is academic: Adams drew from different material. As he points out in his Preface, Sadler's Island is pure invention—no such island exists or existed in the Hudson River at the location indicated—and the crime on which *Sunrise to Sunset* is based, an actual and unsolved mystery, took place in Rhode Island.

13. New York *Herald Tribune, loc. sit.*

14. *Grandfather Stories*, p. 16.

NOTES TO CHAPTER XI

1. Millicent Winton Veeder, *Door to the Mohawk Valley* (Albany: Cromwell Printery, 1947), p. 71.

2. William C. Langdon, *Everyday Things in American Life 1776–1876* (New York: Charles Scribner's Sons, 1941), p. 128. Langdon's Ch. VII, "When Canals Had Their Day," is of general interest and relevance.

3. (Ithaca: Cornell University Press, 1949), p. 10. This volume also contains Andrew D. White's "The Cardiff Giant: a chapter in the History of Human Folly, 1869–1870."

4. The novel was serialized in the *Post*, Jan. 31–March 21, 1959. While this novel does contain elements which are of interest to the canal enthusiast, Kelland's apparent lack of knowledge of the Syracuse area will not satisfy the purists among students of regionalism.

5. Thomas F. O'Donnell, *A Dam for Delta* (mimeo script), p. 9. In 1957 and 1958 the play was produced by the Utica College Gaslighters in several upstate communities; it took First Honorable

Mentior. in the A. M. Drummond playwriting contest sponsored annually by Cornell University.

6. *Body, Boots & Britches* (Philadelphia: J. B. Lippincott Co., 1940), p. 222.

7. See *The 1937 [Mohawk] Drama Festival Magazine*, III:2 (July 13, 1937), 6.

8. See, e.g., Edward Everett Hale, *Memories of a Hundred Years* (New York: The Macmillan Co., 1902), and Herbert Quick, *One Man's Life* (Indianapolis: The Bobbs-Merrill Co., 1925). Elizur Wright, *Myron Holley* (Boston: Printed for the author, 1882), devotes seven chapters to the Erie in this biography of a man who (as DeWitt Clinton put it) "devoted his whole time and attention, mind and body, to the canal." The biographer feels Holley to have been the single most important factor in the State's building the canal and one unjustly treated by the State which "saved $80,000 by throwing upon Mr. Holley a burden of responsibility for which it paid him nothing." (p. 327.)

9. *The Erie Canal Centennial Celebration 1926* (Albany: J. B. Lyon Co., 1928), p. 17.

10. Hazel A. McCombs, "Erie Canawl Lore," NYFQ, III:3 (Autumn, 1947), 212.

11. From a contemporary account of the 1825 celebration; quoted by Carl Carmer, " 'O the Ee-rye-ee was risin'," " *American Heritage*, III:3 (Spring, 1952), 10.

Index

(Unless otherwise noted, all place names refer to New York State.)